Barking Up th

Cover design: Artwork by Kathleen Harryman

For more information, please contact: Jeffrey Brett at
magic79.jb@outlook.com

First Edition published: June 2019

Second Edition published: March 2021

Barking Up the Wrong Tree

For Jenny

With Love Always

Copyright © Jeffrey Brett 2019

Barking Up the Wrong Tree

An Unexpected Surprise

With the descent of the evening sun casting long shadows over the estate the day was almost done leaving Lady Olivia Ashleigh time to reflect and gather her thoughts. Checking the time with the clock on the mantel the minutes seemed to be dragging on by.

'Where could they be,' she pondered, 'and why were they taking so long.'

Standing beside the tall window of the drawing room with only the echo of the clock for company each precise movement of the Swiss mechanism was like the falling of the blade descending the guillotine making her wait that much more anxious.

Large, although impressive the manor house at Willow Beck sat imposingly in the centre of the estate, the family home of the Ashleigh family. Built in stone it had outlived generations of the residents in the nearby village. At night the floorboards creaked and when the whistled, the odd ghost could be heard wandering the long passages, especially underground.

For the umpteenth time she gently thumped the wooden window jamb.

'Just where could those young men have got too?' she contemplated. Unusually she could feel the tension rising up her neck although she dismissed the sensation blaming the recent wet weather instead. 'I am far too young to have such a condition.' She checked the clock once again. They were late and it was worrying.

Somewhere in the large hall outside she heard a creak. Smiling to herself she thought nothing of it. 'Good evening Lawrence,' she said, 'I trust that you've had a good day!'

Lord Lawrence Ashleigh, the late husband was no longer around due to his sudden demise. Some said his going was an ill-fated departure, whereas others said it was long overdue. Whatever the reason it meant that Olivia Ashleigh had responsibility to oversee the estate and daily its affairs.

As you would expect with a house so large, extensive land and an underground cellar running virtually the length of the house there were challenges, least not keeping the field mice from the pantry. But Olivia had found a way to cope. She did however like punctuality.

Drumming her fingers on the paintwork she watched the sun falling between the branches of the trees that lined the back lane which ran adjacent to her land. Falling slowly it left in its wake a bronze covering above the heads of the rose bushes surrounding the bay window where in one corner the stems were under attack from weeds. She made a mental note to inform the gardener, Charlie Luft. When the clock chimed out the hour, she turned away needing something to help steady her nerves.

Like anxious mice holding onto the stems of bent wheat the two young men in the back of the lorry readied themselves as the driver took another sharp bend.

'For gawd's sake Tommy steady on please,' cried Samuel. *'My old man will murder me if this lorry gets returned damaged.'*

The trio had been travelling nearly all day covering the many miles from the vineyard in the Luberon Valley in Western Provence, taking the afternoon ferry from Calais to Dover, before skirting sheepishly around the Kentish coastline passing through the borders of Essex and Suffolk, and finally with relief taking familiar country lanes back to Willow Beck.

Changing down a gear Tommy Jenkins could see the tall chimneys of the manor house. He called back telling the other two that they only had another half a mile to go.

'Cor we ain't half gonna cop it,' said Robert Perry looking across at Samuel Byrne, 'we're behind schedule and her ladyship don't like waiting around.'

Samuel Byrne, the farmer's son steadied himself for another bend. 'Stuff her time keeping, I'll just be glad when we're there. We've been thrown about the back of this bloody lorry like a couple of skittles.'

Robert Perry the only son of Reg Perry, the village constable rubbed his calf muscles which ached. He was looking forward to a good long soak in a nice hot bath.

'Will you pair stop belly aching,' Tommy responded as he slowed the revolutions of the engine ready to take the turn left, 'and hold onto those flamin' crates, we've come this far without a hitch. I reckon if we pull together we can unload this little lot in under half n' hour.'

Samuel looked across at Robert who was sat opposite. 'What's his hurry?' he quizzed.

'He has a date with Alice under the church clock at ten.'

Samuel Byrne was amused. He laughed shaking his head. 'I don't know where you get the energy Jenkins.' Robert who was still vigorously rubbing the back of his legs watched Samuel enjoy the moment.

Puling the wheel of the lorry straight Tommy smiled. 'The trouble with you two is you don't eat properly. I watch my calorie intake and what I eat, instead of gorging the rubbish that you morons put away.'

Robert Perry and Samuel Byrne screwed up their faces. It was ages since they'd had something to eat. 'There ain't nothing wrong with a hearty fried breakfast,' replied Samuel. 'Oatmeal doused in milk with grapes or grapefruit is what my grandma eats, but only because of her dodgy false dentures and her constipation.'

Jumping down from the back of the lorry they grabbed the wheelbarrows that had been left at the side of the house by Charlie Luft. They were surprised that he wasn't there to greet them back. In the drawing room Lady Ashleigh was relieved to see the headlights of the lorry streak across the freshly mown lawn. An hour and ten minutes late, she could forgive them glad that they were home safe. She poured herself another sherry. *'I am as parched as a hog's arse on a winter's day,'* she muttered to herself.

Pulling the heavy curtains together she switched on the lamp beside the piano before heading for the kitchen. In the hall the odours of a fresh baked apple pie filled the ground floor. Pushing open the kitchen door she found Janet Simpson, the house busy at the gas stove. 'They're home Janet.'

'I know m'lady, I heard the familiar laughter. Those buggers would laugh to a pudding crawl.'

Olivia Ashleigh tapped on a water pipe which disappeared under the kitchen floor to the cellar below. Several seconds later she received a corresponding signal. Janet passed over a wickerwork basket which was put in dumbwaiter and sent down.

A minute later the sample bottles arrived having been hoisted back up.

Olivia caressed the neck of the bottle as Janet took the custard off the heat.

'These look perfect,' she exclaimed she read the labels. A connoisseur of wine, she recognised a quality Cabernet Sauvignon. Cradling the bottle as though it were a new born baby she danced around the kitchen arriving at the drawer containing the corkscrew.

Plunging deep, she twisted, yanked and pulled hard. After a few tugs the belligerent cork relented. The more resistance that the cork gave the better the wine. Then with a loud plop it came away from the neck of the bottle.

'Let it breathe Olivia,' she murmured to herself as Janet handed her a glass.

'It's a good colour m'lady, a deep red and you can smell the fruit.'

Olivia Ashleigh poured into two glasses. 'Sheer exquisite luxury,' she purred believing that it had breathed long enough.

Sipping slowly, they felt the velvety liquid slosh its way down the back of their throats. First came the hint of smooth blackcurrant closely followed by a woody aging where the wine had been stored in wooden barrels at the vineyard. With a quick tap on the pipes they sent down the unopened bottle. It would be added to the stock in the cellar.

Taking a jug of pouring cream from the fridge Olivia Ashleigh placed it beside the pitcher of hot custard and apple pie. She made sure that there were sufficient bowls and spoons. Checking the kitchen clock they had been back half an hour and any minute now the lorry would have been unloaded, the wine stored and the cellar door locked. She watched as Janet finished her wine.

'That slipped down a treat m'lady, the boys did well.' Olivia agreed. They turned to look as the hinges of the pantry door creaked badly in need of some fresh oil. The last up was Robert Perry who bolted the door. He joined his fellow travellers at the old oak kitchen table.

'Am I glad to see you three,' she said, as Janet cut them generous portions of the pie. 'You were beginning to make my insides do somersaults. I thought that you had come to a sticky end.'

Tommy looked up from his plate. 'We nearly did your ladyship,' he sniffed catching the influence of cinnamon, 'there was a new face on the customs line at the Dover check-in. His uniform was pressed razor sharp as though he'd just come from the training academy.'

'He was as keen as Colman's Mustard.' Added Samuel as he watched Janet heap his plate with pie. 'And he had a beak that would have made Concorde envious. Luck would have it the car in front of ours was occupied by a couple of foreign looking blokes, real dodgy characters they were and up close they looked like they'd been in a hit and run accident. They were that ugly that the sniffer dog was more interested in them rather than us.'

Tommy continued. 'Having cocked its leg against their rear tyre the dog must have caught a whiff of something suspicious. It did a double circuit of their car before launching itself at the passenger. Poor bugger almost turned white with fright. The Hounds of the Baskervilles had nothing on the mutt. Trying to restrain the dog we got waved on through.'

Olivia smiled passing the jug of cream. 'Had they been in an accident?'

Robert grinned. 'No. What Samuel meant your ladyship, is that they were both wearing turbans!'

'Oh, I see,' she replied. She poured wine into their glassed. 'Turbans as opposed to bandages. When my late husband Lawrence was the British High Commissioner in India he could identify the different tribes by the way in which they wore their headdress or how it was patterned. Afternoon teas were always such colourful affairs.'

Tommy passed the cream to Samuel. *'Best take some before she puts the jug back in the fridge!'* Robert frowned suggesting that they stop being impolite. With a flick of his head he indicated that time was marching on and that Annie would be waiting under the clock.

'So how much did you manage to secure?' Olivia Ashleigh asked.

'A gross with a dozen bottles in each box m'lady.' Replied Robert.

Olivia Ashleigh saw Janet's jaw drop open. 'How on earth did you manage to acquire a hundred and forty four boxes?' she asked.

'End of season sale m'lady or least I think that's what it was,' Samuel replied. He rolled the pie to the side of his mouth to speak. 'One of the porters at the distillery took me to a shed out back where he showed me a stack of boxes. He said it was one of their best wines, but they needed to shift it quick.'

Olivia Ashleigh was intrigued. Samuel continued.

'I'm not that good at the lingo m'lady, but he said it was something like *'stock de fin de saison, pour un bon prix'* or something like that. He said we could have it dirt cheap as long as we had the cash. We bought the lot.'

Lady Olivia Ashleigh moved away from the cooker and sat herself down at the table. 'What he said dear Samuel was that the wine was the end of season stock and available at a good price.'

'Oh, I thought *bon prix* meant it was a top grape.' Robert and Tommy said nothing.

'So how much did you pay in total?' she asked.

Samuel was on a roll as he wiped the custard from his lips. 'As we agreed m'lady five hundred euros. You said to get a middle of the road red wine with a decent label, so we did. Did you see the image of the chateau on the label, it looks real posh.'

Olivia Ashleigh did the sums quickly in her head. Twelve dozen boxes, each containing twelve bottles with a retail value of around ten to twelve pounds would fetch between seventeen to twenty thousand pounds. She looked at the tree young men sat around her kitchen table. They had secured the lot for just under five hundred pounds allowing for the exchange rate.

'And this man at the vineyard, did he give you bill of sale?' she asked.

'No,' replied Samuel, 'I did think that was a bit odd. One minute old Henri was there showing me the wine, then next like Houdini he'd disappeared and done a runner with our five hundred. We loaded the lorry and did the same.'

'This Henri,' she asked curiously. 'I take it that he did work at the vineyard?'

Samuel grinned and shrugged his shoulders. 'Well he looked French. He spoke the lingo okay and he was wearing an auction house jacket. I took it that he was legit and above board m'lady.'

Olivia Ashleigh put her head in her hands and slowly, very slowly she began to laugh. When she pulled her hands away from her face, her eyes were damp and full of exuberance.

'My guess is that Henri was a scam artist, a confidence trickster and that he was never an employee of the wine auction or any member of the chateau distillery, By the grace of St Christopher you have not only acquired a very good quality wine at an extraordinary ridiculous price, but you've returned safely to England and dodged customs.' She moved to the end of the table. 'There is no bill of sale so the authorities will have no record of your ever being there. Unless somebody has the registration of the lorry this trip never took place.' She raised her glass. 'You did good boys, real good!'

Samuel looked at Tommy then Robert. 'What if we'd been stopped at customs with a load of good stuff and no bill of sale, we'd be banged up in some French pokey by now.'

Tommy agreed. 'We would have been up the Wensum without a paddle that's for sure.'

Janet breathed in deep making the three of them turn her way. 'Well good fortune smiled down on you this time and you got away with it, so stop your bleating. Who wants more pie?'

The air in the kitchen was thick with a mix of relief, bewilderment and astonishment.

Many of the villagers believed that since the death of her husband, Olivia Ashleigh had turned eccentric and perhaps a little daffy, but she was an astute business woman and nothing like stupid. The thoughts inside her head were moving faster than the winning greyhound at the Yarmouth dog track on a Monday night. 'Did use your father's lorry Samuel for the trip?' she asked.

Samuel looked up from his extra helping of pie. 'Yes m'lady. Although we switched plates before we left. We used the registration of a tractor down at old Horace Butler's farm. I'll change the plates over before he uses it next.'

Lady Ashleigh laughed admiring their pluck. Not only brave, they were devious and smart.

'My goodness that should confuse the police if they begin making enquiries. And the lorry, it's not sign written?'

Tommy responded first. 'No m'lady, Samuel's dad don't spend good brass unless he has too. I told Mister Byrne that I had to pick up some spares for my horse drawn carriage that I'm doing up. He thinks that the three of us went to Southend and stayed overnight.'

Olivia Ashleigh tapped the edge of the table thinking. 'The mileage might be the only drawback. Would he notice?' she asked.

Samuel shook his head quite adamantly. 'I doubt it. The only thing that my old man ever notices is if his stock is putting on weight. We could drive to Scotland and back and he'd be none the wiser.'

The lady of the house looked at her empty wine glass. They could never go back not least to the same wine distillery at Luberon or any other distributor in the region. Future trips would need to be planned. It was all a matter of staying one step ahead of the French authorities. She was still thinking when another thought popped into her head.

'And when you drove back through the village did anybody see you enter Willow Beck?'

Robert replied. 'Only old Bob Crutch, but I wouldn't worry about him none m'lady. Bob's always been a bit shell-shocked ever since my uncle ran his tractor over that unexploded bomb. Happened that old Bob was out ferreting at the time and he had his hand down a rabbit hole nearby. The blast clean killed the rabbits watching and sent the old boy slightly deaf, plus a touch gaga.'

Samuel circled a finger at the side of his head to indicate as such. 'Not that deaf m'lady that old Bob don't recognise some sounds, only you wanna be around the village and see him duck when a car goes past with the exhaust backfiring.' Janet was the first to join in the laughter.

When the laughter stopped Olivia Ashleigh offered the cream around again. 'I remember that unfortunate incident which nearly killed your poor uncle. I went to visit him at the hospital. He looked like an Egyptian mummy bandaged from head to foot and Bob Crutch never heard a word I said when I stopped at the end of his bed.'

'My dad weren't too pleased about the tractor neither m'lady. The insurance agreed that it was beyond repair, but it belonged to a neighbouring farm. That's how I got the idea about swapping over the number plates. He still complains that old tractor gave him lumbago.'

They left their empty crockery in the sink for Janet to wash thanking her for the apple pie. Making sure of the normal terms with Olivia Ashleigh she added a bonus. She waited until they had left before she went below stairs to check on the latest consignment.

She checked the boxes in the cellar finding extra where besides the wine, they had acquired good quality brandy, doubling the resell value and adding extra to the profit margin. Olivia was proud of her young musketeers and the estate cellar was looking positively full again. Come the morning she send Janet into the village to get the word around to local publicans, hoteliers and restaurant owners that fresh stocks were now available.

Picking bottles at random to check for continuity she acknowledged that the trio had been lucky at Dover customs. Using a duster Olivia wiped clean the bottles that she had touched. Smuggling or contraband as she preferred to call it, was centuries old and ignoring the risk it was traditionally exciting. Looking around at the latest booty the bank manager would be pleased and once again she had managed to balance the estate finances.

Sorting the brandy from the wine she left double-checking the sturdy padlock before slipping the key down the cup of her brassiere. She was about to kill the light in the passage when a movement up ahead caught her attention. Peering through the gloom she thought she saw a shadow move through the door midway along the passage. Going through the door which hadn't been opened for some time the passage led to the vicarage nearby.

Olivia scoffed believing the shadow was probably the ghost of a dead clergyman as the passage had once been used as a secret escape during the reformation of Henry the Eighth. So far nobody had located the key. She felt a chill invade her bones as she shivered. The current vicar, one Victor Higginbottom was a lecherous old bugger who liked his regular tipple of sherry.

Ascending the flight of steps back up to the kitchen she remembered Charlie Luft telling her about rumours that he'd overheard whilst frequenting the pub in the village about the vicar, many concerning his odd nocturnal habits, his liking for alcohol rich fruit cake and his housekeeper.

A recent fitness fanatic, Higginbottom had gone on line and availed himself of an expensive rowing machine. Olivia Ashleigh had made it policy never to be alone or available when the vicar had come calling at her door. She would send Janet instead to speak to the reprehensible little man.

Engaging the large bolts top and bottom she secured the pantry door. It wasn't until she switched off the pantry light that she realised the kitchen was in virtual darkness except for a single low wattage bulb over the cooker hood.

Like in the cellar she saw something move only this time she was able to arm herself with a heavy metal colander.

'It's alright m'lady, it's only me…' Janet called out as she stepped into the light. Reaching for the light switch the cook illuminated the kitchen.

'Goodness gracious Janet,' exclaimed the lady of the house, 'you near scared me to death standing there in the dark. Whatever possessed you to do such a thing?'

'I am terribly sorry m'lady, I'd clean forgot that you down below. I thought that you had retired to the lounge or your bedroom.' Wedged between the stubby fingers of her right hand was a doorstep of a sandwich consisting primarily of cheese with pickles.

Olivia Ashleigh walked across to where Janet was stood flushing pink with embarrassment. She pointed at the cook's midriff.

'I see the temptation of midnight snacking hasn't improved. Perhaps I should contact the vicar and send you over to visit Victor Higginbottom. I am sure that he'd let you use his new rowing machine.'

Janet felt a cold shiver pass through her shoulders. She put the sandwich back down onto the plate on the worktop. 'I would rather run naked through Willow Beck m'lady. He makes my skin crawl when he comes visiting the house. Many a female in the congregation has complained about Victor Higginbottom and his persistent Sunday wandering hands syndrome.'

A smile suddenly appeared on Olivia Ashleigh's cheeks as she didn't want to be seen as the ogre. 'Maybe we need something to distract us both Janet. Other than the wine side-line, life around here can be a little boring. At times it was more interesting spying on Lawrence.'

Janet nodded, but her mind was on her being caught red-handed. She blamed her big bones on her parents as they had never thought of dieting. She envied her mistress who was not only beautiful, but slim and very feminine. Her lumps and bumps went in and out in all the right places even at forty five, whereas Janet's body had looked down at the scales and screamed.

'I miss the master,' she replied.

17

'You miss the midnight trysts you mean when you two and Charlie would sneak down to the kitchen.' Janet looked shocked that her mistress had known about the three of them getting together when she was in bed. 'Lawrence would come to bed stinking of port, raw onions and cheese.'

Janet lowered her head in shame.

'I know that if it hadn't been for you and Charlie, my husband would never have managed the stairs.' She picked up the plate on the side giving it to Janet before walked over to the fridge. 'Is there any of that bread left that you baked today. Waiting around for the young men to return has made me peckish.'

While Janet cut two slices for her mistress, Olivia left the kitchen going to the study. She came back with a decanter of port. 'If you can't beat them, join them!' She poured generous amounts into two tumblers.

'I always wondered how Lawrence got through so many bottles of port in a month.' She chinked glasses with Janet and toasted her late husband. Janet did the same.

'I have always wondered how his blood ran so thick when that misguided bullet shot him through the heart that fateful day. He should have righty leaked pure alcohol.'

Janet spluttered as the port caught the back of her throat. It needed Olivia Ashleigh to help slapping her back to relieve the constriction. 'I would like to think that the master died a very happy man m'lady.'

Olivia Ashleigh smiled hearing the owl outside hoot. She took it to mean that contrary to local superstition their luck was about to change.

Two for the Pot

Armed with pad and pen Janet waited patiently as Benjamin Chapple moved the bottles first to the left, then to the right of the bar display trying to decide how many he needed to order.

'What are you up too Benjamin?' she asked, the irritation lingering long enough in her tone to prompt a response.

'I'm almost there,' he replied passively. Janet looked up at the bar clock knowing that she had other calls to make. Flicking the end of the pen back and forth between her teeth she hinted that she was poised and ready to take his order.

Benjamin rubbed his chin thinking. He needed to place an order and be quick about it before his hesitancy was reflected in the price.

'I was just them shifting about, trying to make some extra space. I'm still undecided whether I can fit two bottles of brandy on the shelf or just the one.'

'Two,' Janet precipitated. She moved next to where he stood to move the bottle again. 'Although with a little adjustment here and there Benjamin there's be adequate room for three.'

The wily landlord scanned his eye over the shelf one more time. Maybe she was right and three would work. 'If we did make it three, how would that rest in my favour?' he asked, ever the opportunist.

Janet Simpson grinned. At last and they were almost there.

'This is the best cognac for miles around and our stock comes direct from a highly reputable supplier. Today's price would be thirty five pounds a bottle, thirty for two and twenty seven fifty for three.'

Doing the maths in his head Benjamin calculated that he would save over twenty pounds on taking the three. He was about to agree when Janet delivered the appetiser of her offer. 'Make it worth my while Benjamin and take four bottles, and you only pay a hundred!'

He could already envisage the return on bar sales recouping at least five times the cost of the four. Holding out his hand they shook on the deal.

'And Charlie, he'll deliver as usual later this evening?' He rang up a *No Sale* transaction on the bar till removing five, twenty pound notes.

Janet marked up her ledger. She pulled in the tip of her tongue that had been patiently sat at the side of her mouth. 'When have you ever known Charlie to pass up a drinking opportunity? I'll make sure that he parks around back and out of sight of any prying eyes.'

The landlord of the Angler's Arms lay the new crisp notes on the bar top for Janet to count.

'And this brandy is the real deal, a genuine brand?' he asked watching Janet hoist up her jumper where she had a money wallet strapped to her waist band.

'Direct from the vineyard yesterday and to your front door with no import tax to pay.'

Pulling down the hem of her jumper Benjamin wondered who in their right mind would ever attempt to rob Janet Simpson. Built for comfort not speed she was a formidable lady, although on a good night undeniably sexy.

Janet slipped the pad and pen into her pocket, gave Benjamin a wink of confidence then walked to the door. Her first sale had been a success. Standing behind the bar Benjamin Chapple watched her walk past the saloon window. He couldn't explain the feeling deep in his gut, but it was always there whenever Janet Simpson came to visit. It was still there when she left. Confident that he had secured a good deal he went backs to his thoughts of the two of them lying naked on some white sandy beach in the tropics.

Janet Simpson rubbed her hands together with glee. She was not only a good cook, she was a wry old devil when it came to selling. Charlie had often said that she had a shrewd mind for business. Inside the pub Benjamin was about to adjust the record on the previous night's takings by a hundred pounds when to his surprise Janet reappeared before the bar. Once again she had her order pad and pen out. 'Silly me, I almost forgot the wine and we an excellent red from the same vineyard, a steal at only twelve pounds a bottle.'

Before Benjamin Chapple could reply, Janet had her sales pitch already prepared.

'Think about it Benjamin, the customer would get little change from twenty pounds and you'd be eight pounds better off. You'd positively have the customers eating out of your hands for more, I guarantee you!'

Once again that nagging in his gut reappeared. He sensed another bargain and defeat. 'Do you have a best price?'

Janet paused, inhaled and like a seasoned sales rep she pondered. 'This particular brand retails for around twenty two, but to you I'll do it for twelve.'

'But that's what you said before.'

'Janet feigned innocence. 'Did I really... my what a silly ass I am. I should have said fourteen, but never mind twelve is still a good deal trust me. How many cases would you like?'

Checking that his wife Marge wasn't within listening range Benjamin leant over the bar top. *'Six,'* the order left his lips as a mere whisper. *'Although I don't have the ready cash to hand. 'I'll be going to the bank later and will have the money for when Charlie comes in this evening.'*

Janet marked up her book with six cases. 'Always a pleasure doing business with you Benjamin. Give my regards to Marge.' She left the pub having secured an order for just shy of a thousand pounds.

Feeling the morning breeze on her face Janet was glad to be out of the manor house kitchen. She happily waved at people that she recognised, but walking and not stopping for a chat was vital as the midnight sandwich, onions and port was still weighing heavily in her stomach. It had been almost two in the morning, having shared memories that they finally retired to bed. With a discreet belch of gas Janet contemplated the idea of a new diet regime.

Sensing that he had done well with the order Benjamin Chapple made himself an extra special creamed coffee. He was still rearranging the display bottles when he felt a presence nearby. Normally Marge wouldn't appear before ten.

Benjamin was looking forward to Charlie visiting later that evening to hear of his escapades as an old war veteran where he had served as an SOE operative. Loyal to the Lady Olivia Ashleigh, Benjamin knew that Charlie was also her friend. Although he had never asked, Charlie had strong hands, hands that could kill a man and make it look like a genuine accident.

He was still lost in his thoughts when Marge suddenly appeared from the kitchen at the rear of the pub. She was approaching with a disapproving tut-tut accompanied by a shaking of her head. She immediately noticed that the bottles on the display had been moved around.

'What have you been up too?' she asked, the suspicion in her expression narrowing the gap between her eyelids. She put a tin of polish and a duster beneath the bar top.

'Nothing that would really interest you Marge,' Benjamin replied, sensing that it was safer not to make eye contact. 'I was just rearranging some of the stock and giving them a wipe down before we open for trade at lunchtime. A good landlord should always present his bottles at their very best. You never know who could walk in through the door!'

Marge sniffed not believing a word of what her husband said. Having endured their marriage for longer than she cared to remember, it had been even longer since they'd cuddled or kissed. As sharp as a new pin she rarely missed a trick especially where it concerned her husband.

'And what exactly did that infernal woman want here this early in the morning. As soon as my back is turned, she slips in through the front door like some lost, wheezing eel armed with her pad and pen wheeling and dealing her wares. Have you two lumps of lard got a thing going between you?'

Marge sniffed the air once again checking that the atmosphere in the bar area was the right ambience before they opened the doors officially.

'I take it that you're referring to Janet Simpson,' Benjamin replied indignantly. 'Don't be daft Marge and you know that I've only ever had eyes for you. I have my standards.' He reached under the bar for a box of peanuts.

Marge scoffed back. Standards indeed. She only had to look at his waistline to see how standards had slipped. With the silence increasing the tension Benjamin continued, feeling that he ought.

'She popped in to discuss the catering for the forthcoming garden party at the vicarage. We don't want to duplicate anything. That would affect our profit margin.' Unable to reach his handkerchief Benjamin sneezed a sure sign and habit when he was lying.

'If you're buying cheap, shoddy liquor on the side and not from the brewery as per our agreement there will be hell to pay Benjamin Chapple, mark my words!'

A regular church attendee Marge believed that the good lord would watch over his flock with a keen and appreciative eye. She left to check that the snook was meticulously clean in case Victor Higginbottom called in needing a small sherry.

A believer of the faith, Marge was banking upon her reverence with the vicar being rewarded in heaven one day unlike that of her conniving, scheming double-dealing husband. Returning from the snook she eyed him suspiciously.

'One day Benjamin Chapple the good lord will summon you to his throne, where he will cast down apt punishment for your sins.'

He watched as she went to check on the small dining area. He mumbled to himself having finished loading the peanut tree. *Saints and sins indeed. The bloody devil himself would go on holiday if she turned up.'*

Although a little plump in certain areas, although nicely proportioned as far as he was concerned he was still thinking about Janet Simpson. Since their days at school he'd always had a soft spot for the cook.

'What was that you muttered?' asked Marge, looming towards the bar like an uninvited spirit.

'Nothing dear,' he sheepishly replied, 'I was just thinking out aloud and how this place could do with a fresh lick of paint. Perhaps also removing some of the old tack and pictures.'

Marge was waiting for the sneeze, but it didn't materialise.

'The last time this pub was decorated was when my dear mother sadly passed from this life and into the next. If you recall we held the wake here.'

Benjamin Chapple knew it was dangerous to grin. It had been worth the cost of the decoration to have the wake. He looked at his wife wishing he could arrange another.

Peering in through the restaurant window Janet managed to catch the attention of the Italian as he busied himself setting out the tables for the lunchtime trade. As far back as she could remember there had always been a hotel in Willow Beck although the restaurant area had changed hands many times down the years. Nowadays however *The Dumbleton Keep* was firmly on the map and a sought out place to dine. During the last decade, the hotel owners had successfully introduced an Italian cuisine bringing in Antonio Vincenzi as the manager.

Reluctantly the Italian smiled and waved back at the woman outside. Receiving a visit from Janet Simpson was like the head of the Mafioso coming for lunch. Not only insistent with her offers the big lady had an even bigger bosom that could not be ignored. Smiling graciously he unlocked the door and let her in. Paying for protection was probably much easier than dealing with the cook from the estate house.

Stepping aside Antonio made a point of displaying the gold ring on his left hand. Despite it being there the woman insisted upon hugging, crushing and kissing him on both cheeks. Unable to resist her advance he gasped for air in-between breaths, feeling her shudder as sensual thoughts pulsated through her body. Fighting to be released the restaurant manager could hear again the warning given by his late mother telling him to be wary of women like Janet Simpson.

'Ciao Antonio,' she greeted releasing him from her embrace, 'and how is my favourite little Italian?'

As far as Antonio knew he was the only Italian for miles around. When the order pad and pen appeared he felt his resolve go into hiding. The visit he accepted was going to cost him dearly.

*****

Olivia Ashleigh looked at the shadow which had been cast by the arm on the sundial.

'Janet will be back soon. I hope she's had a successful morning.'

Charlie Luft who was bent down on his knees looked up from his digging in autumn dahlias. 'She has a canny streak that others can't resist.' He gently set aside a big fat juicy earthworm that had been dug up by accident. Plunging his finger into the soil he made sure that the worm found the hole. 'I expect that I'll be going out for my usual tipple this evening?'

With the shooting rifle safely hanging over the crook of her arm she nodded back responsively. 'Only if you feel up to it Charlie. A lot depends on Janet and how many orders we've secured today.'

He wiped the sweat from his brow with the back of his hand.

'Right you are m'lady.'

He hoped that Janet had done well. Driving the old black Rolls Royce Phantom around the village was a mission that he enjoyed. He would deliver the orders from the boot making the Angler's Arms his last call. At one time the luxurious model had been his late master's pride and joy, but Olivia had always considered the Rolls too ostentatious and she preferred to be seen using the land rover instead.

Whatever time Charlie got back from his deliveries Janet would be waiting to ensure that he had a doorstep sandwich waiting for him. Like her, he liked cheese and pickled onions, the bigger the better.

Watching the lady of the house and the gardener talking Barbara Jenkins stood out of sight behind the curtain at the first floor window. Aunt to Tommy Jenkins she had recently taken the vacant position of house maid. Although she couldn't quite hear what they were saying they did seem to have a familiarity about them that she had not found working in other houses.

Not long in service at the manor house, Barbara had been grateful to Janet putting in a good word with her ladyship, an employer who she found to be fair and very friendly. Olivia Ashleigh she deemed was always smiling as she walked about the house although more often than not with a glass of red wine in her hand.

Barbara enjoyed her position at the big house and working with Janet, a friend of her mothers. The money was good and it made a pleasant change from the smell of stale beer plus having to endure the lewd jokes passed around between the regulars at the Anglers Arms. Of course there were none when Marge, the landlady was present.

Pushing the duster along the top of the walnut dresser Barbara was careful not to disturb any of the framed photographs or other precious mementoes. One photograph in particular fascinated her. It was of Lord and Lady Ashleigh taking afternoon tea in the grounds of some posh place. Barbara thought it looked like India.

Everything about the photograph looked grand, the tall white painted cane cushioned chairs and the pair of them surrounded by luscious leafy green palms. At the side of the tiled courtyard uniformed servants waited discreetly ready to serve their need at a moment's notice.

Lightly brushing over the other ornaments made Barbara let her imagination run riot believing that she was there with them in the photograph. With a flick of her forefinger and thumb she could call upon a servant and have coffee delivered. India she scoffed was a far cry from the reality of Willow Beck and the only elephant that Barbara had ever seen had been at the zoo as a young child.

Barbara was still dusting when she suddenly gasped clutching her chest. 'What on earth was that about?' She went to the window to check. Never keen to hear gunfire she always considered a volley of shots to signify death. It surprised her to see Lady Ashleigh holding the hunting rifle to her shoulder. On the far wall by the vegetable patch lay a dead pheasant, the single shot perfectly executed. Ducking quickly from sight behind the curtains once again Barbara felt her heart beating strong.

In the aftermath of Lord Ashleigh's inexplicable death the verdict had left doubt surrounding the incident although the rumours throughout the village had remained divided. Killed by a single gunshot to the heart allegedly meant for a passing deer the shooter had never been found. Some in the village believed that the lord of the manor house had been murdered, whereas others especially in the corridors of power in Whitehall were still in debate, wondering if his death was in some way related to his time spent in India.

Looking from behind the curtain Barbara took another peek.

As you would expect, the police had carried out a thorough investigation, although neither rifle nor shooter had been found to suggest foul play. The coroner, Jeremy Makepeace had no option, but to record a verdict of death by misadventure. Barbara looked over to where the pheasant was lying in full glare of the sun, she gulped. Was it possible, she wondered?

Back in time for coffee before lunch needed to be prepared Janet found Olivia Ashleigh and Charlie Luft in the vegetable garden at the rear of the house.

Hearing Janet's familiar voice Barbara was tempted back to the window again. Between them there followed a lot of counting on fingers and Janet referring to a small pocket book. Maybe, she thought they were planning another garden party. A social highlight on the village calendar where the afternoon one summer's weekend was loaded with delicious cakes and mixed game pie. Nobody in their right mind ever refused an invite.

Barbara had been to one afternoon party and she was looking forward to being invited back again to another. Best of all was the opportunity to exchange gossip. She was still thinking about sampling another slice of game pie when another shot rang out from the garden below.

'That's two today,' Olivia Ashleigh remarked succinctly, 'if I can bag us another before sunset, we'll have enough for a fair sized pie.' She reloaded the rifle, leaving it cocked over the crook of her arm. 'You did very well this morning and Charlie is looking forward to going out this evening.'

'It was a good morning m'lady and better than expected,' Janet responded. 'Benjamin Chapple at the Angler's Arms knows a good bargain when he sees one and the little Italian, Antonio Vincenzi, he never refuses an offer. All-in-all we sold five bottles of brandy and ten cases of wine.'

Olivia Ashleigh smiled enthusiastically. 'I think that with lunch today we should celebrate the occasion with a nice bottle of red.' Barbara wondered what all the congratulatory back slapping was about.

'Do you think you can manage this evening or will you need a hand Charlie?' Olivia Ashleigh asked of the man still kneeling.

'No, I'll be okay m'lady, it's nothing that I've not handled before.' He grinned looking up at Janet. 'Although, I might be back later than normal.'

With his keen eye Charlie had spotted the curtain twitch at the first floor bedroom. Like any good spy his head had barely moved, only his eyes.

'Mrs Jenkins is taking a keen interest in us from the bedroom window.' He yanked up a bunch of freshly grown carrots from the ground cleanly slicing through the vegetable with a single stroke of his gardening knife severing the green from the orange storks. Barbara Jenkins quickly ducked away from the window, turned and ran to the door wanting to be in another room should they come looking for her.

Olivia Ashleigh saw the curtain twitch. 'I don't think we need worry ourselves too much about Mrs Jenkins. I saw her watching us. I think shooting the two pheasants might serve as a warning and besides we're too far away to be overheard.' She looked at Janet. 'However, in the circumstances perhaps it might be prudent to keep a close eye on our housemaid. At least until we have got rid of the stock in the cellar.'

The trio laughed knowing that with a couple of lunchtime wines inside her stomach Barbara Jenkins would lose control of her tongue and freely she would tell them everyone's business in the village. Charlie picked another bunch of carrots handing them over to Janet.

'Coffee first before lunch,' Olivia Ashleigh suggested, 'and let us invite Barbara along as well. It'll give her time to ponder over whether we saw her watching us.'

Taken During Exercise

There was no reply at the front door so David Gambitt, the Church Verger for St Ridley's went around back of the vicarage where generally the kitchen door was nearly always left unlocked.

Systematically making his way through the downstairs rooms he arrived at the study hoping to find the vicar inside as David was keen to hurry Victor Higginbottom along. The vicar was already late for morning service.

Pushing open the door the verger was immediately confronted with a vision that he did not expect to see. Rubbing the shock from his eyes he hoped that when he took his hands away the scene would be different again. It was still the same. David Gambitt wondered who to call first, another witness, the bishop, the police or an ambulance.

Lying askew with his head awkwardly pressed flat against the mesh guard of the rowing machine was the vicar. His outstretched legs either side of the centre bar had stopped twitching five minutes before David Gambitt arrived and from the blank stare on Victor Higginbottom's face it was quite evident that he was dead. With his tongue hanging limply to the side of the mouth the vicar or his spirit was on its way to meet his maker.

David Gambitt stepped into the room. The closer he went to the dead man he could see the vicars lycra shorts which were bunched down over his knees. Knelt down and patting the vicars hand was the housekeeper Martha Matthews. David tried hard not to focus his attention on her naked bleached white buttocks that resembled the rear end of a Hereford cow.

Suddenly aware that they were not alone Martha screamed and let go of Higginbottom's hand. In a flurry of embarrassment and confusion she fumbled with her bloomers realising that the front of her blouse was also open.

'*Martha,*' the verger cried disdainfully, his eyes glued to her bust and bum, '*what have you done to Victor?*'

Moving quickly behind the study desk where it offered protection Martha began pulling herself together. With her out of the way David Gambitt looked again. He couldn't fail, but to notice the vicar's proud erection. It seemed to be pointing up the celestial staircase to heaven.

Reassembled Martha saw the verger looking. Stepping away from the desk she took a yellow duster from her skirt pocket dropping it gently over the vicar's manhood. David grinned, now it looked like a geometric pyramid from ancient Egypt. Fighting back tears of anguish Martha sighed wanting a moment to gather her thoughts and explain. David checked the time with his watch the church service was due to begin in five minutes.

'You must believe me Mr Gambitt, I innocently came looking for the vicar to give him his breakfast. I was trying to revive him when you walked in.'

David Gambitt noticed that the frilly hem of her bloomers was peeping below her skirt, she was as sexy dressed as undressed. He felt his heart racing just looking. Martha sensed that the silence meant she needed to expand her account and innocence.

'All week long, I had been telling the vicar how dangerous it was to use the machine so vigorously, but he would insist on going as fast as possible. Back and forth, back and forth first thing in the morning and last thing at night. He told me that it helped him unwind.'

Checking the carotid artery the verger traced the vicar's metal cross and chain which he wore whatever the occasion. One end was entangled in the mechanics of the machine, the other wrapped tight around the vicar's neck. David Gambitt looked up at Martha. 'He must have been going at a fast pace and the chain throttled him. As the police tell us speed kills!'

On the coffee table next to the piano was an untouched assortment of breakfast fruit, toast and black coffee. David Gambitt pointed at the bottom of Martha's skirt. 'You're still hanging proud my dear.'

Martha readjusted her bloomers protecting her modesty. 'It's this damn cheap elastic that they use nowadays,' she heaved up the offending underwear until it was no longer on show. 'Nothing ever seems to stay up for long these days.' Looking at the vicar, David Gambitt thought differently.

Ignoring the look of acceptance on the dead man's face, it looked very much as though the vicar's final prayers had been answered in more ways than one. Having feasted his last moments on Martha's chest he had died a happy man. The verger watched curiously as Martha began searching the floor looking for something that she had lost. Gambitt asked if he could help.

'I'm a button missing from my blouse.' They looked, but it was nowhere to be found. 'I had to loosen the blouse, so that I could begin mouth-to-mouth resuscitation.'

Replacing a loose strand of hair that had come away from her headband, Martha was finding being in the same room as the dead vicar upsetting. She sat herself down on the edge of the weights bench.

'There is no point in distressing yourself Martha.' Said David. 'I'll simply tell the bishop and the police that I found you trying to revive the vicar.'

Of course the truth would never really be known not unless Martha confessed hers sins. Placing a comforting hand on her shoulder the verger saw an opportunity arising from the ashes of a tragedy. Walking through the thoughts flashing through his mind, he was sorting the chain of events.

Martha had arrived with the breakfast, whereupon the vicar had demanded sex. A torrid session had ensued and by an odd quirk of fate, in the heat of a passionate embrace the vicar had become over excited throwing his head back, thus making the cross fly back beyond his head landing amongst the mechanics of the rowing machine.

Unaware of his sudden predicament Martha was beyond help herself believing that his sudden holding of her buttocks, the gasps, moaning and groaning, along with the intermittent breathing was because Victor

Higginbottom was reaching the peak of no return. Being throttled at one end and exercised hard the other the vicar was in no fit state to repel her advances. Looking down at Martha, Gambitt saw only a lonely individual, a frightened woman who needed an ally. She saw the verger looking down at her breasts. She quickly folded her arms across her chest.

'I don't think that helps the situation Mr Gambitt,' she declared glaring up at him.

'I was just thinking about how we can protect the vicar's dignity. Once rigor mortis sets in, it could be several hours before gravity takes a reverse effect.'

Martha looked at the dead man thinking her duster would need washing. 'What are we going to do David,' she pleaded, 'I will be seen as a harlot, a trollope. God will never forgive me.'

David Gambitt knew the moment had arrived.

'Well Martha,' he grinned, 'the secret of what really took place can stay in this room or join the many other rumours in this village. The alternative is how I benefit personally from these unfortunate circumstances.'

Martha recognised that she was trapped and with no escape. Whatever the outcome she would not leave the study without her trusty yellow duster. She stared back at the verger, a bachelor for most of his life she recognised the expectant glint in David Gambitt's eye.

Sha had her own alternative. 'We could just pull up his exercise shorts and leave the room accepting that a tragic accident had occurred with my arriving too late to help.'

David Gambitt saw his chance of being with Martha slipping away.

Martha however was equally the opportunist. 'Perhaps once this unhappy episode is dealt with we could become friends David, very good close friends!' She snatched his hand placing it firmly over her left breast.

The verger felt his heart suddenly race. 'That was just what I had in mind. A latter day Adam and Eve and with the serpent gone dead and buried, the secret would be ours forever.'

Working together they yanked up the vicar's shorts having a little difficulty with his erection, but lycra had been designed to allow for maximum give and with a jiggle here and there it managed to keep everything discreetly hidden. Taking a step back to admire their efforts the yellow pyramid had become a mini Darth Vader.

Martha removed the breakfast tray taking it back to the kitchen where she added more water to the kettle and switched it on. Coffee helped her think. Alone in the hall David Gambitt called the police.

'What do we say about the vicar's predicament?' she asked as they sat drinking coffee together.

'The police are no fools, even Reg. I'll use my influence and say that the vicar went about his exercise vigorously, so much so that rumour had it he was one of those autocar-exotic partakers only this morning the excitement was just too much.'

39

'And the village bobby would believe that?'

David looked confident. 'Without a shadow of doubt. Reg Perry is very broadminded.'

Martha put a hand on his knee and gave it an encouraging squeeze. 'I can see that our friendship is going to be exciting, as well as adventurous.' He smiled back, the morning had certainly not started as he had expected, but all said and done it was ending well. He watched as Martha cut a generous slice of her home made fruit cake putting it on his plate.

'Did they say how long they would be, before they arrived?' she asked.

'It depends on how fast Reg Perry can cycle over here.' He broke away a corner of his cake. 'Don't worry Martha we're already home and dry on this matter. Reg values his quiet time on a Sunday so he'll be keen on putting this matter to bed as quickly as possible. He'll probably have a roast waiting when he gets back home.'

Martha could feel the tension ebbing from her body. She was enjoying her coffee when a sudden rapping on the kitchen made her scream. David Gambitt almost chocked on the cake that had become lodged in his throat. She slapped his back hard as she stood the elastic of her bloomers giving way once again. After several seconds of coughing and watery eyes she was relieved to see that he was okay.

'You should be more careful. How would I explain two deaths in one morning to the police!' she turned to see that the person knocking was none other than Percy the vicarage gardener. He was very excited and pointing in the direction of the study.

40

'*The vicar,*' he cried out, '*he's having difficulty with his machine!*'

Martha invited him in, but knowing that his boots were muddy he only ventured as far as the kitchen door. 'Is he dead?' Percy asked, surprised to see them calmly taking coffee and cake.

'I'm afraid so,' replied the verger, 'a regrettable accident whilst taking morning exercise. Reg Perry is on his way.'

Percy removed his cloth cap lowering his head respectfully.

'It was bound to happen sooner or later. I'd see him prancing about, real peculiar it was. Why only last spring I see him in his study dressed as the devil.'

Martha kept her eyes low so that neither man could see. She vividly remembered the morning having dressed as an angel. It was a game that they both liked to play. *Opposites* the vicar had called it. The game was designed to see which was the most powerful of the elements, although it always ended with sex.

David Gambitt asked Percy to go the church and explain to the parishioners who were probably still gathering that there would be no morning service nor evensong. An official notification would be pinned to the door of the church that afternoon explaining why.

'Was there a large congregation today?' Martha asked, after Percy had left.

'Quite an expectant audience. Strangely enough much better than of late.' He paused for thought. 'It's like they knew that something unusual would happen today and that's why they came.'

Martha excused herself wanting to change her underwear before Constable Perry arrived. She had never liked nor indeed trusted the policeman, but it was important that he didn't see anything remotely suspicious.

Ten minutes after receiving the call Reg Perry parked his bike against the vicarage porch and rang the doorbell. Removing his ankle clips he slipped them into his tunic pocket. Martha was there to open the door.

'Now then,' he began, clearly agitated having been called away from his allotment, 'what's with this garbled message that I received from the station, something about Victor hanging himself?'

Appearing at her side for support David Gambitt took charge escorting Reg through to the study with Martha following close behind. They watched as the policeman did several circuits of the rowing machine, checking the deceased from different angles. Reg stopped every so often to record certain particulars in his notebook before resuming his examination. On top of the piano he noted the decanter of sherry and a half filled glass.

'Who exactly found the vicar like this?' he asked, pen poised.

'I did,' replied David, lifting up his hand. Reg told him to put it down as nobody else was present. David Gambitt turned surprised to find that Martha was no longer present.

Reg pointed down at the vicar's lycra shorts. *'So what have we here?'* he mused.

'Over excitement I'd say Reg.' replied Gambitt.

Reg nodded. 'I would say Victor Higginbottom has rowed the boat across the lake to fetch the sword for the last time, wouldn't you!' Habitually he licked the end of his pen, leaving a thin blue line down the centre of his tongue. Kneeling beside the vicar he prodded the upper arm only to find that was completely stiff. 'Was he like that when you found him?' he asked, looking up at the verger.

'Do you mean dead or erect?' David Gambitt responded.

Reg grinned. 'Both, I'm not fussed which came first although it'll save time knowing which so that I can record both answers simultaneously.'

David Gambitt recognised the importance of saving time hearing the echo of voices as people were leaving the church nearby. 'Yes, on both counts,' he replied, 'and obviously something aroused Darth Vader.'

'Autoerotic asphyxiation,' Reg mumbled, 'it rarely fails to excite!' He noticed that the verger looked impressed by his quick deduction. 'Compression of the neck inducing partial asphyxiation to heighten sexual pleasure, only on this occasion the vicar must have already been in heaven when his chain got caught in the mechanism of the rowing machine.'

From his tunic pocket he produced a small digital camera from his tunic pocket. He took several photographs.

'That should keep the Inspector happy.' He said putting the camera away.

'What's your verdict Reg?' Gambitt asked wondering what had happened to Martha.

'I can't really see anything abnormal with this man's death David, other than the silly bugger chocked himself setting the speed control on fast. I'll make out my report and pass it along the line. The Coroner is very busy at the moment and will probably agree with my report.'

Sniffing hard he detected the familiar odours of roast beef cooking in the oven. Reg checked the time making it a few minutes after eleven. Soon he'd be settling down to his own Sunday dinner. 'Does Martha still make fruit cake at the weekend?' he asked.

They went through to the kitchen where Martha had already boiled another kettle. Cutting the constable a slice of her best homemade fruit cake he took his place at the table.

'The vicar had an unfortunate accident,' the verger declared as Reg took his first bite. Martha smiled back weakly. Chewing on the cake which was good Reg reached for his notebook.

'And where was you Martha, when the vicar was exercising?' he asked.

'Upstairs making the vicar's bed and getting ready his bath. The vicar always took exercise before facing the congregation.'

Reg made a note of the reply. 'He should have used a bike like mine, much safer and easier to control. This will mean a new shepherd in Willow Beck.'

Accustomed to seeing dead bodies in all manner of poses and circumstances Jack Duggan the Funeral Director was not a man to judge. He discreetly asked his assistant to fetch some string.

'What use is string?' asked Martha somewhat puzzled.

'We'll need the string to tie it down,' Jack replied. 'It'll stay that way for at least another couple of hours!'

'Reminds me of a bloke I arrested once,' Reg responded. 'He'd overdosed on Viagra.'

'Oh...' replied Martha. 'Please be sure to comb his hair,' she asked of the funeral assistant. 'The vicar was very particular about always looking his best.'

Patting his tunic pocket Reg winked at David Gambitt. 'I've got all the hard evidence that I need and there's no denying what the old bugger was thinking when he popped his cogs.'

Martha huffed loudly and left for the kitchen to check on the beef roasting in the oven. 'I had best inform the bishop,' said David Gambitt as they heard the kitchen door close.

'Yes, he'll need to be told. I guess now wouldn't be the right time to take a statement.'

David Gambitt nodded back. 'Martha will come around soon Reg. She's a tough old bird and probably seen a lot worse in her time. Having served the vicar for a number of years I'm sure that she'll miss him though. I only hope the replacement isn't as eccentric.'

They watched as the corpse was lifted from the floor and carefully put in the black body bag, smiling when the string slipped its knot and the vicar refused to lie down. Reg Perry saw Percy watching through the study window. 'I had heard that Martha was as barren as a windswept field.'

David Gambitt shook his head avidly.

'You know the village Reg and rumours often have little foundation. Have you never seen the photographs of Martha when she was a young woman, why she would turn the head of many an admiring young man. Rumour had it that her late husband Joe found it difficult to keep up with Martha' insatiable appetite. Like the vicar he died with a smile on his face.'

'Are you suggesting that she killed poor Joe?' Reg asked his brow frowning.

'No. I was merely implying that our Martha is a real dark horse and that at one time with the stable door left unbolted no young stud in Willow Beck was safe.'

Standing in the framework of the kitchen door Martha watched as Jack Duggan and his assistant loaded the black bag into the back of the van. They had only reached the end of the vicarage drive when she saw John Steele, the Bishop walking towards the rear of the house.

'A sad occasion,' he declared greeting the verger and policeman. 'I trust dear Victor passed peacefully?'

David Gambitt was the first to respond. 'He died with a smile on his face your Grace. The lord will take care of his needs in heaven now.'

Bishop Steele looked skyward and crossed himself. 'And the parishioners, have they been told?' he asked.

'Yes, I sent word to cancel this morning's service. I wasn't sure about evensong.'

The bishop nodded back approvingly. 'A wise decision considering the unfortunate circumstances. Our prayers today will be with God and Victor.' The bishop caught a whiff of the beef cooking in the oven. He sniffed long and hard.

'And Mrs Matthews, has she been looked after?' he asked.

'In more ways than one,' replied David Gambitt, and the good lord in his infinite wisdom always cares for members of his flock.' Steele thanked them for their help in the matter as he walked towards the kitchen door.

'I will avail myself to dear Martha and stay for dinner. Together we can work out what is required now at St Ridley's vicarage.'

'He got here rather quick don't you think?' said Reg, noting the time of the bishops arrival. David Gambitt thought so too. Trumpington Salle where the bishop had his official residence was a good twenty five miles away.

'When I called his housekeeper she told me that Steele was out an about.'

Spinning the pedal of his bike to the correct position Reg was preparing to leave. 'God moves in mysterious ways even when it involves one of his own.'

David Gambitt agreed. He had banked on staying with Martha for Sunday lunch, but when he saw the kitchen door close he saw his chances of dinner and sex dwindling fast. Replacing his bicycle clips, Reg mounted the bike. 'Do you think he knew about Martha and the vicar?' he asked.

'I'm sure he does.' David Gambitt replied. 'John Steele and Victor Higginbottom go back a long way. They went to the same school. Were in the same scout troupe and both joined the religious college the same year. The rumour amongst religious circles was that John Steele was appointed Bishop because he knew somebody in Downing Street and that the select committee felt compelled to honour his appointment.' He watched as Martha cut John Steele a slice of her best home-made cake. He continued despite his frustration.

'I was never completely sure nor did I have any evidence, but there existed an underlying tremor of transgression whenever the bishop and vicar were together.'

Reg was interested as he steadied the bike with one foot the other on the pedal. 'You mean like a scam?'

'I was never sure.'

Reg scoffed. 'It wouldn't surprise me, nothing does these days. The police is the same. Officers scratch one another's back, whereas the only back I scratch belongs to my wife.' They took one last look back at the vicarage kitchen before heading for the gate. The grave stone which had been ordered by John Steele was a fitting tribute to Victor Higginbottom.

'Here lieth a true man of the lord,

Taken before his time,

Always upright

A man to whom his flock could depend.'

The rumours continued throughout Willow Beck fuelled no least by the passing of the vicar, but in time like ghosts some would disappear. The same could have been said for the vicar's rowing machine which mysteriously disappeared overnight, although David Gambitt suspected that the bishop was now the proud new owner.

Morning Coffee

Barbara Jenkins took her seat at the kitchen table nervously holding onto the handle of her coffee mug knowing that their eyes were watching her every move. Had they been aware of her watching them talking in the garden earlier, she couldn't be sure.

'I am terribly sorry if my shooting startled you,' Olivia Ashleigh introduced breaking the awkwardness of the silence, 'although I am surprised as I would have thought that a country girl such as yourself Barbara, would be used to such sounds.'

Barbara Jenkins smiled back trying not to blush. 'Normally m'lady I am, although for some reason today the shooting put my nerves on edge.' Charlie eyed her suspiciously. The housemaid's reaction normally meant guilt. On the side and ready to be cleaned lay the dead pheasants. 'In days gone past I'd go with my father and uncles on a shoot. They'd hunt mainly for game. Guns tend to scare me.'

Lady Ashleigh nodded looking at Charlie who she knew would be studying Barbara closely.

'The next time that I take my rifle out into the garden or the nearby wood, I'll be sure to tell you first so that you're aware that there could be the sound of gunfire on the estate.'

'Thank you m'lady.'

'So what do you know then Barbara,' piped up Janet, 'what's new about the village?'

Eager to change the subject Barbara was eager to please. 'I did hear the other day a snippet of gossip going about that Margaret Chapple might have a fancy man in her life.'

'Does she indeed,' Janet Simpson grinned back, 'now that is interesting. Somebody connected with the brewery perhaps?' She noticed the gossip had Olivia Ashleigh and Charlie Luft interested as well.

Barbara's eyes fluttered like the wings of a butterfly, her eyes full of surprise. 'I think it's true. Annie Crabshaw told me?'

'Ah…'said Janet. Coming from Annie, it has to be true!' Charlie thought Janet would have made an excellent SOE agent and that she had dangled just enough of the carrot for Barbara to nibble upon.

'Well,' Barbara continued, sensing that the more she told, the more she would be accepted into their inner circle, 'it would seem that Marge has been seeing the delivery driver every Tuesday night instead of going to bingo in the city and Annie Crabshaw cleans the pub when Marge has her lie down after the lunchtime trade. Every Tuesday morning Marge has her hair done and after her lie down she takes a long soak in a hot bath filling the tub with salts of peach. Rumour has it that her fancy man is Bert Tonks.'

'The drayman?' Janet asked. Barbara nodded.

Olivia Ashleigh pushed the biscuit barrel across to Barbara offering more chocolate ginger nut crunch. This snippet was certainly worth knowing and could favour their own endeavours. Any connection with the brewery could be very handy.

'And the publican, Mr Chapple is oblivious to this romantic liaison?' Olivia Ashleigh asked, taking a biscuit for herself.

Barbara pushed the remainder of the chocolate delight into her mouth. Chewing quickly and gulping hard she swallowed the melted mastication.

'According to Annie m'lady, Benjamin Chapple seems quite happy with the arrangement. My husband reckons that his interests are focused on the horse racing results where the odds are better.' Janet offered Barbara another biscuit to compensate for the last which she'd hardly tasted.

Charlie who had been listening and observing was saying nothing. He knew Bert Tonks, big muscly man and cheeky disposition. The drayman's wit would appeal to Marge. He too saw an opportunity in the affair.

'I had also heard,' prompted Janet pushing the conversation in a different direction to test Barbara's wealth of gossip, 'that when the undertakers removed the late Victor Higginbottom from his rectory they had trouble fitting him into the body bag. Do you know anything about that?'

Feeling the rush of hot blood race to her cheeks and chest, Barbara fanned herself. 'George Gadd, the mortuary attendant told me that they had to tie it down with string, only his thingy kept popping back up having slipped the knot.'

'Tying what down exactly?' asked Olivia Ashleigh looking at Charlie.

Tying an imaginary knot with her fingers to help demonstrate how Barbara Jenkins muttered what. 'You know m'lady, his thingy. George said it was like Saturn Five on the launch pad and waiting for lift off.' Olivia Ashleigh smiled back at her housekeeper. It had been a long time since she had seen a naked man.

'Did George say who else was at the rectory that morning?' asked Janet. She took another biscuit passing the barrel to Charlie, knowing that it would eventually end up with Barbara again.

'David Gambitt, Reg Perry and Martha Matthews the housekeeper. The Bishop, John Steele arrived as the undertakers were taking the poor vicar to the mortuary.'

'Reg Perry,' Janet echoed. She exhaled emphatically sat next to Barbara. 'I bet the constable could tell us a tale or two.'

Again Barbara was forthcoming. 'Reg is very discreet about his police work. He spends most of his time over the allotment preferring the quiet life to fast cars and the early morning drugs raids. The last time I spoke with Reg he told me that Willow Beck more or less runs itself.'

'So he's not very active then?' asked Olivia Ashleigh.

'Oh he stops the odd motorist m'lady, mainly the tourists passing through and the odd overzealous youth, but he says it's only to help balance his quota of convictions and keep his sergeant happy.' She dunked her biscuit in her coffee. 'He likes a tipple though does our Reg when he's not on duty.'

'Beer or spirits?' enquired Janet.

'No, wine mostly. His wife Emma reckons Reg considers himself to be a connoisseur when it comes to the old grape.'

'Does he indeed,' Janet smiled. She puffed up her cheeks resembling a hamster. 'Who would of thought of our village bobby as a wine expert?'

With three chocolate crunch biscuits already devoured and another on offer, the three of them were sure that the extra glucose intake would help Barbara remember more. She didn't disappoint.

'Reg was quite the tearaway when he was Roberts's age. My Sid said that quite often he would have to help Reg home from the pub three sheets to the wind. It wasn't until Reg crossed paths with Emma that he straightened himself out. Sid reckons it was Emma who made him join the police.'

Janet refilled Barbara's coffee mug, anticipating that the housemaid was on a roll.

'Did any of you hear the rumour going around about Reg and that a couple of years back he had been reprimanded for accepting illegal game birds out of season. Reg got off with a warning and ever since he's kept his nose clean and deep in his allotment where he can't come to the attention of the Divisional Superintendent.'

This was music to Olivia Ashleigh. The fact that the village constable had a slightly tarnished human resources record could prove an advantage. She herself had seen minor indiscretions being swept under the carpet in the diplomatic service. Such matters were hardly ever raised again unless to an individual's advantage. Smiling to herself she thought it was time that they were acquainted with Constable Perry. Looking at the dead birds an alibi on the side of the law could be a useful asset.

'You are a very useful mind of information Barbara,' said Lady Ashleigh, 'and your little anecdotes make our coffee breaks so much more absorbing. We must do this on a regular basis.'

A wide smile spread across Barbara's Jenkins face. 'Oh, I've many more m'lady where they came from.' She looked up at the kitchen clock realising that she still had Janet and Charlie's rooms to clean.

Olivia Ashleigh also noted the time. 'Wonderful, perhaps you'll keep them for another occasion Barbara.' The housemaid thanked them for coffee, made her excuses and left. Checking to see that she had indeed Charlie sat back down again.

'Back in the nineteen forties we would have said gossip and people like Barbara were a dangerous mix. She's like a busy bee wanting to pollinate the whole orchard.'

Olivia Ashleigh grinned agreeing. 'This particular bee, I think we can use though Charlie. She has a lot more to tell and keeping abreast of the village could prove advantageous to our little enterprise.' She pondered for a moment as she nibbled around the edge of a biscuit. 'When we were living at the embassy in India my husband would tell me, keep some secrets close and those that could be useful let slip. Soon the fish nearby will come closer to take the bait. Fish you see will nibble at what they cannot hear or smell, but curiosity is a fiendish hook.' She noticed the vacant look Janet's face. 'A penny for them?' she asked.

'I was just thinking m'lady how that toffee-nosed mare at the Anglers Arms could so easily topple from her high and mighty throne. At school Margaret Glenister walked from classroom to classroom with her nose stuck in the air and a tight cork stuck up her…' Charlie coughed quickly to prevent Janet from saying where.

'Maybe we need to find out a bit more about this Bert Tonks the drayman. Leverage can be a useful tool in negotiations.'

Charlie Luft grinned. 'You would have made a find SOE agent m'lady.'

Olivia Ashleigh found the compliment extremely gratifying. 'I would spend many summer's with my Aunt Bessie, a grand lady, spirited and so wise. She taught me a lot and the most important lesson how to use snippets of information to your advantage. We need to keep a close eye on Barbara, Reg Perry and the landlady, Margaret Chapple.' She put down her coffee mug. 'Maybe it's time that we looked at expanding our operation.'

'Like what m'lady?' Janet asked.

'I'm not entirely sure. I'll give it some thought this afternoon. Something however that will give us an edge over any competition.'

Charlie scoffed. 'Forgive me for asking m'lady, but what competition. We sell locally and there's nobody else abouts with our stock availability?'

'I was thinking of the supermarkets Charlie although we would need a way in.'

Charlie's weather beaten face creased into a grin. 'Planting up in the vegetable garden this morning I was having similar thoughts. We would need a diversion.'

'Like what exactly,' asked Janet who was always keen on any extra cash.

'Well for a start, we could spike a few bottles of their red.'

'Sabotage,' Janet muttered, 'whoa, hold on tonto that's serious time inside Charlie.'

Olivia Ashleigh breathed in deep. 'I like your thinking Charlie. It would need careful planning.'

Charlie turned back to Janet. 'How many publicans do you know who water down their beer or spirits to make them go a little further? We would only be making a few bottles bad that's all. Nothing drastic that would put anybody in hospital. After the first mouthful they would tip the rest down the sink as drain cleaner. In the meantime we seize the opportunity and grab a piece of the bigger action.'

Olivia Ashleigh nodded, Charlie had thought it through. 'Go on,' she encouraged, 'tell us some more.'

Knowing that he already had his ladyship's backing Charlie explained. 'It's easy Janet. We visit a supermarket and buy two bottles of their best red then we come back here. Using a syringe we extract some of the wine up through the cork, replacing the deficit with a poor grade vinegar. I can seal the bottle using melted wax and nobody is any the wiser. Word will soon get around that the supermarket have invested in a bad batch of wine. That's when we arrive and offer a good quality product. The supermarket manager takes in on a trial basis and before you know it, we're supplying a regular order and we're quid's in, so is the supermarket.'

'And you can guarantee this?' Janet asked.

'Ninety nine, point nine percent. Wine connoisseurs take their drinking seriously. They're the first to complain and before you know it, their comments have been escalated up the line from shop staff to the store manager, head office, the buyer and eventually the vineyard. We can help avert a confidence crisis and being local we are the solution to a serious problem.'

Janet however needed convincing. 'And how do we meet with demand. We struck lucky Charlie with the last batch that they boys brought back. They'll not find another imposter at every vineyard and two dodgy foreigners at the customs shed.'

Olivia Ashleigh palmed her hands up and down above the table top like a fluttering butterfly.

'We can easily overcome the stock issue. What do you think about imported cheese, a good quality cheese?'

Janet immediately was thinking of her late night snacking of cheese and onion sandwiches. 'It's a good idea m'lady.'

'Think of it as sort of coup Janet. If we can get into a supermarket with our wine, why not cheese. I am sure that on our travels we can invest in a good product or two. Willow Beck Manor has throughout the centuries always managed successfully to find solutions to overcome obstacles. We will seize the initiative and go forth in our entrepreneurial attack on the supermarkets.' She fisted the air triumphantly sensing the spirit of the contest ahead. Charlie did the same and moments later Janet joined them.

'We will overcome, that's our mission statement.'

'A mission statement m'lady, what's that?' Janet asked.

'We take the fight to the battlefields and like NASA we blast off, we discover new territory and return triumphant and all the richer.'

The last bit Janet did like although she did foresee a problem.

'Our present customers don't keep records about what they buy from us and we don't charge value added tax or import duty. How would a supermarket manager include our stock without somebody further up the chain of command smelling a rat?'

Olivia Ashleigh encouragingly patted Janet's arm.

'Don't worry yourself with the trivial details. I already have an idea brewing inside my head and remember that my Aunt Bessie taught me how to be very resourceful.'

Charlie Luft thumbed up at the troubled cook. 'Where there's a will, there will always be a way found to skin a wily old fox.'

The Evening Run

Charlie parked the black Rolls Royce alongside the rear door of the pub before going inside to find Benjamin Chapple. He was ever watchful for the suspicious Marge who had a knack of appearing when she wasn't wanted. In the boot he had the landlord's wine and brandy order.

He found Benjamin pulling a pint for one of the local farmers, Jack Pulmer who was sat in the public bar digging out the ash from his pipe. Charlie liked Jack although with his rustic weather-beaten face and wild woolly hair Charlie thought that Jack resembled an uncanny likeness to a grizzly bear in tweeds.

'Evening there Jack,' Charlie greeted, 'weather's been kind to us of late.'

The farmer acknowledged with a solitary nod as she paid the landlord for his ale. 'Aye, but we wouldn't miss the sun for a day or so hereabouts. Them there fields could do with a damn good downpour.' He replied.

Benjamin gave Jack his change, rolling his eyes at Charlie. 'There is no pleasing you farmers. If you don't get the sunshine you moan that the crops don't grow and if you don't get rain, you whine about the seedlings not coming through. I likes both sunshine and rain only in moderation.'

Swallowing his mouthful of ale Jack had heard the argument many times before. 'If it weren't for the likes of me and some others around here landlord, you wouldn't have any vegetables on your dining table. I'm just saying that we needs both sun and rain, sometimes together, but when the time is right for us. A farmer has to sow and reap as the season dictates, not by what that dopey vicar used to spout from his pulpit on a Sunday morning.' He took another sip before going on. 'Although I heard from a very reliable source that the man reaped what he sowed even to the end.'

Charlie grinned to himself. Word was slowly getting around about the unusual demise of Victor Higginbottom. He didn't think it would take long.

'I also heard,' Benjamin Chapple replied, leaning over the bar and pressing his face closer between the two men, 'that we have a lady vicar arriving soon.'

Charlie watched Jack pick up his beer mug, clutching onto the tankard in case she suddenly appeared.

'A woman vicar,' the farmer emphasised, 'I hope she's nothing like that dopey mare we see on the telly. They're getting in everywhere lately. Why we've even got a female couple running the old Watersend Farm over at Stopham. Married as well or so I've been told.'

Charlie scanned the interior of the pub expecting Marge to suddenly pop-up from behind the duke-box or wherever. His furtive looking didn't go unnoticed by Benjamin.

'Don't worry my friend she's not here. Marge has got the bug for playing bingo of late and has started to spend a lot of her free time down at the Mecca Hall in the city. I can't quite see why she gets herself all tarted up to go, but least ways she's out of my hair.'

'In somebody else's hair and bed,' thought Charlie as he grinned back. All the same it was handy that Marge was out of the way.

Jack butted in. 'That's just what I'm saying about women. They have their time and place. Cooking, washing, playing bingo or bringing up the children, not spouting religion from a pulpit or running a bloody farm and driving a tractor!'

Charlie was aware of a table nearby where four young women were all listening in on Jack's outburst. He quickly changed the subject. 'I see that *'Star Gladiator'* won the three thirty at Kempton this afternoon, did you have a flutter landlord?' With Jack muttering on the quartet resumed their conversation. Rubbing his hands gleefully together Benjamin Chapple promptly produced the winning ticket from his shirt pocket.

'It was streaks ahead of the field and won by a good three lengths. The nag came in at eleven to one. I made a tidy one hundred and twenty pounds plus my stake money.'

'Probably more than Marge will get at bingo tonight,' Jack quipped, grinning at the table of young women. It wasn't money that Marge was going to get to grips with, but Bert Tonks thought Charlie. Jack turned the win around to the weather again. 'A hundred and twenty pounds. I'll be lucky to make that in a week if we don't get some rain soon.'

'Talking about nags Jack, how's the missus is she well?' He refilled the farmer's glass.

'Same as usual and still suffering from lumbago. She's been to the doctor, but that daft bugger reckons that there's now't left in the medicine cabinet that will help only she's had it all before.'

Benjamin Chapple wiped the bar top dry where Jack had spilt some of his froth.

'Until Marge took up bingo on a Tuesday evenings she was always complaining about back pains, now by some miracle they've suddenly disappeared!' Putting the cloth back next to the sink the landlords thoughts were momentarily elsewhere. 'Come to think, she's stopped moaning about most things unless it involves me!'

'That would be because of the adrenalin rush Benjamin,' Charlie insisted. 'It's surprising what a win can do to lift the spirits.' Benjamin agreed placing his glass beneath the optic and filling it halfway with whiskey.

Finishing his ale Jack belched loudly. 'Maybe, I should think about sending my Edna along to Tuesday bingo as well. We could do with some extra cash and it would stop her persistent bleating. I get enough of that from my sheep.'

Leaving Jack to mull over the bingo idea, Charlie and Benjamin went out back of the pub to begin unloading the cases of wine and brandy. They used the rear stairs to the cellar below. 'Does Marge ever come down here?' Charlie inquired, as they stacked the boxes.

'Only on the very rare occasion. She doesn't like it down here, not since I put out the vermin traps.' Charlie looked around. Several traps had been tripped although there was no sign of any dead mice.

'And the bait, what are you using?' he asked.

'I'm not and there's no mice down here Charlie. It's only a ploy to keep Marge from snooping around down here. What I do with the stock is my concern and not hers. It's bad enough when Bert Tonks or his young assistant has to come down here to check on the brewery kegs.'

'Does Bert have a big round?' Charlie asked, counting down the boxes that had been delivered.

'Big enough I guess. It starts in the city and ends up somewhere along the coast. Marge keeps the books and she knows when we have brewery deliveries.'

Benjamin didn't know why Charlie should be so interested in the drayman, but his philosophy in life was simple. Each man had his reasons for asking, to do what pleased them most and lastly to die. Running the pub, betting on the horses and keeping out of Marge's way was Benjamin's survival plan. As long as his wife didn't find out about his dealings with the manor house everything was as karma had intended.

'Did you hear about how Victor Higginbottom died?' Charlie prompted, returning to the subject before putting down the last wine box.

Benjamin smiled, a smile that only men can produce. 'I'd heard that he was being serviced by Martha at the time, whilst taking morning exercise.'

'The original sermon on the mount,' Charlie laughed, 'we must have the same source.'

Benjamin did a quick recount and satisfied he took the remainder of the money owed from his trouser pocket.

'Reg Perry was in here the other night drowning his sorrows. It was fortunate that Marge had a headache and went to bed early. It was Reg who told me about Martha and poor old Victor. What with the new vicar arriving I hear Martha is keen to move across to Trumpington Salle.'

Charlie looked surprised. 'She's going to keep house for the bishop?'

'So it would seem.' Benjamin watched the gardener count the money. 'Martha apparently has an insatiable appetite that needs satisfying.'

Charlie smirked. 'And this new lady vicar, does anybody know anything else about her?'

'Only that Willow Beck is her first parish and that her name is Mary Anne Nelson.'

It was an interesting name thought Charlie. He wondered if she was a distant relative of the famous Lord Nelson. A new vicar however was good news, possibly corruptible and in time she could be moulded by her ladyship. 'We're thinking about expanding, importing cheese,' Charlie added, 'would you be interested Benjamin?'

Benjamin Chapple grinned, affectionately patting his stomach. 'I like anything French Charlie. It has that *je ne sais quoi* air of mystery about it, which is both pleasing to the eye and the palate.'

'Good, we'll keep you posted when we get some in.' He looked at the time. 'I'd best cut along as I have another order to deliver before I head back.' Charlie was about to climb the stairs when he remembered something else. 'Other than the brewery and the manor house, do you ever get your alcohol elsewhere?'

Benjamin Chapple shook his head looking slightly puzzled. 'Not unless we find ourselves running low on stock. As a last resort we head to the nearest supermarket for emergency stock, why?'

Charlie gave a shrug of his shoulders. 'No reason really, I was just ruminating that was all. I wondered how our wine compared with the stuff sold in the local supermarkets.'

'It's much better and cheaper.' Benjamin replied shutting the cellar door, slipping the padlock through the hasp plate and giving it one last tug for luck. It was the answer that Charlie had hoped to hear. He promised the landlord of the Angler's Arms that he would be back later for his usual tipple. Benjamin laughed. Charlie only made deliveries when it was Reg Perry's night off.

*****

Antonio Vincenzi peered through the window of the restaurant seeing the shiny Rolls Royce parked outside.

'You have come alone?' he asked, his dark eyes deep with apprehension.

Charlie looked around before he replied adding to the moment. 'Does Janet frighten you that much Antonio?'

66

'Si - si,' the Italian was ashamed to admit, *'she is built like my mama, only bigger.'* He emphasised the point by spreading his fingers wide, curving the two ends in to create two huge breasts on his own chest. 'That woman scares me Charlie. When she sees me, she crushes my ribcage in a cuddle and my beautiful Gina, she is always wanting to know how I get bruises working in a restaurant.'

Charlie made a fist and thumped the air. 'You need to be firm Antonio. Demonstrate some of that spirited hot-blooded determination that you Italian's possess. To stop a foe in their tracks you have to show strength. Take control of the situation and make her think twice before she attacks you.'

Antonio caught sight of himself in the reflection of the darkened window.

'I am like Daniel and she the lion Charlie.' He sighed, an exaggerated expression of hopeless defeat. 'Can you image where she would tell me she had a thorn if I asked where?'

Charlie laughed. 'I admit she is a big girl.'

'I dare not ask if she would like to stay for a coffee. There is no saying what she would do to me and I have to think of my Gina.'

'We're thinking of expanding into cheese as well, would you be interested?'

Antonio helped unload the boot. *'Si – si Charlie as long as Janet does not pressurise me into buying too much.'*

Charlie pocketed the cash. There was never any receipt.

'I'll make a special point of telling her to be gentle with you in future.' He told Antonio that they would be in touch as he started the engine. Before pulling away from the rear yard of the hotel Charlie looked back at the Italian, his slim figure made no taller by the thinning patch on top of his head. Janet had positively terrorised the man. If only the restaurant manager knew about the other women in the village who also had the hots for him and his smouldering dark eyes. He slipped the gear into first and started to pull away.

'You're right Antonio, she is definitely a big girl.'

Charlie was on his way back to the Angler's Arm's when he caught sight of young Robert Perry walking on the opposite pavement. He called across to the policeman's son.

'Hello Charlie,' Robert acknowledged, 'been out on your rounds?'

Charlie Luft engaged the brake and switched off the engine, getting out so that they could talk. 'You lads did very well on that last trip. Her ladyship is working out a bonus when we tally everything!'

Robert was happy to hear it. 'Things got a bit hairy at Dover, but we had luck on our side Charlie and by the grace of God we managed to get away without causing any fuss.'

Charlie liked Robert and considered him to be the brains of the trio.

'We are thinking of expanding the business and adding cheese to our shopping list. Trouble is the French might have CCTV of the lorry so we might need to think of another way of getting a shipment back home, have you got any ideas?' Charlie asked.

'What about using Bill Symons,' Robert was quick to suggest. 'Bill was a tug boat captain at Felixstowe until he took retirement. He has a boat for pleasure and it's a nice craft, a seagoing vessel or so I've been told.'

Charlie Luft looked at Robert Perry and suddenly a big grin creased his cheeks. Not the least interested in joining the police force, unlike his father, Robert liked the excitement of smuggling illicit goods.

'Bill Symons,' Charlie mused, 'that's a damn good idea Robert. I would not have thought about a boat.'

'Of course, it would mean bringing him on board Charlie. He'd have to be in on the cut and it would need her ladyship to approve the idea.'

Charlie rubbed the bristles on his chin. He was already thinking ahead.

'And we could either hire or buy a cheap van over in France. Having picked up the alcohol and cheese we could unload it onto the boat and leave the van down some back street where the gendarmes hardly ever ventured. It's a good idea young man.'

'If we sailed at night and arrived early we could avoid customs or the coastguard. Coming back we could use one of the creeks along the North Norfolk coast. You could meet us Charlie with the Rolls. Who'd suspect the roller would be full of contraband.'

Charlie gratefully slapped Roberts shoulder. 'You've a quick thinking brain young man. You'd have made a good spy.' Charlie's smile disappeared. 'Your old man would have a dizzy fit if he ever found out about your involvement.'

Robert responded with a grin. 'My grandad weren't no saint Charlie. Back in the fifties, he and his mates were always getting done for poaching. I know because grandma told me. My dad has never mentioned it.' Charlie nodded, minor indiscretions must have been a family trait.

'Come up to the manor house tomorrow and we'll discuss the proposal with Lady Ashleigh.'

The Saucy Belle

Bill Symons was surprised although amused to receive an invite to afternoon tea at the manor house. An easy going man, he was known at the Angler's Arms to be a little guarded and slightly suspicious when offered a way to make money. Having replaced the receiver of the phone it had been some time since he had been anywhere near the large estate or indeed the church next door.

Having freshly baked a walnut fruit cake for the occasion, Janet had prepared the table in the kitchen where they could sit comfortably around the ancient oak table and talk. The seating arrangement was designed to have the retired tugboat captain sit near the warm cooker range and next to Olivia Ashleigh.

'Thank you for accepting our invitation Mr Symons,' introduced the lady of the manor, 'I'll not beat about the bush, we invited you here because we have a business proposition which we think might interest you and benefit us into the bargain.'

Bill Symons rubbed the underside of his nose with the back his forefinger, a cautious habit that gave him time to think. 'Please call me Bill or Captain. I don't like formality, it's unfriendly.' He added a smile to show that he was.

Olivia Ashleigh smiled, she liked his approach.

'Alright then… Bill it is. To begin with Bill can we have your assurance that anything discussed within this house will remain strictly confidential between the four of us present.'

Symons stopped rubbing his nose. 'Discretion is my middle name.'

Olivia nodded satisfied that his word was his bond. It was unfortunate that Robert could not have been present as it was his idea, but Reg had asked for help in setting up the one and only speed trap in the village.

'Traditionally,' she began, 'the manor house has been a symbol of wealth and a place where people in the village could come if they needed help. That said, the church next door was always deemed too cold and uninviting to offer salvation other than spiritual, and unless seven loaves and a basket of fish suddenly appeared before the altar, promises do not feed stomachs.

'To help the needy the lord of the manor needed a healthy income. My late husband, his father before him and generations going beyond and down the ancestral line found a way around importing certain goods to help bolster the financial chest without paying revenue to our corrupt government.'

Bill Symons grinned again. 'Basically you mean smuggling!'

Olivia smiled sat next to him.

'In the very loosest use of the term, I suppose we are Bill. Although we prefer to see ourselves as enterprising entrepreneurs.'

Bill appreciated the subtle difference. 'Why me?' he asked.

'Because we're looking for a man with experience of the sea and a boat to become an equal partner in our operation.'

Bill Symons liked their honesty. Looking up at the clock it had taken less than two minutes to get the crux of the invitation. He broke away a piece of the walnut fruit cake that Janet had especially baked for him.

'And I take it that my part in this enterprise having been invited here today, would be to sail across to France, collect the goods and bring them back to Willow Beck.'

Charlie who was older than Bill knew from conversations with Benjamin Chapple that the retired tug boat captain was a fine seaman. Some about the village deemed that Bill had salt water running through his veins rather than blood.

'You know the North Sea probably better than anybody else around here Bill,' Charlie replied heaping praise at the man sat opposite, 'and we need a man of your experience and calibre to slot into our future plans.'

Bill looked at Janet giving her a wink. 'This cake is very good. Should I agreed to join this merry band of entrepreneurs, considering the risks that I would be taking, as part of the agreement I would want a fruit cake made fresh for every trip.' Janet clasped her palms together. The captain had a certain twinkle in his eye that made her insides shudder.

I'd make you a cake at Christmas and another on your birthday if you say yes to our proposal.' She asked if he liked rum and raisins.

Bill laughed looking at Olivia Ashleigh. 'Is the Pope Catholic.'

'And just when is your birthday?' Janet asked, fishing for the captain's age.

'December twelfth every year, although I never disclose which year other than it's been a secret for longer than I care to tell.'

'You're Sagittarius,' Olivia Ashleigh said popping a walnut slice into her mouth. 'A star sign known for their straightforward, possibly assertive approach. With a hint of restless anticipation, although not uncommonly adventurous with a desire for ambition and unafraid of a new challenge. Most of all though you are honest and you expect others to be the same.'

Sitting next to her Bill was close enough to detect the perfume she was wearing. He liked it. 'I reckon that about sums me up, ticking most of my boxes.'

He raised his finger before anybody present added anything else.

'Before I agree and sign on the dotted line, most importantly who will be the crew and who collects the goods?'

'We use three young men from the village,' Janet replied offering more tea.

'A mariner never refuses tea lass.'

Charlie rolled off the names pushing his mug forward for Janet to fill. 'Robert Perry, Samuel Byrne and Tommy Jenkins. They're good lads although I can't vouch for their sea legs as they've only ever been on the cross-channel ferry.'

Bill nodded. 'Well we'd soon find out. The *Saucy Belle* is my boat. She's a Broome Admiral, a very sturdy and reliable vessel. She would easily make it to France and back.'

Olivia Ashleigh liked the captain's forthright approach and his attitude which was much like her own. 'You would be very well compensated for your part Bill. The cake we could all enjoy.'

Bill Symons frowned creasing his weather beaten brow. 'The policeman's son. Now there's a strange choice. Isn't that a bit risky?'

Charlie responded first. 'It was young Robert who suggested that you join us. He's a shrewd lad, intelligent and he has ambition. It's not that he doesn't respect his father nor indeed the law, it's just that like us he's not into politics and sees this little venture as a profitable adventure.'

The captain clamped his fingers together as though about to pray. 'And Reg would never suspect his son as being involved should he ever get whisper that something was going on. It's ingenious.' He drummed the tips of his fingers on the table top. Suddenly his thoughts turned into a smile. 'Alright, I'm with you.'

They stood up shaking hands, the agreement was made. Quite unexpectedly the captain kissed the back of Olivia Ashleigh's hand much to the amusement of Janet and Charlie.

'Being an equal partner, does this allow me the opportunity to take afternoon tea with you more often than once a year?' he asked.

It had been a long time since anybody had kissed her hand or indeed her lips. Olivia Ashleigh steadied her breathing before she gave her reply. 'That would please me captain, if you would.'

Sat next to Charlie, Janet gave him a nudge. They both thought that the grieving period had run its course and it was about time that her ladyship was back out on the road looking for a romantic adventure of her own.

'We're pleased to have you on board captain,' said Charlie, nodding confidently.

'So what plans have you made for the next trip?' asked Bill.

'That really depends on when you are available,' Olivia replied, covering her kissed hand with her other.

'Anytime would suit me.' Bill sniffed, this time rubbing the underside of his nose sensing the call of salt water. 'However, I'd need to consult the charts, checking on tides and weather. Dunkirk would be my choice of harbour and offer the shortest route across the North Sea.' He smiled. 'I would need to check that my passport as well and make sure that it's valid. Other than that the *Saucy Belle* is always ship-shape and ready, and at your disposal.'

She watched from the privacy of the bedroom following the progress of the old tugboat captain as he walked back up the drive to the road. Bill Symons had a confident stride. She felt it had opened up a new chapter in her life just by meeting him.

Gently caressing where he had kissed the back of her hand the sun was warm on her face coming in through the bedroom window. Suddenly the future looked that much brighter.

Olivia Ashleigh watched until he turned and was lost beyond the front hedge.

Turning away from the window she was found herself confronted by a framed photograph, a black and white image of her late husband taking part in a game shoot in the fields nearby. Picking up the photograph she studied the man, his stance and the others stood nearby. Feeling her heart flutter wildly as she turned once again and looked along the drive. She felt no shame thinking about another man. Bill Symons was unlike any man that she had ever met and none, not even her husband had ever kissed the back of her hand.

She replaced the photograph.

'Time to move on Larry,' she whispered to herself, 'time to plan ahead and live again!'

The Night Crossing

They let go the mooring lines as the *Saucy Belle* drifted gently away from the grass bank with the sun already a bright yellow orange dipping low over the nearby treetops.

On the crossing with Bill Symons was Samuel, Robert and Tommy. Olivia Ashleigh had given the retired tugboat captain five thousand pounds from which he could deduct his expenses including fuel and harbour tax, with enough ready cash available to haggle the purchase of a cheap van, wine and cheese.

Before departing Charlie had discussed with Bill how they intended infiltrating the wine sold at the local supermarket in the hope that they could reduce some of their cellar stock. Bill promised to return with the next batch of wine and cheese.

Guiding the boat down river they waved at dog walkers on the bank with Bill acknowledging those that he had known for years. He calculated that it would take most of the night to sail across to Dunkirk. There was a high moon and the tides were in his favour. He had picked their departure when the coastguard went for their supper. They passed a lone fisherman concealed amongst the reeds.

'Out for a spot of night fishing captain,' the angler called out as Bill guided the boat beyond his rod.

Bill Symons waved as ever the jovial sailor. 'Something like that Harry. We'll have that jar together when I get back.' Harry thumbed his finger into the air, it would be a drink to look forward too. Hidden from sight the trio waited until Bill gave them the word that they could come up on deck.

'I hate being cooped up like a chicken in a damn hen house,' Samuel remonstrated as dark cloud started to blot out the moon. Leaning through the doorway of the cabin Bill issued a warning.

'Make sure you three keep your eyes peeled for signs of any river police or the rangers. Those buggers appear like an owl hunting mice, fast and silent!' He manoeuvred the boat around a boat load of holidaymakers trying to moor their boat for the night. Bill thought that they should have been tied up a long time ago.

'Do they patrol at night?' asked Samuel, eager to be up top with the captain.

'All night sometimes lad. There's no rhyme or reason to their thinking. It all depends on how many are using the river.'

Robert nodded at Samuel. He knew some officers that patrolled the river. His alibi was that he was spending a couple days up at the Kelling Heath camping site with Tommy and Samuel. Emma Perry was pleased to hear that her son was getting out and about, getting some fresh air and adventure. 'You don't want to end up like you father,' she had told him, 'becoming lazy and uninteresting.' Robert smiled to himself. She would have a fit if she knew that it was French air he would be breathing.

'How far before we reach Yarmouth?' Tommy asked as he scanned the nearby bank and the fields beyond using a pair of binoculars.

'About another hour by my reckoning. You'll know when we pass the *Anchor's Rest* where we turn sharp port before heading out into the North Sea.'

Samuel Byrne who preferred his feet on firm ground could feel his lunch swimming about in his stomach. 'I don't mean no disrespect captain, but are you sure that this old tug will hold up to the rigors of the sea. It can cut up rough out there?'

Bill Symons grinned back having expected the question from at least one of them. It surprised him that it had taken so long to be asked. 'Have no fear lad, this here boat is a genuine Broom Admiral, built solidly from mahogany and good English oak. The *Saucy Belle* is forty three long and boasts a beam of over ten and a half feet. Together we've been to Belgium and France more times than I care to recall. Set your mind at peace and we'll make the crossing without a hitch. I checked and the weather forecast is good for tonight.'

Tommy Jenkins tapped the wall of the cabin which sounded solid. 'Why the *Saucy Belle*?' he asked.

Keeping a watchful eye on the river ahead the captain stroked the wooden surround of the wheel. 'She's named after a lady that I once knew.'

They each detected the romantic propensity in the way he aligned the boat to a lady.

'A special lady by any chance Bill?' Tommy pursued.

'Aye lad she was once and a woman like that never really leaves your heart, not without first cutting her initials in deep.'

'Did you marry her Bill?' Samuel pressed winking at Robert and Tommy.

Bill Symons took a moment before he replied. Time enough to have the memory of her smile reappear. 'No lad, you see at the time I was married to the sea and a man can only have one mistress at any given time.'

He gripped the wheel and pointed at a shaft of light coming around the bend further ahead. Pulling the boat into the river bank he ordered Tommy to drop the anchor over the side. 'Be quick lad,' he said, 'otherwise they'll notice our dispersive.'

'Our what?' asked Samuel.

'Our wash, a ripple which would indicate that we were moving.'

'Who do you think it is Bill?' Tommy asked feeling his heart thumping inside his chest cavity.

'The sun went down early this evening so by rights the only people on the river at this time will be the river police or the rangers. Best you three get down below and keep down low where they can't see you. I'll sit up top here reading a paper and with a bit of luck they'll just go on by without stopping.'

Samuel hid in the toilet, Tommy in the forward bedroom and Robert concealed himself in an empty blanket box. Clutching the cross and chain that his mum had brought him for his eighteenth birthday Robert prayed that they would get out to open water without being stopped. Minutes later the wash left behind by the passing cruiser made the boat rock back and forth. Inside the toilet Samuel felt queasy. They heard Bill talking with the cruiser crew before he gave them the all clear.

'Was it the patrol?' Robert asked.

Bill grinned. 'No, it was only a honeymoon couple desperate to find a place to stay for the night. I told them about a pub that I know further up river. With any luck they should just make it before the light fades completely. It was their navigation light that we spotted.' He laughed seeing their relief. 'Let's get that anchor back up and then we'll head out towards Yarmouth, it's not that far now!'

Ever the inquisitive policeman's son Robert was keen to know why the boat had *'Saucy'* in the name.

Switching on the navigation lights, Bill winked at Robert. 'That's the thing lad, you can never tell what a woman is thinking. Belle was good at keeping secrets, but I never knew what she was thinking come the next morning. You'd be wise to remember that.'

'Did she want to marry you?' he asked.

'Aye that she did.' He watched for other signs of river activity hearing the anchor land on the deck. 'She told me that she would wait around until I was retired.'

'And now that you are retired?'

Bill responded shaking his head with slow deliberate movements. 'Alas it wasn't meant to be. My lovely Belle died two years before I handed the keys of the tugboat over to a much younger man.'

There the questions stopped.

Leaving Bill to his thoughts the trio watched as Great Yarmouth harbour came into view. On either side of the river were a range of buildings, people walking and public houses. The harbour lights many said having been out all day to fish resembled an angel sleeping having watched over them while they battled the waves for their catch.

Looking back at the receding coastline which was disappearing fast the boat had become blanketed instead by a darkness that seemed to grip them on all sides. A good sign as Bill pointed out was that the sea was calm. Every so often however the eerie silence would be peppered by the sound of slapping pockets of green water leaving in its wake a spray which washed across the deck. The only one not enjoying the experience was Samuel who kept blowing his cheeks out to resemble a stuffed hamster.

'How deep is here Bill?' asked Samuel, leaning over the gunwale.

'In the middle lad I'd say about three hundred feet, but it can vary depending which bit of water you are sailing. It don't really matter though as generally it's all wet and bloody cold on top surface. Has somebody put the kettle on,' he asked, 'only it's time we had ourselves a brew.' Surprisingly Samuel volunteered to make the drinks preferring to be below deck where he considered it was safer and where he couldn't see the sea. He was joined by Tommy leaving Robert to talk with Bill.

'Did you see the coastguard as we left Yarmouth?' Tommy asked.

Filling the kettle Samuel gave a shake of his head. 'No, only those blokes enjoying a drink at the Anchor's Rest. Do you reckon this is going to be easier than going by road?'

'I think the captain knows what he's doing and at least this way we shouldn't meet any customs official's enroute, not least until we reach Dunkirk.'

'Yeah, and look what happened the last time we went there in great numbers.'

'That was different Samuel and now there are only four of us.' Tommy sat himself down on a long settee happy to find that it was surprisingly comfortable. It was the length that he found surprising. 'How did Bill get this down here,' he pondered. 'It's far too big to fit through the cabin door?'

Samuel looked at the padded seat then back at the door. 'Probably took it apart, then put it back together again.' Looking around at the interior of the cabin there were wooden cupboards dotted here and there, each an ideal place to conceal illegal contraband. 'I bet Bill never imagined the *Saucy Belle* being involved like this.'

A sudden creak of wood made them turn where they saw Bill standing in the doorway. 'Certainly not with you lot I didn't. I remember when you three were in short trousers and not interested in girls.' He reached over and took one of the mugs scooping in two spoonfuls of sugar. He sat himself down. 'Being a tugboat captain isn't just about pulling and shoving huge container ships in and out of a port all day, sometimes you can get called upon to help out with ships in distress or other sorts of calamities.' He watched Samuel add coffee to the four mugs. 'Ships that get abandoned in a storm and leave their cargo behind, unattended.'

'So you've done this kind of work before?' Samuel asked, as Tommy took a coffee up to Robert who had been left to steer the boat.

'In a manner of speaking, I have. You see the law of the sea is a lot different to that on land. When a distressed boat is left abandoned the cargo can be salvaged. You just have to evaluate the risk involved.'

'Like what?' Samuel was interested to know what cargo before he went risking his neck.

'Alcohol, goods with a high insurance value and gold.'

Bill Symons watched as Samuel's jaw dropped. 'Gold, what on the North Sea?' Samuel replied.

The retired tugboat captain grinned wide. 'Aye lad, there's a lot of sandbanks along the east coast and many an unfortunate mariner has felt the hand of doom stretch out and suck a boat under with an incompetent master at the helm. If you don't know the tides, respect the water and the Southern Bight they can be a mighty treacherous place to be wandering about especially come the dark.'

'Does Robert know what he's doing steering?' Samuel asked. Beyond the porthole it looked very dark.

Bill however didn't look overly worried. 'Aye, he's doing a grand job. A natural born sailor and as long as he keeps steering south easterly we should arrive as day breaks on the French coast.' He stretched over reaching for a large round tin. 'Here have a biscuit lad, Janet Simpson made them fresh this morning. They're full of honey and nuts, they'll help settle your stomach and stop it from rolling around.'

Samuel took a biscuit to be polite although his stomach was like a witch's cauldron as it bubbled louder than the lapping of the waves on the outside of the boat. Putting the biscuit down beside his coffee, he watched the froth move back and forth. 'Maybe, I'll eat it in a minute.'

Bill watched as Samuel went from a sun kissed almond to a dull shade of green. 'This is your first time at sea isn't it?'

Samuel nodded. He was now holding his stomach. He watched the froth for a few seconds more before leaping to his feet and racing for the steps up to the deck above. Leaning over the side of the boat he emptied the contents of his stomach.

'Will he be alright?' Tommy asked seeing Bill follow. As skipper of the boat he didn't want to have to turn the boat about and look for a man overboard, not in the dark.

'He'll live, although I'll tell you this and that Samuel is no sailor.'

Robert kept his concentration on the task at hand guessing that they were mid-channel as the waves were now a little higher and stronger. With Bill looking on admiringly he was in awe of the young man's maritime expertise. Shoving himself back from the top of the gunwale

Samuel was pointing at something large in the water. Bill noticed that he was unusually quiet.

'What you seen lad?' he asked.

'There...' he said, *'there was a fin, a fucking great big shark fin!'*

Bill went to the gunwale to look. He laughed. 'It was probably only an oceanic whitetip shark, they're often seen in these waters. They're quite harmless.'

Samuel Byrne was even less enthusiastic about being at sea. It was bad enough bobbing about in the dark, but now there were sharks to consider. He realised that he wasn't wearing his lifejacket. Standing in the middle of the deck he watched again for signs of the fin cutting through the surface. He felt his chest would explode if it did. More than on the day when he had seen Evelyn Earnshaw sunbathing naked amongst the sand dunes. 'They don't jump into the boats do they?' he asked.

'Only if they're hungry lad.' Bill was still chuckling to himself when he went back down below where his coffee was waiting. Alongside the wheelhouse Robert and Tommy were also laughing.

'Fuck off... it's not funny,' Samuel replied indignantly, *'you should have seen the bugger, he was longer than my old man's tractor!'* His description only made matters worse.

Around twenty past five the first rays of daylight broke through the darkened sky giving the crest of the waves a silvery shimmer as though each movement was encrusted with thousands of white diamonds. Not far away was the French coast. Rising from his hour of sleep Bill Symons stretched recognising some of the landmarks.

Bill was impressed. 'You've done really well young Perry, we'll make a captain of you yet.' Robert was glad to hand over control of the boat to Bill again and take the opportunity to walk around rejuvenating the muscles in his legs.

'After we've tied off, we'll find somewhere to take breakfast, but if anybody's hungry there's bread in the galley if you want toast. We're about forty minutes out from Dunkirk.'

Surprisingly Samuel was the first down to the galley he was joined by Robert. Tommy elected to stay with Bill. 'What made you go to sea?' he asked.

'Being raised as a boy on the Broads I would spend every waking hour that I could on the river with my uncle sailing a small ketch. Braden Water scared the hell out of me, but it was there to be conquered. I've never refused a challenge.

'After I left school I enlisted in the merchant navy where I spent eight years at sea sailing back and forth across and around the globe stopping off at different ports, meeting all kinds of people. We delivered and collected cargo whatever the shape, some human, animal or otherwise. When the chance of becoming a tugboat captain came up, I jumped at it and never looked back. The sea calls even in your sleep. I find it can make the soul restless if I don't get my feet wet at least once a month.'

Tommy sniffed, tasting the brine in the air which invaded the back of his throat. Bill was right and there was something magical about the sea that you didn't find on land. 'I could get used to this life captain, I've really enjoyed the crossing. I like the unpredictability of the sea, it's a different world out here.'

Bill nodded. 'Aye lad, that's exactly what it is a different world only not all land folk see it that way. Many hate the water like young Samuel. Having retired I've amazed myself and grown to like both. That said I'll probably have a Vikings funeral when I go.'

'That's where they set fire to the boat with you in it!'

'That's about the size of it,' he turned the boat portside. 'The thought of letting earth worms have their fill when I'm dead terrifies me.' They watched the compass move on the bulkhead. 'I couldn't be cremated. With all the rum that I've consumed down the years I'd probably explode before the gas meter needs another shilling.' Bill placed Tommy's hands on the wheel. 'Here you guide us in. Take it down to four knots lad and keep your eye starboard only the harbour has some unseen rocks outside of the breakwater. The marina is safe enough it's just the approach that can catch you out.'

Tommy kept his hands steady as he pulled back the throttle dropping from six to four skilfully negotiating the breakwater and into the mouth of the harbour where the water was much calmer. Finding an empty berth he reversed the engine and eased the boat alongside another. 'That is as good as I have ever entered this marina,' he remarked, giving Tommy a congratulatory pat on the back, 'maybe you should take us back out when we leave.'

'I would like that.' Tommy was full of confidence. 'You have to show the water whose boss Bill.'

'You got it lad. Respect is the key to sailing the seas. Now we had best contact Olivia Ashleigh and let her know that we got across safely.' Leaving them to secure the boat Bill went to find a phone box and register their stay with the harbour master.

'He could have used my mobile,' said Robert as they watched him enter the harbour office.

'I think he wants the conversation to be private,' replied Tommy, 'and my aunt Barbara, she reckons that the old girl has the hots for the sea captain.'

Wine, Cheese and a French Van

When Bill returned he came back armed with baguettes, long freshly baked bread sticks stuffed full of delicious cooked bacon. 'This should set us up for the morning until lunchtime. There's also a concessionaire de fourgonnettes half a mile from the harbour master's office, we can easily walk there and find what's available.'

'What's a forgotten whatever?' asked Samuel, adding ketchup to his baguette.

'A van dealer,' Bill replied handing around three plates so that they didn't get crumbs everywhere. 'I think we should something French, it won't arouse suspicion. Anything remotely English will automatically have the authorities jumping all over us.'

Samuel was in favour of Bill' suggestion curving his hands in and out. 'They even have a car where the bodywork comes apart, a bit like a French woman's chemise.'

'How would you know that?' asked Robert raising his eyebrows at Tommy.

'Don't you remember that French teacher we had from school who told us that she was from Paris, why do you think I did so much detention?'

Bill grinned thinking school had changed from when he had attended. 'Well let's keep focused and that we're here on business and blending in with the locals will make our lives easier. Have your passports with you at all times and if stopped by the police, be polite and helpful, don't answer them back. Remember we're here to look for a holiday cottage, not buy wine and cheese, okay?'

They all nodded indicating that they understood. Bill pointed at Samuel Byrne.

'And no adverse comments about how they do their farming this side of the channel. Like the fishermen the famers get very agitated about criticism and centuries old tried and tested ways.'

'Well one thing they get right is pig farming, this bacon is lovely,' he replied, scoffing down another mouthful.

Around nine on French time they walked to the vente de fourgon, where there was a wide variety of local vans on offer.

Francois Dupont, the congenial salesman answered all of Bills questions and half an hour later he and Bill shook on the deal having purchased an olive green coloured Citroen, model H van for six hundred and fifty euro's including tax and insurance. The registration document showed that it had once belonged to a Baker, named Monsignor Henri Fauche. Bill though it was appropriate that it would be used to transport wine and cheese back and forth to the marina.

Heading out of Dunkirk they joined the main highway travelling to Alsace near to the Belgium border where they found the village of Saint

Cambrae having been told by Francois Dupont that they would find an excellent family run vineyard.

'The grass,' Francois said of his recommendation, 'is the greenest in France and the cows they give the finest milk. The soil is rich in nutriments and Saint Cambrae grows the best grapes.' Kissing the tips of his fingers he enthusiastically endorsed everything French. 'I only drink the finest of wine and my cellar is stocked by this vineyard!' Francois also said that if it would help, he would call ahead and arrange an appointment. It wasn't until they arrived at the vineyard that Bill found out that Francois and Victor the owner, were in fact cousins.

Just over six hundred miles west of their location back in Norfolk, a different plan of action was about to be put into effect only with a similar motive.

Janet Simpson walked through the door of the supermarket taking a trolley with her. A regular customer every Monday morning she waved at members of staff that she knew, including Alfred Strong the delicatessen manager, who had once said that they could set the store clocks by Janet's arrival as she was always so punctual.

'The usual?' he asked as Janet pulled her trolley to a halt.

'Yes please Alfred, although make it double as her ladyship is having some friends over for an impromptu cheese and wine afternoon.'

Pulling the wire down and through the slab of cheese Alfred cut away a nice rectangular slice which could be cubed if necessary. Janet asked for a tub of his finest olives and two fresh rollmops. It was all part of the masquerade that would help dispel any suspicion and thus so far Janet had played her part well, watched by Charlie Luft who was waiting patiently in the Rolls parked outside.

Next Janet moved around the aisles choosing French sticks, several jars of pickled onions, a fruity chutney and lastly half a dozen bottles of red wine. At the checkout she paid with cash, smiled at the cashier wishing her a good day before she left. It was that simple.

'Did Alf swallow it?' Charlie asked.

Janet grinned as she took her seat in the back, placing the bags of shopping on the floor beside her. 'Like a dog devouring a juicy bone!'

Charlie chuckled. 'Alf never was the brightest spark in the box of fireworks. He's never got over the fact that somebody told him at boy scouts that his mother was a virgin when she had him.'

Other customers exiting the store and in the car park heard the laughter coming from the interior of the Rolls Royce. 'Listen to them,' said a middle-aged resentful woman to her friend. 'Not a bloody care in the world and they've never done a decent day's work in their life. The upper class are all the same.'

Charlie drove to the next supermarket where Janet was again consistent with her shopping list, buying instead ingredients for an evening dinner party adding the same six bottles of red. When she settled herself in the back seat for the second tome Charlie drove them back home to the manor house.

Stage one of their plan had been initiated. In the kitchen Olivia Ashleigh was eager to hear how the shopping expedition had gone.

'Like a dream m'lady,' Janet replied, as she emptied her shopping bags, putting away the meat and rollmops in the fridge and the rest in the pantry. On the kitchen table she placed the twelve bottles of red wine.'

'Where's Charlie?' Olivia Ashleigh asked.

'Garaging the car m'lady.'

The younger woman grinned, happy that all had gone well. 'And as agreed, the message that we are entertaining guests fell upon the right ears?'

'Just as though it were signed and sealed in heaven. There was nothing really out of the ordinary that we don't normally purchase, except maybe the rollmops. I thought I would add them as a treat for Charlie.'

Olivia Ashleigh grinned. 'And there I was thinking that you were sweet on Antonio Vincenzi.'

Dropping her head down to hide her eyes Janet couldn't help conceal her feelings any longer. 'Charlie is like an enigma m'lady. He's deeply silent like the thinker and yet under that exterior shell he's a lost soul waiting in line to get his wings. A sort of dark horse amongst the clouds. He just needs a woman to look after him, that's all.'

With that the door of the kitchen opened and in walked Charlie. 'Who's a dark horse?' he enquired, latching onto the last bit of the conversation.

'Margaret Chapple,' Lady Ashleigh suggested, 'we were just discussing how the landlord could be so naïve.'

Janet Simpson whispered 'thank you' and in return received a roll of the eyes from Olivia Ashleigh to suggest that there were times when girls had to stick together and protect one another, especially where affairs of the heart were concerned.

'Benjamin would be better off without Marge,' Charlie agreed, voicing his opinion on the subject. 'There's little enough honesty about in the world today without wives being downright unfaithful.' He saw the bottles lined up on the table. 'Have you heard from Bill and the lads yet m'lady?'

Olivia Ashleigh filled the kettle.

'Bill telephoned as you was getting the car out of the garage this morning. They arrived safely and were seeing about a van soon after registering with the harbour authority. We did right bringing Bill Symons on board. The captain has a level head on his shoulders and suddenly I feel more relaxed and that he is there to look after those young lads. There's no deny that they've done well on the last few trips, but luck and good fortune can only last so long!'

Checking the seals around the top of the wine bottles Charlie seemed satisfied that removing them wouldn't present much of a challenge. Taking his multi-purpose knife from his pocket he checked the attachments,

'Towards the end of the war we would tamper with the bottles that were intended for the big houses outside of Paris where the German Officers had their private quarters. If we couldn't win the battle on the streets by fair means, we made damn sure that some of them buggers never left the building, not least until after it was all over!'

Olivia Ashleigh gently patted the back of Charlie's hand. 'We don't want to be over exuberant with our tampering of the wine, just enough to have people complain about the quality.' She added. 'Bad wine is one thing, but interfering with a person's natural bodily functions crosses the line of decency and could prove very uncomfortable for the individual affected, not to mention the rest of the household would suffer as well.'

Charlie understood. He produced a small polished tin from his pocket. It was both old and scratched in places with small dents around the lid. As expected they were keen to know about the tin.

'It wasn't damaged when I jumped form the plane, but got damaged when I fell through the branches of a large tree having parachuted into France. If it hadn't been form the parachute becoming entangled around the branches I would have been seriously injured or died that day. To cover my tracks I set fire to the parachute as I couldn't untangle it from the tree, but I ended up burning down half a wood. The Germans who came to investigate thought that the fire had been started by lightning. I was lucky that it was raining hard that night.'

From inside the metal container Charlie removed a medical glass syringe, where the numerals down the side were imperial rather than metric and the plunger was real silver. He pulled a small bottle from his pocket showing it to them both.

'It's a poor grade vinegar that has slowly gone to seed. Mixed with the contents of the bottle it will soon be completely unpalatable. We just have to wait for the right moment then *bang* we step in and offer our own wine. Simple as that.'

They watched as he skilfully removed the plastic seal from the bottle neck before drawing a small amount of vinegar up into the syringe. Then pushing the needle through the cork he made the smallest of holes. With a measured amount the first bottle was already going bad. Charlie replaced the plastic seal adding a gentle heat from the gas stove rubbing the edge around the glass neck until it was difficult to tell that the seal had ever been removed. When the process was complete he passed the bottle over to Olivia Ashleigh for examination.

'I would challenge any supermarket manager to tell me that anything looks different.' He said.

Olivia Ashleigh and Janet both examined the bottle, it was perfect and looked as good as new. Possibly better, having been stored in the warehouse of a local supermarket, placed on the selling shelves and picked up several times by prospective customers who would debate choosing a cheaper brand with a sour kick like a mule or select a much more refined bottle.

'It's good Charlie, real good,' Janet was full of admiration over his endless talents. She finished off making the coffee.

There was no invite for Barbara Jenkins this morning to join them for coffee. Later Janet would take her a cup and tell Barbara that they had to hold an urgent meeting concerning the arrival of the new vicar, settling on the arrangements to make her welcome to her new parish. Within the hour all twelve bottles were injected, contaminated and resealed.

Marking the box so that it didn't get mixed with any of the good stock they sat down each bottle until at last all twelve was ready to be returned to the supermarkets. Putting them in a box so that they wouldn't get mixed with any other stock, they sat back to relax and await news from France.

*****

'This is a hell of a bone shaker,' complained Samuel as they made their way to the village of Saint Cambrae.

'Well sit on your jacket,' Bill advised, as he checked the map that Francois Dupont had given them, 'and for gawd's sake stop moaning.'

Samuel couldn't be sure if the bubbling once again in his stomach was due to sea voyage, the rich bacon baguette or the constant rattling of the old van. He was concerned that his insides would erupt before they reached their destination.

Like so many villages that they had passed through the buildings were whitewashed, the churches old and roadside cafes were romantically quaint, although there were few shops.

Exiting from the side door Samuel was especially glad to breathe in the fresh air of the countryside rather than exhaust fumes and brine. An old woman walking by carrying a wicker basket filled with various fruits stopped to look at him. She mumbled something incoherent before going on her way, *'les touristes, ils sont tous les mêmes'*.

Coming up beside Samuel, Bill put a hand on his shoulder. 'See, you've already made an impression Samuel. She said… 'Tourists, they are all the same!'

'Bloody cheek,' Samuel replied indignantly, 'I'm no different to anybody else in this world.' Bill agreed with the woman and Samuel did look a dishevelled mess. He was in need of a shave and a shower and his hair resembled nothing short of a badly constructed bird's nest.

'Best you stay with the van,' Bill advised. 'We'll scout around. Make sure that nobody steals our prized possession.'

Samuel kicked the back tyre. 'What this heap of crap, nobody with any sense would come anywhere near it, let alone want to steal it!'

Tapping the side panel Bill demonstrated that the van was solid and well-made. 'It just needed a good run out. After the first five miles the oil settled and the exhaust stopped smoking. That's what you could do with to stop your stomach rumbling.'

'What oil or a run?'

'A big greasy fry up. It would line your stomach and make you feel less hostile.'

'What I really need is a good lie down.'

Bill suggested that Samuel perch himself on the grass bank beside the van where the shade would prevent him from getting sunstroke should he fall asleep. As the three of them dusted themselves down they saw a man approach with his hand outstretched. Victor Dupont was pleased that they had made the journey in unexpected good time.

He was proud of his lot and quickly explained that what had once been a pig farm with a century of history attached had been successfully transformed into a thriving and reputable vineyard. In his wisdom however Victor had kept back six of the pigs for his own domestic use.

'It is better than having a dustbin,' he said as he gestured that they follow. 'They are happy to live on the scraps which makes excellent ham, pork and bacon. At the weekend I take one truffle hunting.'

Bill Symons was the first to shake the Frenchman's hand, hoping that his strong grip was an indication of their honesty and intention to do business. 'Your wine comes highly recommended my friend.' He introduced Tommy and Robert to Victor. The wine producer was pleased to see that they have chosen wisely.

'Francois is a good salesman and a Citroen is reliable, a traditional workhorse. You should check the oil before you leave, but otherwise it will run smooth for many miles. I myself have one out back.' Bill grinned thinking it was probably a better model. 'Let me give you gentleman a tour of the Saint Cambrae vineyard and perhaps as we walk I can explain some of the history attached to the estate.'

Victor as they quickly learnt was passionate about his vineyard, his grapes and his concerns regarding overzealous selling.

'People who have no real interest in wine, buy instead nasty cheap products that they can obtain from retail outlets without ever understanding the benefits of a good wine.' He clutched his chest. 'Health can be improved by drinking a good red. I think of my heart as healthy not just each day, but in the bedroom too,' he paused raising a closed fist, it gives a certain ooomphh to the occasion.' Bill liked Victor's marketing strategy.

Victor winked at Tommy and Robert. 'One day *mon amies* you will remember my words, when you are older like me.'

They continued to follow as he showed them the shop and the barn where most of the wine was stored, pressed, bottled and labelled before being boxed. Robert noticed the pigs in the pen, they were huge. Victor noticed Robert watching.

'We rotate between pig and grape. We allow our pigs to forage for a season them move them elsewhere on the estate. We then grow our grapes in the field where the pigs have turned the soil. The wine produced here is rich and fruity. It is an age old tradition from the time of the Revolution, when poor country folk saw vineyards as the extravagance belonging to the aristocracy.'

While Tommy and Robert listened Bill was busy checking through the wine shelves.

'My ancestors, the Dupont family saw the uprising as an advantage that they could profit from protecting some of the vines which they kept hidden and instead they let the pigs on the farm eat that years grape crop. When the pigs were slaughtered the meat was thought to be

102

exquisite. We had more pigs, but they went to market recently, now we've just the six left, but they work hard.'

'Pigs and grapes to produce wine, that's an odd mix Monseigneur?' Tommy exclaimed.

'Indeed it is my young friend, although a very successful combination. Francois my cousin, he too had the chance many years back to join me here where we would have doubled our annual production, but alas his head was so easily turned by fast women, fine dining and even faster cars. Unfortunately, not the wine. You might wonder why I tell you that, but to appreciate a good wine, you have to be patient. Allow nature to do its work before you sow and reap the benefit. Women and fine dining go together well with a good wine, but not a fast car.'

Tommy failed to see the connection and he'd not seen anything remotely fast back at the Dunkirk van sales plot. In the field beyond the vineyard Bill saw and heard a herd of cows happily grazing in the lush long green grass. 'And the cows Victor, are they yours also?'

'Qui mon amis, although it has not always been easy with such stupid creatures. My eldest son, he runs the dairy farm from which we produce cheese. I have two sons and a daughter of eighteen.' Victor pointed at the converted barn to the side of the wine store. 'Wine and cheese they complement one another, do you agree?'

Bill instantly saw an ideal opportunity appearing. He could make a killing on both with price and quantity getting quality into the bargain. 'We would need to sample some first,' Bill agreed. The Frenchman clapped his hands together gleefully looking skyward. Providence was shining down on his luck this day.

'Perhaps you would do me the honour of accepting an invite to lunch where you can sample both the wine and the cheese. My wife has only this morning baked fresh bread?'

'We would very much like that, thank you.' Bill looked back at the gate where the van was parked just beyond. 'There is another in our party, although he's taking a lie down at the moment. He's not a good sailor.'

Victor smiled. 'Maybe he can join us later, there is always enough food and we never run out of wine!' Tommy volunteered to go and tell Samuel about the invite.

Walking towards the Citroen van Tommy was aware of the vehicle rocking from side to side occasionally. He looked back to make sure that nobody else had stopped it. He was about knock on the side door when he heard instead whispered voices coming from inside. One he recognised as Samuel the other was local and belonged to a female. Putting his ear to the metal panel he listened.

'Oh Sammy,' sighed the girl lustfully, *'your skin it is so muscly and so smooth, unlike the boy's here. They are all pimply.'*

'Not half as much as yours,' he heard Samuel reply, his voice both masterful and wanting, and with a tinge of frustration. 'I seem to be all fingers and thumbs today, I can't undo the clasp.'

Sighing the girl smacked his hand aside.

'Why the problem always, boys cannot undo the clasp of a brassiere. Knickers yes, they come down so easily, so fast and without any fuss, but a brassiere it causes such a puzzle.'

Tommy didn't know whether to laugh, walk away or give advice. He was still deciding when the van stopped moving. 'After we remove my brassiere, you will show me much respect, yes?' the girl asked. Tommy was willing Samuel to reply, but there was a silence, a pregnant pause.

'Chantelle, you're the first girl that I have ever seen naked, of course I'll respect you!'

'You lying toad Byrne,' thought Tommy. Next came a low feminine cry of alarm followed by a masculine groan of pleasure as the van started to rock again.

'How do you know my name?' Chantelle asked.

'It's tattooed on your shoulder,' Samuel replied, forgetting the rumble in his stomach.

'Ah yes of course my tattoo. You know my father he does not know of it... not yet anyway.'

There was a loud thud followed quickly by another as Samuel kicked off his boots. Moments later it went deathly quiet. Tommy wondered if he should check to see that they both okay. He had his hand on the door handle when the moaning resumed. When a long sigh followed by a cry of content filled the interior he decided to turn and walk away. Samuel he decided wouldn't be interested in lunch, not now.

Walking back to join Bill and Robert, Tommy was shaking his head. Samuel had some front, he really did. He had only been in France a few hours and already he'd shagged a French girl. He found the others in the cow shed where sterile preparations were being made to milk the cows.

'Your friend,' asked Victor, 'he is not going to join us for lunch?'

'No, he's lying down in the back of the van and taking things easy. I wine with cheese might perhaps be a little too rich for his palate at the moment.'

Victor nodded. He was grinning at Bill. 'The pleasures of being young. Why I remember when I could burn the candle at both ends mon amis and then go back for more. Now I find I have ulcers instead to keep me awake.' Tommy went to stand beside Robert.

Bill agreed. He also appreciated the passing of the years. 'I would have thought living in a peaceful village such as Saint Cambrae would have been idyllic and not caused you much stress.'

'Ahhh… that is the problem lies Bill. My young daughter Chantelle. Already she is eighteen and finds life here very boring. She is always looking for adventure beyond our gate.'

Tommy felt the cough suddenly grip his throat. Robert helped by slapping his friends hard on the back. 'I am very sorry,' Tommy apologised, 'it must have been a loose husk floating somewhere in the air.'

Victor also helped slapping his back. 'That would be my neighbour Pascal. He is already out in the fields sowing his corn crop. Occasionally the *Mistral* sends us a warning and that it isn't too far away. We have the breeze, but the big wind, it never comes this far north.'

'What's wrong?' whispered Robert checking to see that Bill and Victor were busy discussing the milking process.

'It's Samuel, he's in the back of the van with Victor's daughter!'

Robert looked beyond the milking shed door at the green van parked outside the gate. *'Bill will kill him if he finds out.'* Robert ran his fingers through his hair wondering how to avoid a monumental volcanic eruption. Tommy was still watching Bill hoping that he hadn't noticed the girl leave the van. 'I suggest we say nothing and hope that he never finds out. If Lady Ashleigh finds out she'll never trust us again. Samuel's exploits could ruin everything.'

To their surprise Bill turned suddenly with a question. 'What do you think lads?' he asked.

'More than impressive,' responded Robert, 'the cheese should be good quality if this milking shed is anything to go by.' Bill smiled back, pleased that they had been paying attention. Not too far away they heard a bell sound.

'Adele, she always rings the bells to signal that lunch is ready. Come my friends, now you sample what we, the pigs and the cows help produce.'

Seated around the farmhouse table in the sunny courtyard Victor introduced his wife, Adele. She was younger than her husband and as Bill noticed very attractive. 'Have you seen Chantelle?' she asked Victor.

'No, not since early this morning. She's probably with one of the boys from the village. You know what she is like when the sun is out.'

Tommy lent in close to Robert so that he could not be heard. *'Blimey, I wonder what floats her boat if it's raining!'*

Adele produced a tray of various cheeses, cut bread and pickles. She left the choice of wine to Victor. Laid out on the table were smaller glasses than usual realising that they had to drive back to Dunkirk.

'This...' Victor said placing a bottle before Bill, 'is one of our best sellers. You will see that the label it says Chateau Cambrae, but that is only for commercial use.' He poured out a glass to each so that they could taste and savour the flavour.

Bill patiently sniffed the wine letting the odours infuse his senses before he took a sip.

'That is good, really good Victor,' he was impressed. 'Fruity, with a slight kick, not unpleasant though and it lingers nicely on the palate.'

Victor smiled at Adele. 'You see my dear. A man who appreciates the importance of our soil.'

'It's really lovely,' Tommy added finishing the contents of his glass, 'is it just red grape?' he asked. Sat alongside Robert was equally impressed.

Victor was grinning like a Cheshire cat. 'I can see that I cannot fool your palate my young friend. We add a little extra in the fermentation process. A small amount of resveratrol, a phytoestrogen. It not only helps process a unique flavour in the wine, but it can also benefit health benefits protecting against age related diseases. It is as important in the benefit of young women, boosting their estrogen levels.'

'How's that,' asked Robert thinking about Samuel lying with the grape producer's daughter.

Adele responded for her husband. 'It can affect the balance of female hormones and help them get pregnant!'

Tommy almost chocked on the wine, but this time he managed to clear the obstruction. Chantelle probably drank a glass of red every evening with her meal night before she went out.'

It was fortunate that Victor laughed seeing the funny side of Tommy's embarrassment. 'It can also tickle the back of the throat to one who is unaccustomed to the taste.'

Bill however wasn't so easily fooled. He glanced at the van wondering what was keeping young Samuel. Also missing was the Dupont's daughter. On the boat over he had studied each of the young men and noticed how each was different from the other.

Robert Perry, as expected was slightly suspicious of most things, but an intelligent lad thinking through a problem. Bill liked that he had integrity. Tommy Jenkins was also a thinker, although more robust he was for getting on with the task at hand and as far as Bill knew the only one of the three to have a steady girlfriend. Which left Samuel as the odd one out in the group. The son of a farmer, Samuel was good on land, but not on water. Bill had already witnessed his lack of grasping reality, his carefree spirit and how the lad would rush recklessly into an adventure not thinking about the consequences. Bill had still to make up his mind about young Samuel Byrne.

They tried other wines, some white although mainly red, agreeing that the Chateau Cambrae was by far the best. Bill thought it would please Olivia Ashleigh. He set about negotiating the price with Victor. They came to the agreement that the greater the quantity, the lesser the cost per bottle, the same going for the cheese. The two men shook on twenty four boxes, each containing twelve bottles together with a dozen cheese bricks. Victor let them have the lot for two thousand, four hundred pounds which Bill happily paid cash. The captain of the *Saucy Belle* told Victor that they would be back for more.

When the forklift arrived with the loaded pallet Samuel was happily sat beside the van chewing on a blade of grass. At last he had a smile on his face and colour in his cheeks.

'I'm glad to see that you're feeling better,' Bill said as he walked towards the van, 'help us load this lot and we can be on our way.' Like a rabbit escaping from a chasing ferret Samuel was up in flash. Full of renewed vigour he grabbed the first case. Coming alongside Tommy had something to whisper. *'I hope your girlfriend doesn't have a taste for wine!'*

Samuel frowned back. *'Why?'*

Tommy laughed. *'Time will tell, Samuel Byrne. Time will tell!'*

He wouldn't elaborate as he went to fetch more boxes. Samuel thought about asking Bill, but the older man kept on giving him funny looks. Odd glances of suspicion. Samuel thought it best to keep quiet. Checking his watch Bill calculated the journey time back adding in the extra hour difference.

'If we get back to Dunkirk before sunset, we might just catch the tide in time to sail back tonight.'

Samuel paled thinking about another night crossing and the sharks. He would be pleased when they were back in Norfolk.

They waved with Bill thanking Adele and Victor Dupont for their hospitality.

Tommy thought that he had caught sight of a curtain move at the window of an upstairs room in the house. He guessed it was Chantelle watching. Looking across at Samuel, who sat on the nearside of the van interior, he had not seen the girl nor had he looked to see if she had watched him leave.

Who Dares Wins

As always the case, the return journey back to the marina at Dunkirk was quicker and less hazardous. Having checked the oil the engine did well. Bill was pleased with the old bakers van which had been unceremoniously christened by Samuel.

By his reckoning Bill Symons believed that the wine would sell for around fifteen pounds a bottle and with a reasonable mark-up on the cheese, they could easy double their profit margin. It should please Olivia Ashleigh, Charlie Luft and Janet Simpson. Looking in the rear view mirror he was surprised to see that Samuel was still wide awake keen to see the passing countryside, although unusually he was quiet and not joining in the chatter between the other two lads. When Samuel saw him looking he moved forward and occupied the seat next to Bill.

'You seem a lot more attentive than the outward journey to Saint Cambrae,' Bill remarked. He watched attentively as a French driver contemplated overtaking on the inside.

'I feel a lot better now thanks,' replied Samuel, 'but I'm glad that I skipped lunch.'

Tommy had stopped talking with Robert. He glanced over at Samuel, but their friend up front didn't look back. Robert whispered to Tommy. *'He'll come unstuck one of these days. Pretty soon his luck is going to run out!'* Tommy shrugged although he was convinced it would. Since their time at school together Samuel had always led a charmed life. *'Don't bank on it,'* he replied, *'he falls in muck chest high and manages to rise up like the phoenix smelling ever better than when he went in.'*

'Bill will lynch him, if he finds out what happened while we were having lunch!'

Tommy grinned. *'Aye, I reckon he would at that.'*

Keeping his head down Tommy liked Bill Symons. He admired the way that the man handled the negotiations with Victor and buying the van, and how nothing seemed to fluster his resolve. Looking at Samuel, of course even the most placid of people could turn if provoked. Knowing about Samuel shagging Chantelle in the back of the van could be one such occasion to evoke such a reaction.

By the time that they reached the marina the sunset had slipped below the nearby rooftops and dusk was already shrouding the harbour in a muggy darkness. Bill parked the van alongside the *Saucy Belle* where unloading would be that much easier and less suspicious. Luck was on their side too as the harbour master had only minutes beforehand gone for his supper and their arrival had gone unseen.

'Store in where there's space,' he ordered, 'and behind the long settee you'll find secret panels. I made them just in case I ever needed an occasion such as today. Make sure you distribute the load evenly though only listing to one side the harbour master might wonder why.' They had just secured the last panel back into place behind which was the cheese when a harbour official walked the wall checking the names of the boats moored for the night. Bill gave the signal, tapping the control bulkhead three times.

'Bonjour Monsieur,' the official said coming across Bill who he found studying his charts in the wheelhouse, 'are you planning on leaving the marina this evening?'

Bill made out that he was surprised to see anybody about. The van had been parked between two others, probably owned by fisherman. 'Welcome monsieur, please do come aboard. We arrived this morning, but one of our party has been a little off colour all day, so we're undecided yet if we are staying or not.'

Bill made out that he had been studying the weather reports as well. The harbour official checked Bill's charts.

'Conditions at sea are favourable tonight, although a night crossing might upset your friend all the more.' He advised. He bent down and waved at the three young men below.

'I thought we were leaving soon?' Samuel whispered. The other two put a forefinger to their lips. *'Sccchh. We are, but Bill's trying to stall the port official. Just act normal if he comes down into the cabin.'* Tommy moved over to the galley kitchen where he began putting things straight. Robert and Samuel took a book each from the shelf. They settled themselves either side of the cabin, evenly distributing their weight.

'Is that your van parked on the quayside monsieur?'

'Qui monsieur, a very pleasing purchase from a local dealer. We thought that it would be handy in case we decided to go touring further inland. Unfortunately, with one of our party feeling queasy we might have to come back another time.'

'Queasy?' the official repeated, unsure of the term. Bill mimicked somebody vomiting to which the official raised his hand in acknowledgment. *'Ahhh vomissement, qui monsieur I understand.'*

The official noticed that the charts that Bill was studying were old, although very detailed. 'You've sailed these waters many times before?' he asked.

'Qui,' replied Bill, standing aside so that the man could see the charts better. 'I was a tugboat captain before I retired.'

'Ahhh, un capitaine de remorquer,' he grinned, holding out his hand for Bill to shake, 'so was my father. It is good to meet another captain.'

The similarity of occupation seemed to immediately sway any suspicion on behalf of the official, he looked down below deck and smiled at the captain's companions.

'You are lucky to be sharing such and an adventure. Bon voyage mes amis.' Stepping back onto the quayside the official caressed his hand along the rail of the cabin top. 'This is indeed a fine vessel monsieur, an Admiral Broom if I am not mistaken.' Bill joined the harbour official also running his hand along the woodwork.

'Constructed entirely from mahogany and oak. As good a boat as any built these days.'

Anton Martine agreed as he admired the craftsmanship. 'Indeed, I would agree with you captain and so would my father. He would like to see your boat if you ever return to Dunkirk.'

Bill Symons smiled as the Frenchman stood back to admire the boat in its entirety. 'We have friends in Alsace that we will be visiting on our next trip. Perhaps we can take your father out on trip around the bay. Keep a look out in the harbour masters logbook for the *Saucy Belle* monsieur.'

Anton Martine said that he would. He left the marina happy and content, and later he would have something special to tell his father when they met up for a drink.

Going back down below deck Bill found the three of them still reading. He was pleased to see that they had remained calm throughout the official's visit.

'Are we going back tonight?' Samuel asked.

Bill was undecided. 'I am not sure. Our friendly port official didn't appear suspicious, but officials can be cunning devils. They can put on a convincing smile, although at the same time planning to examine the boat thoroughly later.

'Curiosity is a strange human behaviour. It casts doubt on both sides. It might be more prudent if we went into town, had ourselves an evening meal and then find somewhere convenient to park the van. That way staying overnight might show that we've nothing to hide. Sailing now we might find ourselves stopped by customs before we got clear of the harbour.'

'Keeping a poker face,' said Samuel. Tommy looked at Robert raising his eyebrows to below his hairline.

'That would mean leaving the boat unguarded Bill. What about the wine and cheese that is stored on board? Robert asked.

'That's the chance that we'll have to take lad if we're to make this trip several times again. Sometimes the more daring you are, the more you get away with.'

They headed into town locating a restaurant around back of the town square where unusually custom was light for the hour. Taking in the terrain Bill spotted a convenient area big enough to park the van. After being shown to their table Bill said that he had a phone call to make.

'He's phoning her a lot, ain't he?' Samuel queried leaning across the table.

'Well maybe they've got things to discuss,' replied Tommy, wondering if he should call his girlfriend.

Samuel screwed up his face. 'Blimey, Ashleigh's old enough to be my granny and Bill ain't that far behind.'

Robert didn't think that Lady Ashleigh and Bill were as old as Samuel described. 'Don't your grandparents share the same bed anymore?' he asked, keeping his finger on the menu where a particular meal had caught his eye.

Samuel looked at Robert as though he'd just swallowed a live frog.

'How would I know that,' he replied. 'One of them has rickets and the other arthritis. I don't listen at the door if that's what you mean. It'd be like a clacker board malfunctioning on the bed.' Samuel put down his menu, deciding that he would wait for Bill to return before ordering as he didn't understand most of what was on offer.

Tommy had already decided on what he was having. 'Well you weren't exactly doing so bad yourself at lunchtime today. The van looked like it was having a dizzy fit when you and Chantelle were humping back and forth inside.'

'Sssshh!' Robert ushered, seeing Bill weave a path between the other tables. *'He's coming back, so keep your trap shut about lunchtime!'*

Bill took his seat next to Samuel. 'Have you all decided yet?'

'No,' replied Samuel, 'I don't understand the menu, it's written in French.'

Bill quickly scanned his eye down the page. 'Well you have a choice of fish, veal or steak, with either chips or salad.'

Samuel was ravenous having not eaten since early that morning. 'I fancy a nice big juicy steak!'

Bill checked the menu. 'You do realise that steak here can mean horse.'

Samuel looked back incredulously, unsure if he was jesting.

'You're having me on aren't you captain. I'm not eating any bloody horse, however hungry I might be.'

Bill grinned. 'Well choose something else.'

Going back down the menu that he didn't understand Samuel chose a fish course instead. He shivered. 'I could have been eating the last nag home at the Longchamp Race Course. At least with king prawns, rice and a garlic sauce I know what I'm getting.'

'Right,' said Bill, 'and what about you Tommy, Robert, what are you having?' They both opted for veal with a side order of creamed potato and vegetables. Bill ordered a steak au poivre with buttered vegetables.

When the meals arrived, they all looked more appealing than Samuels, where the chef had mischievously placed a sprig of rosemary central to the crabs head. Looking down at his plate Samuel thought the crustacean was staring back up at him lying on a bed of hot rice.

'Eat it slow,' Bill advised Samuel. 'Should we decide to leave Dunkirk tonight, munching through king prawns at haste, will have them come back and bite you later.' The dread of meeting another channel shark Samuel did as advised.

'Did you get through to Willow Manor,' Robert asked, adding butter to his bread roll.

'Yes and Lady Ashleigh is very pleased with the arrangement with Victor.' He leant in a little closer, 'and they went to the supermarket today. Charlie has done his bit so our purchases will arrive just in time.'

A waiter suddenly appeared at their table with a complimentary bottle of wine.

'Compliments of Madame Charron,' he said, pouring a little into Bill's glass and waiting for his approval. Robert frowned wondering why.

'What's that for?' Samuel asked suspiciously. Bill thanked the waiter nodding his approval.

'Before I made the call home I spoke with the restaurant owner, a Madame Charron. She agreed to us leaving the van around back of the restaurant providing that we pay her a nominal fee each month. I gave her two hundred euro's and an assurance that we would be back sometime soon. The wine is a show of her gratitude. Two hundred euro's for a small space that's hardly ever used is good business.' They raised their glasses to salute the large lady sat at the bar wearing a feather boa. Leaning sideways towards Samuel, Bill added, 'and for an additional extra two hundred, I said that I would throw you in for the night!'

Bill had to slap Samuel's back hard to prevent him from choking as the others laughed. Tommy looked at Robert. They wondered if Bill knew about Samuel's lunchtime exploits.

Regaining his composure Samuel had suddenly lost his appetite.

'Tell me that you're kidding me captain, she looks like my Aunt Dolly and the old bird's had plastic surgery.'

As tommy and Robert laughed Bill leant close to Samuel. *'Well… rumour has it that you've a taste for French women!'*

Samuel glared across the table at Tommy and Robert, but neither would give away anything.

'Don't blame them,' said Bill, 'they didn't tell me, you did.'

Samuel turned quick to ask how. 'When you volunteered so readily to help load the van your tee-shirt was on inside out!' Tommy and Robert had to stop eating their food to continue laughing.

Indignantly Samuel tried to excuse the error.

'Well you parked the van under a bloody tree where there wasn't a lot of light in the back. I was dressing when she told me that she thought she heard somebody coming so we got dressed a lot quicker than expected.' Samuel stopped talking, thinking. *'Fuck, I hope Mr Dupont didn't notice!'*

Bill joined the others laughing.

'Well I'm sure we'll find out when we go back in six weeks' time.' Bill winked at Madame Charron. 'And maybe your little filly might not be as little as she was today.'

'How did you know that it was Chantelle in the back of the van?' Samuel asked.

'I might look old to you Samuel, but I've been around the block more times than you've had horse steak for your dinner. Let's look at the facts. Firstly, you were both missing from lunch and secondly, I saw her sneak back into the farmhouse. Lucky for you neither her father nor mother saw her. Lastly, putting the tee-shirt aside, you had rosy cheeks and a certain glint in your eye.'

Samuel blew out having been caught out. To make matters worse Bill suddenly produced Chantelle's bra.

'In your hurry to get dressed I found this. One of you must have thrown it clear in your moment of passion. It was down beside the driver's seat.' Samuel felt the weight in the back of his neck get very heavy as his head fell forward in shame. To make matters worse he'd seen Madame Charron looking his way. She had smiled at him, heaved up her chest and was running her tongue seductively across the lipstick stained rim of her glass. Samuel wanted to hide his groin in the seat cushion.

Placing a hand encouragingly on Samuel's shoulder Bill was exuberant, feeling very successful with the outcome of their first adventure together.

'Maybe the next time we come back to Dunkirk instead of paying Madame Charron to look after our van we should just send you upstairs Samuel for a couple of hours. Look upon it as an inter-continental entanglement of diplomatic relations and helping our cause.'

Samuel wasn't amused and for once the halo of luck had slipped.

Around ten they left the restaurant and the van out back heading back to the marina on foot. The town was relatively deserted except for the odd couple out to watch the stars overhead. Back at the boat Bill checked the quayside for any signs of unwanted activity. He was relieved to see that all was peaceful. Since the end of the meal Samuel had been unusually quiet too.

'What are we doing Bill,' Robert asked, as Bill checked the charts one more time.

Bill looked at Samuel who hadn't stopped moaning about his meal, Madame Charron and how they had not let up about his brief encounter with Chantelle. At least his face had some colour. 'Do you think that you could you suffer another night crossing?' They asked. Feeling the damnation of his actions burning deep in his soul, Samuel was reluctant to refuse. 'I'm good,' he replied. 'As long as I can take a lie down. I think that crab is still swimming around inside my gut.'

'Right then,' said Bill, 'if you will both give me a hand we'll get under way and head out before any other buggers come snooping.'

Leaving Samuel below deck Tommy and Robert went with Bill to help cast off. With the engine chugging throughout the length of the boat Samuel was happy to be leaving Dunkirk. He heard Tommy and Robert up top regrouping the mooring lines. The water for now seemed much calmer than when they had arrived.

He lay down for about half an hour, but was unable to get the taste of the shellfish from his mouth. Calling up he asked if anybody else wanted a coffee. Getting no takers Samuel made himself a mug taking it through to the forward cabin where there a bed. He had just put the mug down when he froze thinking that he'd heard a noise coming from his end of the boat. He checked around, but nothing was out of place and the other three were in the wheelhouse. *'It must have been a piece of flotsam,'* he muttered to himself, settling down on the mattress.

They had been at sea for almost an hour when the bow of the boat suddenly went up, crashing back down with enough momentum to wake Samuel from his slumber. Sitting up he dangled his feet over the side rubbing the sleep from his eyes as he yawned wide. A moment later he was sniffing the air which had a funny aromatic odour. He sniffed again *'curry'* he said nodding. He could feel his stomach gurgling at the thought.

When the shadow sneezed Samuel realised that he wasn't alone. Reaching behind he fumbled for the light switch which he didn't find. *'Who's the fucks there,'* he cried raising his right fist defensively.

A voice responded piercing the darkness. 'Please do not be afraid sahib, I am Rakeesh and a friend.'

Remembering where the cabin switch was Samuel flooded the space with light.

Sitting on a wooden chest opposite his bed with his knees pulled up into his abdomen was a young Asian man, not much older than himself. The stranger looked worse than Samuel felt. His eyes were full of concern and his face was gaunt.

'Where the fuck, did you come from the genie's lamp?' Samuel asked. He blinked twice to make sure that he wasn't dreaming.

Rakeesh smiled back showing two lines of perfect dentistry. 'I am from Delhi sahib. I have been walking many days to reach the sea.'

Samuel let forth a low whistle. 'All the way from India, get away with you and how come I didn't see you when I came to take a lie down?'

'Because sahib, I did hide in the wardrobe. Rakeesh has been ducking and diving since leaving Delhi.' Looking at how thin Rakeesh was in his rags Samuel believed the stowaway could lie under a bed sheet and not be discovered.

'What are you doing here,' he asked, 'aboard the Saucy Belle. Bill, our captain will have a fit when he sees you!'

Rakeesh templed his hands. 'I am making my way to England where the streets are all paved in gold and the grass is always green!'

'Yeah right,' Samuel replied, 'and my Aunt Fanny is the Queen of England.'

Rakeesh looked surprised. 'Queen Fanny. She is your auntie, yes sahib? A truly noble woman and she reigns over all your beautiful land. You must be a prince.'

Samuel felt his head drop forward. 'No, my Aunt Fanny isn't a relative, although my Aunt Dolly thins she's the queen, but she's loopy enough to be queen. Come to think of it old Liz don't have a lot of say in matters of state these days, not since the Magna Carta.'

Rakeesh smiled showing off his pearly white teeth. 'Yes, I saw that film with Michael Caine. And your queen she is married to this man Magna Carta. I have heard of him also, a wealthy man with many corner shops, specialising especially in good quality watches, diamonds and jewels.'

'No you prat,' Samuel chuckled, 'that's naffing Cartier!'

'Yes sahib, that is right. He is the son, Charlie Boy and married to Camilla. He came to visit India only recently.'

'Fuck me...' muttered Samuel under his breath realising that they weren't getting very far. 'I think you and me had best see the captain.'

125

Like a nodding dog Rakeesh wobbled his head. 'Yes, that is good sahib. Captains are always good men, wise and knowledgeable. I had a book once when I was a child, it was called *Captain Scarlet.* He was a good man. He fight off evil.'

Samuel helped Rakeesh stand. 'Well one look at you and he's gonna think that you're a bloody mysteron, besides a mystery.'

'Ah,' Rakeesh exclaimed warily, 'the mystery voice that nobody sees, this is not so good!'

When they stepped up from the cabin below Bill Symons looked first at Samuel then the grinning Asian who followed. 'Where the bloody hell did you find him,' he asked, holding onto the wheel, 'in the tea caddy?'

'No captain, he was hiding in the wardrobe.'

Bill Symons sighed long and hard as he shook his head. 'You go to bed with some funny friends young man.' He didn't give Samuel time to reply, instead he turned his attention to the Asian standing beside the cabin door. 'You look half starved, when was the last time that you had anything to eat?'

'I don't know sahib.' Bill knew it to be true.

Giving the responsibility of steering the boat over to Tommy he suggested that they went back down into the cabin where they could get the stowaway some food and then begin unravelling the mystery as to how he got on board.

Making coffee all round and a sandwich filled with cheese of which they had plenty, they sat and watched Rakeesh devour his food with as much dignity as the occasion would permit. Holding onto the coffee mug with his free hand his eyes looked extremely sunken, although grateful.

'Thank you sahib captain, you are a good man. You must know Captain Scarlet.'

Bill looked at Samuel who said he would explain later. Remembering his visits to India way back in the seventies, during the reign of Indira Ghandi, Bill recalled a country divided, although welcoming of foreigners despite certain underlying tensions.

'How did you know that this boat would be going to England, only there were dozens in the harbour, you could have picked any number and got it wrong?'

'I heard you sahib, when you was talking to the man from the boat house. I heard you speak good English.' Bill thought Rakeesh probably meant the harbour masters office. 'And the tall man, he was looking for me.' Bill thought he was referring to Anton Martine.

Rakeesh told them how he had left Delhi five weeks beforehand and been travelling on the long dusty roads ever since, avoiding highway robbers and criminal gangs, hitching a lift with whoever was kind enough to stop and help. Using a donkey, a lorry even a pedal bike, he had eventually arrived in Dunkirk. 'I am now close to my destination.' He said.

'Which is where exactly?' asked Bill, although he had a good idea.

'England, the land of Queen Fanny!' Rakeesh replied eagerly.

Samuel jumped in, seeing the apprehension in Bills eyes. 'We've already had this discussion Bill, trust me you wouldn't want to go there.'

Bill agreed. 'And when we get to England where do you intend staying, you will need a place to live, to work and earn money to feed and buy clothes?'

Raising a forefinger Rakeesh already had a plan in his mind. 'Many moons have come and gone since I worked as a young boy in the house of a very important man. A great man he once told me that to fulfil my destiny, I should broaden my horizon. Before he left India he gave me a photograph, telling me that if I was ever in England to look him up. I think he lives in a big house called Ashleigh Castle.'

Rakeesh promptly produced from his shirt pocket a very old black and white photograph which was badly cracked around all four corners. The people in the photograph however were undamaged and clearly recognisable. Rakeesh handed over the photograph to Bill Symons. 'Here sahib, you look,' Rakeesh prompted.

Bill took the photograph. He slipped on a pair of reading glasses so that he could look properly, but what he saw made the colour in his face fade. 'And you know these people Rakeesh?' he asked.

'Yes sahib that is the master and his mistress.'

Bill grinned. Lady Ashleigh as a mistress was a thought. He passed the photograph over to Robert and Samuel. 'You might recognise the lady standing behind the chair of her husband,' Bill implied.

'Bloody hell,' Robert exclaimed. 'That's Lady Ashleigh and her late husband Lord Lawrence.'

'Yes, yes,' replied Rakeesh eagerly, *'Lawrence of Delhi.'*

Next came a very important question, although Bill Symons believed that he already knew the answer. 'Have you got a passport?'

Rakeesh lowered his head ashamed to look any of them in the eye. He shook his head from side to side creating at the same time a sort of circular motion. 'A passport costs many rupees sahib of which I cannot afford.' He reached inside his shirt pocket once again producing another small picture. 'I do have my embassy pass card with my face on it, it is a good likeness I think.'

Robert saw the image. 'That's like saying that Ho Ching Fat from the Chinese Restaurant in Adlington looks remarkably like his brother and his second cousin.' Bill nodded agreeing. He wondered how they would get past British Customs with a boat load of contraband plus an illegal immigrant. He took another look at the identification card, handing back the photograph of Olivia Ashleigh. She was a lot younger in the photograph although still very striking.

After thinking through the problem he told them what he intended doing.

'I was going to chance our arm and sail back in through Great Yarmouth taking the Yare to where we could meet Charlie, but Rakeesh here could take some explaining. Given the change in our circumstances we should continue heading up the coast. I know a spot just shy of

Blakeney where the estuary flows conveniently into several deep tributaries, deep enough to take the *Saucy Belle*. We'll call ahead and get Charlie to meet us somewhere along the Morston Valley Road.'

Realising that he wasn't going to be dumped overboard Rakeesh was full of enthusiasm again. *'It is how my master, Lawrence of Delhi would say it and who dares wins!'*

Bill Symons looked curiously across at Rakeesh. The Asian grinned back. For the past hour he had been going through various scenarios and excuses should they be stopped by the police or customs. An Asian fisherman out on the estuary at five in the morning was hardly common place in Norfolk. The Ganges or Brahmaputra maybe, but not South of Blakeney Point.

Riding the waves of the Channel the Saucy Belle wasn't that far from the English coast. The conundrum was more baffling than negotiating a thick fog at sea. Bill wondered how he was going to explain Rakeesh to Olivia Ashleigh, Janet and Charlie. Checking the parting of the night clouds Bill gauged that it would be at least two hours before daylight hit the green fields of Norfolk, maybe two hours or longer before Lady Ashleigh got out of bed. Two hours was time enough for him to come up with a plan.

Bill watched Samuel holding onto the cabin door his musings elsewhere back in France. At least Samuel wouldn't go before a court whereas harbouring an illegal alien was a serious offence. He noticed that the sea was getting a dirty muddy colour and choppy.

Extra Hands

Olivia Ashleigh heard the crunch of gravel beneath the tyres of the Rolls as it moved slowly up the drive heading towards the lane at the end. She had considered going with Charlie to meet the *Saucy Belle*, but it was still very early and arriving unexpectedly might send out the wrong signals with the three younger men on board. She was keen however to see Bill.

After the last call from him she had been experiencing butterflies in her stomach, a feeling that had decided to remain dormant. Had the sea captain captivated her that much she wondered, perhaps time would supply the answer. Slipping into a lace chiffon dressing gown she went back to the window to look out, but the front of the house was silent and quiet. The only movement she did expect was Janet would probably be up and making her way down to the kitchen.

'Did Charlie wake you too m'lady?' Janet yawned turning the handle of the tap to fill the kettle.

'It didn't really matter. I'd been on and off all night. I'm always the same when they go on a wine run, only this time it's different and there is the added danger of the sea. I trust Bill Symons, but the channel can cut up rough.'

Janet grinned back although she made no comment. The dark lines under Olivia Ashleigh's eyes suggested that she had been doing a lot of thinking under the stars. 'Would you like some toast with your tea m'lady?'

Olivia Ashleigh looked up from her thoughts. 'Yes please Janet, that will help settle my insides. Perhaps coffee instead of tea.'

'They'll get back safe and sound, I guarantee it m'lady. Bill knows the sea like he knows a good woman when he sees one. Other men on the river tell me that he was born with the spirit of the sea running through his heart.'

'We did right, didn't we, bringing him on board?'

Janet placed four slices of cut bread under the grill. 'It was a wise choice on your part m'lady. Bill is a good steady man and he knows his way around a problem without much fuss. You'll see and everything will be hunky dory when they return home with the goodies.'

The smell of toasting bread soon filled the air as Janet went to the larder to fetch the butter dish and home-made jam, orange with thick chunks of peel and laced with a splash of brandy. Her own recipe.

'And Mr Symons has never been married, I recall you saying the other day?'

Janet smiled to herself. With her back to her mistress experience had taught her that when a woman started asking questions about a certain man, they were becoming romantically attached and interested in that individual.

'Only to the sea m'lady. However, with time on his hands since taking retirement, he can at last relax and give himself over to other pursuits.'

Olivia Ashleigh spread the jam thickly over her toast. Munching down she bit through the crunchy bread enjoying the taste of the orange as it melted in her mouth. 'What other pursuits?' she asked.

'He is partial to cricket, fishing and playing bowls generally although he likes to take his boat up the river quite a lot.'

'So he made an exception by going across to France?'

'Most definitely m'lady. And if I am not speaking out of turn, I would say that you influenced that decision.'

'How so?'

'Well m'lady, it's no surprise that we all miss the master, but as the saying goes life must go on and you are still a very attractive woman. It would be foolish for a man such a Bill Symons not to notice or at least show his hand soon.'

Defensively, but self-consciously Olivia replied. 'Our arrangement is purely on a business basis.'

Janet's eyes dropped to the where her lady was sat the opposite side of the table. 'And the chiffon dressing gown m'lady. You've not worn that particular gown for a long time, in fact the last time was on your silver wedding anniversary. You only wear it for special occasions.'

Olivia Ashleigh touched the fabric of her dressing gown nostalgically. She was lost for a response and didn't know why she had put it on that morning. Janet was right and it was only ever worn for special occasions.

'It must have been the first thing that I grabbed getting out of bed this morning.'

Janet added more marmalade to her toast. The dressing gown would almost certainly have been hanging in the wardrobe and not on the back of the bedroom door like her own. She looked at her mistress hoping that the butterflies stayed around for some time. Looking up at the kitchen clock it was still early.

'I doubt that they will be back for another two hours at least m'lady. By the time they've unloaded the boxes and Charlie alters his route back it might be two and a half perhaps. I'll take a shower before they get here. All that salty sea air is bound to have stirred up an appetite and they'll be wanting breakfast.'

An hour later they returned to the kitchen where the coffee pot was bubbling away. Sombrely attired, wearing an oversized roll neck jumper and faded old jeans Olivia had been conscious of not wearing anything too figure hugging or sexy. Janet approved with a nod. *'Let the imagination do the rest,'* she thought.

Before coming down from her bedroom Olivia had checked herself in the mirror remembering her mother's words of caution when she had been dating Lawrence, a young dashing and aspiring embassy official with ambition, legal or otherwise. *'Don't unwrap the package all at once Olivia, let the ribbon come away slowly. That way you will see for yourself the change in a man.'*

Olivia Ashleigh smiled at Janet reading her thoughts. It was time to put her mother's theory to the test.

*****

Bill Symons manoeuvred the *Saucy Belle* bringing it alongside the old wooden fisherman's jetty. He knew this stretch of water well and it was deep enough to accommodate the hull of the boat. More importantly they could not be seen from the main road.

The grass bank alongside was also sturdy enough to take the weight of a laden car. Only an early dog walker might have thought the unloading of a boat suspicious especially if they noticed the Rolls Royce, but Norfolk was a strange county, with odd people and traditions. It was easier to turn a blind eye rather than lose one.

'Right, come on let's get ourselves organised,' Bill ordered as Charlie stepped aboard.

'Did everything go well?' Charlie asked, catching sight of an extra body below deck.

Bill raised his eyebrows to the fold of his beanie. 'Do you mean Samuel forgetting his sea legs or the journey back.' He thumbed his finger at the cabin door which was slightly ajar. 'We picked up a stowaway at Dunkirk.'

A grinning face appeared in the doorway of the cabin. 'Hello sahib, I am Rakeesh, I am pleased to be greeting you!' Rakeesh stuck out his hand for Charlie to take. Charlie grabbed the hand and forcefully pulled the Asian up onto the deck. He looked at Bill Symons for a reason.

'His story is that he crept aboard while we were negotiating a place to leave the van. Rakeesh here also claims to know Lord and Lady Ashleigh.'

Charlie let his hand fall away. *'Does he indeed.'* Charlie could feel the cold steel of the commando knife hanging down the inside of his trouser leg. Rakeesh produced his embassy pass card and handed it over to Charlie.

'Many moons have passed sahib since I was a young boy. My father was in service at the embassy when Lady Ashleigh would take tea in the afternoon garden.' Charlie studied the photograph. 'You see sahib, she is a very beautiful lady.'

'And you stowed away on the boat, why?' Charlie asked his suspicious hairs at the back of his neck standing proud.

'Because of Lord Ashleigh sahib. He say if I ever come to England to look him up. He tell me that England is the land of opportunity and the streets, they are paved with gold.'

Charlie scoffed giving Rakeesh his photograph back. 'If they were made of gold every slab would have been dug up long ago and sold by the gypsy's.' He ran his fingers through his hair wondering how they were going to explain this to Lady Ashleigh. He asked Rakeesh to give the other men a hand to help unload the boxes.

'Putting aside our stowaway for a moment, did everything else go well?'

Bill Symons nodded. 'Yes and we struck a good deal into the bargain. This is the first batch, but there's much more in the offering if we want it.'

Charlie watched the men loading the boot of the Rolls. 'You've done well Bill. We're about ready this end too and we'll hit the supermarkets again either later today or tomorrow.'

Bill Symons didn't want to be involved with tampering with the supermarket stock, although he was wise enough to appreciate how their plan would promote quick sales.

'Have you thought about what we should say to her ladyship, about Gunga Din over there?' Charlie asked.

'Tell her the truth Charlie, that's my best suggestion. Lying won't help and Lady Ashleigh is no fool. We could always say that she suddenly appeared in a flash whilst Samuel was holding the tea caddy. Let's just hope that that bugger grants us three wishes.'

Charlie watched Rakeesh go to and fro loading the wine and cheese.

'I'll give him that, he's a keen bugger. I still don't trust him though. His eyes are too close to his nose.' Bill hadn't noticed.

'I not sure that I believe he just happened to be at Dunkirk the same time that we were due to set sail. He gave me some cock n' ball story about hiding from the harbour officials.'

Sliding the commando knife from his trouser leg Charlie stroked the blade affectionately as though stroking a woman's leg. 'I could make it look like an accident. We could dump the body further up river and let some dog walker find him. By the time he's found the tides will have done their job admirably. Salt water is as back as being tossed about in an acid bath!'

Bill shook his head unenthusiastically. 'They have exhibits like that in the Black Museum at Old Scotland Yard.' He rubbed the bristles on his chin. 'No, killing him would only complicate the issue and implicate everybody here, including these young lads. I suggest we take him back to Willow Beck and let Lady Ashleigh decide.'

As there was only room for the boxes and one passenger in the Rolls they agreed that Rakeesh should go with Charlie, that way he was less likely to do a runner and if he did Charlie would deal with the situation. Bill and the others would take the boat back out to sea again and come inland via Great Yarmouth. Samuel wasn't keen, but he was easily outvoted.

Bill had another idea. 'Let's hope that we get stopped by the harbour master at Yarmouth. Leastways now they'll not find anything on board that shouldn't be there, cargo or human. It'll help also when we go again across to Dunkirk.'

Charlie applauded Bill's rationale. It reminded Charlie of how careful planning was essential when a dangerous mission was about to happen, allowing for reactive contingencies when the unexpected popped up. Making sure that Rakeesh was surrounded by boxes on three sides in the rear passenger seat he released the handbrake, engaged first gear and pulled slowly pulled away from the mooring electing to take the coast road back to the manor house in case he needed to deal with the Asian enroute. On either side of the coast road the hedgerows and fields were thick with bracken, nettles and woodland.

Like a man who had risen incredulously from the ashes of his death Rakeesh grinned to himself. All was going exactly to plan. He was enjoying the ride in the luxury car and the coast looked very peaceful. Soon a storm would come, a storm of his making.

Like his friend Samuel he had not enjoyed the crossing, but it was essential to gain the smugglers trust. Instinctively he knew that one day he would cross paths with Lord and Lady Ashleigh again.

*****

When Janet caught sight of the Asian accompanying Charlie into the kitchen she felt her jaw dropping. *'What the hell... we started picking up strays as well now Charlie?'* she asked. She lay down the mixing bowl that had been cradled beneath her chest and left arm.

Charlie thumbed at Rakeesh. 'He came back with the wine!'

Walking forward Rakeesh held out his hand and at the same time giving Janet a gracious bow. 'I am pleased to meet you maa ji... I am Rakeesh.'

Caught momentarily off guard by his confident approach Janet shook the stranger's hand, after which she wiped her hand down her pinny. She looked at Charlie for a translation.

'I think it means mum or old lady!'

'Bloody cheek,' Janet responded her expression turning to a scowl. 'And where did you come from?' she asked Rakeesh.

'I was born with my mother in a village named Patpar Puril.'

'Oh,' replied Janet, obviously none the wiser, 'would you like something to eat or drink?'

Rakeesh patted his stomach gratefully.

'Please. The sandwich on the boat is still doing swimming around like a whirly pool.' Janet invited Rakeesh to sit at the table. A minute later the kitchen door opened and in walked Lady Ashleigh. Rakeesh immediately jumped up from his chair bowing low.

'*Sahiba!*' he said. He would not raise his head, not until Olivia Ashleigh spoke.

'Goodness, hello Rakeesh,' she replied walking across to where he stood. 'And please do look up, we are much less formal here.' She was surprised to see him in her kitchen. 'It is good to see you again mistress.'

'What in heavens name are you doing here?' she asked, peering across at Charlie Luft. 'He came with the wine and cheese m'lady, a stowaway!'

'A stowaway,' Olivia Ashleigh repeated. 'How adventurous and exciting.'

She took a pace back so that she could get a better look. The last time that she had seen Rakeesh he had been a young boy. With the passing of the years he had grown and become a man.

'And Bill Symons and the others,' she asked, 'where are they?'

'They're sailing back to the river m'lady, where they'll leave the *Saucy Belle*. They'll join us later.'

Olivia Ashleigh nodded approving of the captains caution. 'Perhaps Janet would make coffee while we decide what we're going to do with Rakeesh.' Sitting down Charlie felt the hilt of the knife dig in his side. He knew exactly what he would like to do with the stranger. Like Bill he didn't trust the young Asian.

After taking breakfast leaving Rakeesh with Lady Ashleigh and Janet, Charlie went to unload the car wanting to be alone. It was bad enough that Rakeesh had seen their imported wine and cheese, but there was no reason to have him know about the underground store. Digging his knife deep into the wood frame of the cellar door he would chose to take Rakeesh to the local wood and be done with him, just like the French Resistance had done during the last war.

Drinking his coffee black and unusually passing up the chance of Janet's finest cooked breakfast, Charlie was uneasy around the stranger in their midst. His story that he had walked from Delhi to Dunkirk was in his opinion not only outrageous, but too farfetched to be true.

Just before eleven the other four arrived at the manor house. They looked exhausted, hungry and in need of a drink. Janet supplied tea and coffee as she made them brunch. When Rakeesh reappeared with Lady Ashleigh he was dressed in some of the master's old clothes. Hanging limply from his body the clothes looked as desperate as Rakeesh. Olivia Ashleigh was pleased to see Bill Symons back safe and sound. Sitting

Rakeesh down amongst the other three she settled herself next to the captain.

'Did everything go well?' she whispered. Her voice was hushed, her eyes on Janet as she kept the four young men amused at the other end of the table.

'Everything went really well except for this minor hiccup.' He raised his eyebrows towards Rakeesh. 'He was something that I hadn't banked on bringing home!'

Olivia placed her hand reassuringly over the back of Bill Symons arm.

'We'll sort out why he's here later. In the meantime I am happy that you got back safely. I was worried.'

'What about?'

'I'm sure what Bill, it was just a nagging feeling that kept me awake at night. It's gone now!'

'Charlie told me that you have the doctored bottles ready for the supermarkets.'

Olivia Ashleigh smiled, up close he had nice eyes, soft yet engaging. She kept her eye on Rakeesh. He was watching and looking around as though taking it all in. She too had her suspicions.

'The supermarket,' she replied dividing her attention. 'Yes, we thought we'd make a start with one branch and see how sales affects their trade. Perhaps after you've finished your breakfast you would cast an expert eye over our plan.'

Sitting at the end of the table Rakeesh had his ears pricked. He made space on the wooden bench when Charlie walked back into the kitchen. Charlie saw the offer, but elected to stand alongside Janet as she poured his fresh coffee.

'I kept some breakfast back just for you, in case you changed your mind. You seemed...' she stalled, 'distracted earlier.'

Charlie tilted his head towards where Rakeesh was listening to the others talk. *'Call it a gut instinct Janet and rest assured I've had a lot of practice. I can smell a rat when it lies.'*

Charlie saw Bill looking his way. He nodded back knowing what the captain was thinking. He sat himself down next to Tommy Jenkins with Janet coming alongside. 'Did you hear the cuckoo earlier?' he asked.

'Yes, I did. It's the first that I've heard this year.'

Charlie lent closer to Janet. 'Originally from France, it is pronounced *coucou.* Our English interpretation is that someone who is cuckoo is mad. As a countryman I've always thought that a cuckoo sings when something's not right. And like our unwanted guest at the end of the table the cuckoo travels miles to reach its destination. Nobody, unless you're a bird or animal travels so far without a passport!'

Tommy stretched his arms high and wide as he yawned. 'Time for some shuteye, so with your permission m'lady we'll take ourselves elsewhere and see you all later.' Grateful for their effort Olivia Ashleigh saw them to the door where she thanked them. She had never seen them to the door before.

Walking down the drive Samuel was the first to speak. 'That was the secret warning, wasn't it?' walking centre his eyes went left and right.

'Yes, it was…' replied Robert, 'although I've no idea why, although my money is on Rakeesh. Did you see the way Bill and Charlie were watching him. They don't trust him.'

'And neither do I,' said Tommy. 'Charlie was talking to Janet about the cuckoo. My dad reckons it's a good sign of when something isn't right.'

Samuel sniffed. 'Well he was sat close enough to Janet. I reckon old Charlie has the hots for the old girl.'

Tommy laughed. 'I saw him in the chemist the other day. He acted very sheepish when he saw me walk in.'

'Probably picking up his prescription Viagra.' Replied Samuel. He rudely stiffened his arm shooting it upright. 'Pecker problems I'd say!'

Robert came to Charlie's defence. 'No. I'd say he had no problems in that department. Charlie is as fit as a fiddle and if you saw the bulge down his leg, you'd not wonder why.'

Samuel laughed out loud. 'That's where he keeps his commando knife you fool.' His expression changed. 'Old Rakeesh seemed genuine.'

Robert shook his head disagreeing. 'No. We should watch him closely. There's definitely something fishy about his story that doesn't add up.'

'But he knows Olivia Ashleigh from way back,' Samuel argued.

Robert Perry suggested otherwise. 'Did you notice how eager he was to help unload at Blakeney, it was like he was counting every boat going into the Rolls. I've a funny feeling about Rakeesh.'

Samuel dismissed the caution. 'You have a funny feeling about a lot of people Perry. It's probably because your old man's a copper. Rakeesh and his kind all work hard, why do you think that they own so many corner shops.'

Just talking about Rakeesh had the hairs on Robert's neck stand on end. Whatever Samuel argued in favour of the Asian, he would not be convinced. 'No, I'm with Charlie on this one.'

Tommy scoffed. 'Next thing is you'll be telling us both that you're joining the police.'

Samuel's head went left and right again. 'You're not are you?'

'Not what?' Robert repeated.

'Joining the boys in blue?'

Robert laughed. 'What and end up kicking the arses of toe-rags like you Byrne. You've got to be joking. I would rather take the risk and continue doing what we're doing now.'

Remembering Where, When and Why

With Rakeesh sleeping soundly in the old servant's quarters Olivia Ashleigh took advantage of the situation taking Bill Symons below to the old cellar via the secret staircase hidden inside in the pantry. Their departure was avidly watched by Janet and Charlie.

'They're getting a bit familiar aren't they?' Charlie frowned.

Janet had made them fresh coffee. 'So what if they are Charlie. I should think that after her husband's death the hours drag on by, especially come the cold nights.'

Charlie was taken aback by her reaction. 'I'm just saying that's all.'

Janet nudged his arm playfully. 'Do I detect a hint of the old green eyed dragon Charlie Luft?'

'They're hazel brown with hints of green you silly bugger,' he replied. 'And no, of course I'm not jealous. I'm just watching out for her that's all.'

Janet looped her arm through his. 'She's way above our pay grade Charlie and you shouldn't be envious of the captain. They move in different circles to us.'

Charlie laughed. 'What like the swirling eddy around dogger bank.'

'You know what I mean you old bugger. If you want love you would find it with your own kind!'

Now Charlie was no fool nor a slouch in the romantic stakes, but it had been a long time, a very long time since he had played the field. With his arthritis he was like a retired race horse, rusty over the jumps and his hooves needed re-shoeing.

He scoffed. 'Who would I find to be interested in me at my age?'

Janet's chest slumped forwarded joined by her head as she sighed shaking her head. When she lifted it back up, she pulled his chin her way. *'I would be interested you daft old bugger!'*

Charlie had to sit back in his chair, his eyes growing wide. 'You Janet… really, I'd never have guessed.'

Janet sat herself even closer. 'You might have been one hell of a spy in your day Charlie Luft, only all that standing about on dark street corners to pass messages must have damped your ardour. Had you not been walking around with your eyes shut or knee deep in muck, I've been keen on you ever since I came to the manor house.'

Charlie smiled back. 'Then why do you chase Antonio Vincenzi around the restaurant when you go looking for orders?'

Janet looked intently at Charlie, her heat beating soundly beneath her ample chest.

'I'd give the Italian five minutes before the flames of his passion went out. A more mature man like you knows how to keep an old boiler stoked for much longer!'

In his time Charlie Luft had met some amorous Parisian dancers, some strikingly more beautiful than others who needed to shave at least once a week. Sitting alongside Janet Simpson he felt a stirring in his loins. Wholesome all over she could cook, drink and say it as it was. What was leftover, well that was the mystery that made everything else seem uninteresting. Charlie saw the future suddenly as he had never seen it before.

'A bit like going on an undercover mission only without the cyanide capsule. Perhaps you had best come and see my prize onions sometime.' He left the invite open for her to decide when and where.

*****

In the cellar below the air was heavily infused with the odour of wine. There was a slight dampness probably from the chalk seamed walls. Bill was impressed with the layout.

'I reckon all manor houses should have secret passages beneath their kitchen.'

Olivia Ashleigh grinned pointing to the locked door at the far end of the passage. 'There Bill, the door on the left leads all the way back to the vicarage. It was used by church elders and ministers fleeing the tyranny of Henry's reformation.'

Bill sensed the chill in the air, but they were at least ten feet below ground. 'Old Henry himself would have been proud of your overseas operation.'

The bottles that had been tampered with by Charlie had been put to one side and ready for distribution. Olivia Ashleigh was keen to have the captain cast his eye over a bottle or two. She wanted to see if he noticed anything out of the ordinary. Picking the first bottle at random he gave it a good shake to see that the seal held.

'Don't worry about my disturbing the wine as the contents will soon settle.' He stroked the underside of the bottle watching the wine calm. 'They are good, in fact very good. I would not be able to tell which had been tampered with had you not shown me.'

It was the approval that Olivia Ashleigh had wanted to hear.

'We will need to organise ourselves properly if we're to receive regular shipments from Saint Cambrae.' She suddenly turned and held his arm. 'Will you dine with me here tonight at the manor house. Janet will cook anything that you desire.'

'I'd like lamb with mint sauce please, potatoes and greens. I'm a simple man Lady Ashleigh. I'm happy enjoying life again after spending most of my life at sea. I'm happy to be working with you.'

'Lamb it is then,' she agreed. He saw her eyes flicker in the cellar light. 'And Bill, please call me Olivia. My life of formality died when my husband Lawrence passed away.'

He nodded. 'An unfortunate shooting accident whilst out for game, or so I believe.'

'I was always on at Lawrence not to go messing with guns and wildlife. Neither like one another and as sure as eggs is eggs, one or the other was likely to get hurt. At the inquest, the Coroner assured me that Lawrence didn't feel a thing.' Bill Symons was glad that he hadn't asked for game.

'What about Rakeesh,' he asked, 'won't he be around this evening?'

Putting her closed fingers to her lips she had forgotten about their guest. 'Rakeesh really is becoming a fly in the ointment. I'll think of something to get him out of the way. I think when you go back to Saint Cambrae he should go along as well Bill. Perhaps leaving him inadvertently at the roadside say fifty miles east of Dunkirk he might take the hint that he's not wanted here. Maybe a call to the French authorities that they have an illegal wandering around the countryside with no passport might start a manhunt.'

Bill Symons grinned liking the idea. She was shrewd besides beautiful. He knew her idea would please Charlie especially.

'Can you contact Robert Perry,' she asked. 'See if he and the others are available to take Rakeesh out later. Let them show him the sights of the local countryside. That way he'll be out of our hair.'

'I'll give young Robert a call later after he's had a sleep.'

'That photograph Bill, the one that Rakeesh keeps in his pocket, it's been tampered with. I know that we never posed for any such photograph. Lawrence was never keen on photographs being taken during our afternoon tea sessions. I don't know what Rakeesh hopes to gain coming here now, but I don't trust him.'

They turned out the cellar light going back up to rejoin Charlie and Janet.

*****

Standing in the middle of the village next to the war memorial the three were about to go their own way needing some well-earned sleep when Robert Perry suddenly snapped the ends of his fingers together. *'Bloody hell,'* he exclaimed, *'I've just remembered where I've seen Rakeesh before!'*

Samuel yawned loudly. 'Okay Sherlock Holmes, where exactly?' he yawned a second time.

Robert slapped Samuel's upper arm making him pay attention. 'The customs shed at Dover on our last trip in the lorry. You remember the two Asians in the car that was attacked by that crazy customs dog. The passenger was Rakeesh. I am sure of it.'

Samuel Byrne stopped his yawning as Tommy stopped fidgeting. *'Fuck me Rob, are you sure?'* asked Tommy.

'As sure as I could be without seeing his bloody passport,' he replied. 'Which he said he lost somewhere on his journey from Delhi to Dunkirk.'

Tommy sensed that sleep wasn't top of the agenda suddenly.

'We should get back to the manor house and warn Lady Ashleigh and the others.' Said Samuel. Robert held onto his friends arm to prevent his turning back.

'Let's just stop and think for a minute.' He said. 'How could Rakeesh be at Dover then Dunkirk, claiming that he had walked from Delhi?'

'Because he was never in Delhi,' replied Tommy.

Robert grinned as his head nodded up and down. 'That's right. He was in Dover because we were in Dover and then Dunkirk because we were there too. That's a hell of a coincidence don't you think?'

'And without a passport!' added Samuel who was annoyed for being sucked in so easily by the greasy Asian.

'What are we going to do Robert?' asked Tommy.

Stifling a yawn of his own Robert Perry massaged the drowsiness from his forehead as he thought through the problem.

'If we go straight back and Rakeesh sees us coming back up the drive, he will suspect that something is wrong. He'd know that he's been rumbled. Somehow we need to get a message to Janet or Charlie so that they can alert the captain and Lady Ashleigh.

'I'll do it,' Samuel volunteered. 'I'll take the tractor. I'll make an impromptu visit with a hay bale. If Rakeesh sees me driving the tractor he won't think anything's wrong. I told him that my dad was a farmer. Charlie however will know something's wrong the minute he sees me driving the tractor. He knows I've not passed my tractor test.'

They agreed that it was the best plan leaving it up to Samuel to warn Charlie and the others. Robert and Tommy went home although neither would sleep wondering when the police or customs would come knocking on their door.

As Samuel had said Charlie saw the tractor coming up the leafy lane behind the estate loaded with a large hay bale. Being driven by Samuel it was a sure sign that something was amiss.

'I thought you'd be fast asleep by now lad.' Charlie said as Samuel switched off the engine and jumped down.

'I've something urgent to tell you Charlie, but we need somewhere private?' Charlie suggested the garden tool shed where he assured Samuel that it was the safest place on the estate. Looking into the younger man's eyes, he could see something was troubling him. Inside the shed they took a seat opposite one another.

'So what's got you all wound up like a coiled spring?'

'Our mysterious stowaway Rakeesh.' Samuel told Charlie about the conversation that he and Tommy and Robert had had not half an hour before.

Taking the commando knife from his pocket Charlie launched the long sharp blade purposefully at the bench post on the far side of the shed. The tip of the blade came to rest with a quiver. The throw was accurate and dead centre of the post. Samuel stared in awe. It was as good a throw as he had ever seen. He could see the hatred in Charlie's eyes.

153

'I knew that there was something fishy about that slimy bastard the minute that I set eyes on him.' Charlie went over to the bench post to retrieve his knife. 'I was all for leaving him in the Glaven and letting the tide do the rest, but Bill didn't want to dirty his hands.'

Remembering that Bill Symons knew about his unplanned fling with Chantelle Dupont, Samuel decided it was best not to pass comment on the captain. 'What are we going to do Charlie?' he asked.

The ex-SOE agent-cum-gardener was thinking deep and murderously. He sat himself down beside Samuel removing the dirt from beneath his fingernails with the tip of the knife.

'I suppose in a way Bill was right. The tides around the headland are not always as reliable as they should be and if the fish or visiting seals didn't clean up, then there was every chance that the bugger could end up being found amongst the mud banks. Can you imagine it lad, the police would have a field day gathering evidence. Something however small would bring them to Willow Beck.

He stopping scrapping the dirt from under his fingernails for a moment.

'We need to devise a plan which will draw him away from the manor house and somewhere obscure where we can do the deed properly. Obviously Lady Ashleigh must not be implemented nor Janet.'

Samuel was surprised that Charlie had included Janet.

'Men must always protect the women and children, remember that lad,' said Charlie vehemently. 'Call it chivalrous if you like, but some of the

154

old values must be kept alive. Even in this day and age when so much about is changing.' He threw the knife again at the same post. Again it hit dead centre and was almost alongside the first notch.

'Fuck me Charlie, did they teach you that in the army?'

'No lad, I taught myself. It came in handy on more than one occasion, trust me.' Charlie didn't say where or when.

Thinking about Chantelle, Samuel agreed with Charlie. Somehow he had to see her again. However in the rush to get away from the vineyard and back to Dunkirk he had forgotten to give Chantelle his mobile number.

Charlie plucked the knife from the post. 'Don't look so pensive lad,' said Charlie, 'there's a solution to every problem.'

Samuel snapped himself back from his thoughts. 'I was just thinking about the visit to Saint Cambrae that was all Charlie.'

Charlie's eyes narrowed. 'Why, did something happen whilst you were out there?' Charlie needed to know as everything as he already had a plan going around inside his head of how to get rid of Rakeesh. He didn't want any more surprises to intervene.

'No, not really. I liked Saint Cambrae and it seemed quieter than here in Norfolk, besides bigger.' All that Charlie could hear was the birds singing.

'You can't get much quieter than the countryside lad, especially on a lazy summers day.'

The two of them sat quietly for a few moments each reflecting. Charlie was thinking about the many parachute drops that he had made at night, dropping into occupied enemy territory to help the war effort as Samuel was thinking of his own conquest. Six weeks seemed like a lifetime away.

Charlie was the first to break away from his memory. 'France is bigger lad, I'll give you that. A lot less hurried as well away from the capital and some of those French lasses can be very sexy.' Charlie blew out through his lips as he curved his hands in and out in a downward movement.

'I know...' it was all Samuel was prepared to admit. Sex with Chantelle had been extremely vigorous as well as exciting. More thrilling than with any of the home grown girls in and around Willow Beck.

'Do you know,' Charlie began, his memory not entirely lost, 'I remember one particular mademoiselle. Her name was Mimi and she was a dream come true. Strikingly beautiful she went in and out in all the right places. Mimi was in the French Resistance and she would tell everybody that she was my lover especially when the Germans came visiting the cafes. I would die a thousand times, but Mimi was incredibly brave.'

'Why didn't you stay in France after the war Charlie, why come back?'

'There was no point, not after Mimi got killed.'

Samuel felt his throat suddenly tighten wishing that he'd not asked. 'I'm really sorry Charlie, I didn't know.'

'Of course you didn't lad, nobody knows. It's one of the secrets that never gets around, so keep it to yourself for me.' The ex-wartime agent let go a long sigh. 'Mimi was killed laying a booby-trap mine in the woods for the German patrols only the bloody detonator was faulty. It went off the moment that she made contact. Mimi didn't stand a chance. I came back home soon after that.'

'Is that why you never married?' asked Samuel. Charlie nodded.

'It took me a long time to get over Mimi.' He chuckled. 'Funny thing was that we were never intimate. There was always some other bugger around.' He winked, probably as an image passed through his mind. 'We got damn close on several dark occasions to making it happen, but it never did happen. I reckon we would have made a good couple, had the war not taken precedence over everything else at the time.'

Samuel was surprised to hear Charlie speak so openly about the past and maybe Mimi was why the old gardener spent so much time alone. Samuel understood how on bad days Charlie could be a little terse. Chantelle had left him with a lingering feeling, something that was both pleasing and at the same time concerning. He would encounter many sleepless nights until he saw her again.

'I think that if I'd found somebody like Mimi, I would have wanted to have been with them whatever the consequences Charlie.'

The gardener knuckled the side of Samuels arm. 'Thanks lad, although in a way Mimi never left.' A third time he threw the knife. It landed as deadly accurate as the previous two occasions. 'Now back to that slimy bugger Rakeesh.'

'You said you had a plan.'

'I've several and none of them are legal. Remember though, we can't involve the women. The accident that befalls our mystery guest has got to be executed with the utmost secrecy and it has to look like an accident. All the best murders are inevitably made to look like an accident. Many a killer has gone to his grave without ever being detected.'

Samuel grinned, he liked Charlie's problem solving approach. 'I could get him work on the farm, there's always fatal accident's every year involving heavy plant.'

Charlie grinned but dismissed the idea not wanting Samuel's father involved.

'It's a good idea, but the least amount of people we involve the safer it is for all concerned, expect of course the victim.' He caressed the side of his cheek with the blade. 'And once the police get involved they never stop turning over stones until they've uncovered every grain of truth. With a simple well-constructed accident the facts speak for themselves and all suspicion goes away without any fuss.

'Lady Ashleigh was going to ask the three of you to take Rakeesh out tonight and show him some of the local sights. If you could let me know where you propose taking him we could arrange for an accidental hit-and-run.'

Samuel grinned. 'Somewhere dark and where there a lot of undergrowth.'

'That's the spirit lad. Accidents are always more predictable when they're out in the sticks. I'd just need to know what time.'

'Tommy has a date this evening with Alice, but Robert and me are free. We'll take Rakeesh out.'

'That's good, two's enough,' agreed Charlie. 'What about Copsley Copse up the road from the estate. There are some very nasty bends at the crossroads and wild animals are always coming to grief there. If you and Robert decide to take a leak in the nearby bushes, it'll leave Rakeesh alone long enough for me to drive at him. He'd be like a deer caught in the headlights. Seconds later our problems will disappear in a flash. It could be weeks, maybe months before he's found. By then there'd be little left to identify him by.'

Samuel felt a cold shiver run down his spine. Charlie made it sound so easy. He smiled weakly wondering how many people Charlie had killed in his time. 'What will you use?' he asked.

'Don't worry, I've got the ideal machine lad. It moves like the wind and runs like greased lighting. One whack should be enough.' With Samuel gone Charlie went to the estate garage where he pulled back a large protective dust cover. Putting the cover aside he admired the motorbike that had belonged to Lord Ashleigh. It was the ideal machine with deadly accuracy. Later he would take it for a run to make sure that it didn't need tuning.

Saint or Sinner

Walking up the path towards the vicarage with her suitcase in her hand Mary Nelson's palms were sweaty with apprehension. St Ridley's was her first church and Will Beck her parish. Mary was determined to make a name for herself.

Only the afternoon before she had cordially shared tea with the Bishop who had informed her of the unexpected vacancy.

'It's yours if you want it Mary. The late Victor Higginbottom left the parish high and dry with his sudden departure. I am concerned that without a vicar to hold together our loyal worshippers, Satan will step in and steal them from under our feet.'

'Is the parish divided in its loyalty to God?' she asked having taken another biscuit with her tea.

'Not so much loyalty Mary, but they need guidance. There is a certain underbelly of activity at Willow Beck that needs a calming influence. You would offer such calm in my opinion.'

Mary smiled over the top of her cup. Willow Beck sounded just perfect. 'The devil however, why surely not Bishop.'

John Steele templed his palms together. 'Sin is everywhere Mary. It appears in many guises and like woodworm difficult to eradicate.'

'How would the village take to the new vicar being a woman?' she asked.

The Bishop chuckled keeping his hands together. 'I would imagine that the initial shock will make them sit up and think. Victor had them eating out of the palm of his hand, but in some ways he had become complacent. Some members of the community were quick to take advantage of his gentle disposition. You however would be like a breath of fresh air. A whole new chapter!'

Mary liked a challenge and she needed a different direction in her life. She accepted the Bishop's offer. It was a chance to put to bed certain aspects of her former life. Putting down her suitcase she had arrived to find a note pinned to the front door of the vicarage.

'Please use the kitchen door around back, I'm busy cleaning. Grace.'

Mary smiled. She liked surprises, although the message wasn't quite what she had expected on her first day. Breathing in she picked up her case and walked around back. At the kitchen door she knocked before entering. *'Hello,'* she called out. There was no reply. Elsewhere in the vicarage a radio was playing.

Mary left her case inside the kitchen making her way to where a female was singing out of tune one of her favourite pop songs. Again she knocked only this time on the bathroom door. The singing stopped. A young woman pulled open the door.

Sweeping aside a loose strand of hair she quickly wiped her hands down her apron. *'Hello there,'* she grinned, *'you must be Mary Nelson the new vicar, 'I'm Grace.'* Ignoring that the woman had been cleaning the toilet pan when Mary knocked on the door she was pleased to meet Grace.

'The Bishop John Steele hired me end of last week as the new cleaner. He asked that I clean the place thoroughly today as you would be arriving.'

Mary had noticed how clean the house looked walking up the stairs.

'Are you related,' Grace asked, 'you know, some great, great grand-daughter to that famous sailor who had one eye and lost an arm. Always looked like he was going for his wallet?'

Mary smiled. She had heard the same question many times.

'Maybe Grace although I've never checked my lineage. Most of my relatives seem to have distanced themselves from history settling in America, Scandinavia and Southern Ireland. I guess that somewhere in that mix I came along. I'm not sure that Lord Nelson was a relative only I'm not good on the water. Giving a baptism is as close as I want to get to water. I don't object to coffee or a wine though!'

Grace checked her watch, it was almost time for coffee and a break. 'So where you born then vicar?'

'That's a good question. I was abandoned at birth and everything about me was written on the back of a tourist postcard depicting Cromer Pier. Somebody who helped raise me gave me the name Mary Anne Nelson. The only real thing I do know is that there was a rector a rector in the family three hundred years back. The rest you can draw from your own conclusions.'

Grace squeezed the excess water down the pan and dropped the sponge in her bucket. She stood up. 'Is that why you became a vicar?'

'Not necessarily although you could say that it was a calling of some sort.'

Grace flushed the toilet, picked up her bucket and ushered Mary out. 'Do you fancy a hot brew and a nice piece of fruit cake?' Mary hoped that she would wash her hands before handling the cake. 'That sounds great Grace. I left my suitcase downstairs, but if you tell me which is my bedroom, I'll just change and join you.'

Grace pointed to the door at the end of the landing. 'Best room on the landing. My room is the other end. It's a live-in position. Is that okay?'

Mary smiled back at the housekeeper. 'I would be really glad of the company. God can only spread himself so thin, resting his head wherever he can.' As though on cue the DJ played *'Papa was a rolling stone'* by the Temptations.

Mary elected to take coffee in the study where the comfy chairs were more appealing than the wooden cushion less seats in the kitchen. The bookcase was full. 'Did all these belong books to the late Victor Higginbottom?' she asked.

'I expect they did,' replied Grace, 'although I'll come clean Mary, I never really attended church unless it was for a wedding. The last vicar made my skin crawl.'

Mary nodded back. After taking tea with John Steele she had contacted some of the tutors with whom she was friendly. There were various versions concerning the late Victor Higginbottom although most considered him to have been an eccentric. She had been told about his tragic accident involving the rowing machine.

'I understand that one of the downstairs rooms was made into a fitness centre?'

'The Bishop had the decorators in soon after the vicar's death. It's now just another room for reading.' Grace told Mary that she hoped they'd take morning coffee together except on Sunday's when Mary had her busy day. Leaving the tray to collect later she went back to her cleaning leaving Mary alone in the study.

As soon as study door was closed Mary settled back into the leather tanned Hadfield. She shut her eyes gathering together her thoughts. It had been a while since she had used her gift last but the time felt right.

The first image to appear was of a man struggling. She was shocked to see a large woman kneeling astride of the man as he gasped for breath. Suddenly a huge cross appeared and the vision disappeared. The next was of a beautiful woman. The same age as Mary. The woman was waving as she approached. Mary saw herself smiling, it was a good omen. The other images blurred and it was another hour before she woke. Her coffee had gone cold, but she could still hear the radio playing upstairs. Mary stretched her arms wide. St Ridley's felt right. She didn't feel any demons about and certainly not Satan. Her attention was drawn to a particular book.

Taking the volume from the middle shelf the book was entitled *Temptation of the Damned.* Mary frowned, it was an unusual book to be owned by a man of the church. Replacing the book she went to explore.

Minutes later Grace appeared with her bucket. 'This kitchen has a nice aura. It's inviting. We had as fancy like this at Divination College. I think I'm going to be very happy here Grace.'

'Have you always lived with church people vicar?'

Mary chuckled.

'Gosh no. I was fostered out several times, mostly because the families sold up or moved away. I wasn't part of their long term plans. My last placement was with a real odd-ball family. The man was a long distance lorry driver and thankfully hardly ever at home. His wife was a nurse who worked nights and together they had an unemployed son who his lifestyle buoyant by growing and selling weed. He told me that he was a professional horticulturist. His green patch was at the nearby allotment.'

'Cannabis?' Grace asked.

Mary nodded, picking up the wiping up cloth and drying a plate that stood in the dish drainer. She laughed. 'At the time it seemed funny as most of the amateur gardeners were retirees, men and women to whom a pop concert was a distant memory. Robin, the son who was twenty at the time would ask them for tips on growing. He got their permission to erect a polytunnel with power.

'You can normally smell cannabis.' Mary agreed.

'The power came from a nearby lamppost. Robin told me that it powered his ultraviolet lights.'

'Didn't any of the allotment people think it suspicious?' asked Grace.

'No. Robin told that he was helping with an experiment for the ministry of agriculture, fisheries and food agency. He even made space in the polytunnel for an old lady to grow her tomatoes.'

Grace nodded. 'The leaves look the same.' Mary nodded back. 'My younger brother,' said Grace, 'used to grow them funny tomato plants in dad's old greenhouse. Our old man was always happy when he'd been down there late in the evening and his tomatoes always tasted twangy!'

Mary smiled. She liked Grace already.

'Didn't the police notice the polytunnel, see the lilac glow at night?' Grace asked.

'That was Robin's undoing. He tried to convince them that the lights were necessary for his experiment. When he got arrested so did five other gardeners, three of whom were on the allotment committee. The old lady disappeared with her tomato plants.'

'What an odd family. A bit like mine,' Grace admitted.

'Anyway, I left that evening with just a few clothes in a rucksack and never looked back. I found a job in a factory and lived rough for a time. One day I found myself inside a church listening to the organist play when I saw the light. Here I am. Not a story that'll get me a red book, but the church gave me sanctuary when I needed it most, so now it's time to give something back.'

'Wow,' said Grace. 'You'll fit in just right vicar. Willow Beck needs new blood.'

There were five bedrooms in all and each was visited by Mary and Grace with Grace showing Mary hers. They decided that they would share the remaining three using them as a guest room, a sewing room and the last an art studio as both Mary and Grace were keen amateur artists.

After lunch Mary went back to the study where she felt drawn to the book again. *Temptation of the Damned* had been looked at many times from the creased pages and some had the corners turned down. Mary took the book outside where she dropped it in the rubbish bin. Looking skyward she wanted a new start and ghosts were not invited.

Returning to the book shelf she found another book on a similar vein but when she tried to remove the book she found it mysteriously stuck fast between two other hardback volumes on either side. However much she tried she couldn't budge the book which was strange. She didn't know, but holding the tops of all three books she pulled them back. Instantly they moved and so did a hidden panel in the wall beyond the tall bookcase.

Mary checked hearing the radio playing elsewhere in the vicarage. She cautiously pulled the appendage open a little wider until confronted with a set of stone steps that disappeared down into where not light existed. Rummaging through the desk drawer she found a pencil Maglite. Despite its size it produced a powerful beam.

Mary stepped down pulling the wall opening shut although not closing it entirely. Casting the beam before her she went down reaching the bottom quite quickly where she found herself standing in a long dark passage. All about were thick entangled cobwebs. Holding onto the torch and the cross hanging down from her neck she followed the beam to the other end.

A Road Island Red and Cockerel

Charlie was pleasantly cordial when he came across Rakeesh, telling him that Robert and Samuel would return around seven that evening to take him out as they wanted to show him some of the local haunts.

'Haunts, what is haunts sahib?' Rakeesh was dressed in another of Lord Lawrence's hand-me-downs after his shower

Charlie thought Rakeesh resembled an over-tanned Charlie Chaplin. He was peeved seeing the Asian parading around in his late master's clothes but as Lady Ashleigh had specifically picked them out, Charlie wondered why as they were the late master's gardening shirt, trousers and shoes.

'Local attractions,' Charlie replied. 'Places you'd find interesting and maybe a trip to the pub.'

'Including the church…?' Rakeesh immediately realised his mistake. Charlie made out that he's not heard the comment. It was however a big mistake and proved that Rakeesh knew more about Willow Beck than he was letting on. Holding the gardening twine in his hand he wanted to wrap it around the Asian's neck.

'Just be ready at seven when they call for you.'

Rakeesh smiled at Charlie as the gardener returned to his duties. He wondered where Lady Ashleigh was. With her around he felt more protected. Mentioning the church was a stupid mistake and he should have known better. He thought about later and being with the young men. On the boat they had appeared friendly enough, chatting and laughing and joking. Studying the time on the wall clock next to the shed, he had enough time left before dinner to take a look around.

Walking through the garden everything was meticulously tended, the flower beds symmetrically designed and cut with Charlie's military precision. The shrubs of which there were many were interwoven by colour. It was a typical English garden. Rakeesh continued to amble about sensing that he was being watched. He looked up quickly catching the fleeting movement of a curtain from a bedroom above. Whoever had been watching had not wanted him to know that they were there. Could it be Lady Ashleigh he wondered, or the fat cook, or the housemaid that he had seen cleaning.

Barbara Jenkins was sure that the man hadn't seen her watching him. She'd not seen him at the house before and it was strange that he was wearing such scruffy old clothes, clothes that she had seen hanging in the master wardrobe. He certainly didn't look like a dignitary from abroad. Barbara was taking a second look when the Asian had looked up. *'Yes,'* she thought to herself, *'he looks so much like the cousin of Mr Patel from the corner shop at Cavendish Forde.'* She was still hiding behind the curtain when a voice from behind made her jump.

'Is something wrong Barbara?' Lady Ashleigh asked.

Barbara Jenkins turned holding her chest. 'Oh I'm sorry m'lady. I didn't mean to be prying, but there's a foreign looking gentleman in the garden below. He's acting quite furtive and doesn't seem to know his way around.'

Olivia Ashleigh looked seeing the back of Rakeesh as he turned the corner. 'I don't suppose that he does, especially as he hails from Delhi in India. Rakeesh is a guest here for the meantime. He was a boy the last time that I saw him.'

Barbara nodded looking as well. 'So he's not the cousin of the Patel's at the Grocery Shop in Cavendish Forde?'

Olivia Ashleigh laughed. Not that I am aware of Barbara, although he might indeed be a distant cousin. They can have dozens in their family units.' She was concerned about the direction that Rakeesh was walking having turned towards the exterior door leading to the cellar.

'Would you rather that I did another room m'lady?'

Olivia Ashleigh moved away from the window. 'No, you carry on here Barbara, I have prior appointment elsewhere and after that to see Janet about an engagement later.'

She went down to the study where it was easier to watch Rakeesh and not be observed. She was still watching when to her surprise Rakeesh produced a mobile phone from his pocket. As far as she could tell he was only checking his text messages. *'I wonder where he got his mobile,'* she muttered. She was even more alarmed when he turned and took several photographs of the house.

'He did what?' Janet repeated when told.

Lady Ashleigh went to the sink to fill the kettle. A Scorpio she had a suspicious nature. She especially didn't like people uninvited checking out her house and estate. Lawrence had wanted to install CCTV but she had said that it would offend the integrity of the staff and visitors. Now she wished she had heeded his advice. 'What's your opinion of Rakeesh?' she asked Janet.

'The jury is still out m'lady.' It was a tactful reply, but secretly Janet to say that she thought he was a devious, untrustworthy slimy toad.

Olivia Ashleigh placed the kettle over the gas ring, preferring water warmed over the stove than by electricity. 'Forget the niceties Janet, please be honest. I won't hold it against you!'

'I don't trust him m'lady. He has shifty eyes that are here, there, everywhere. He gives me the creeps the way that he is always clasping his hands and bowing and he needs to see a doctor about that head wobble. Every time he talks it's like a voodoo doll with a spring missing to keep him upright. Have you noticed how his eyes meet in the middle?'

Olivia Ashleigh looked at Janet. 'Yours do.'

'Not like that they don't m'lady. His are way too close to his nose. They look like a cobra who got nudged before he was ready to wake up. My dad always said that people with eyes too close to their nose needed watching.'

Olivia Ashleigh fetched two clean mugs from the pantry shelf adding a heap of coffee in each before pouring in the hot water. Janet felt uncomfortable about her ladyship making her a drink when it should have been the other way around, but Olivia Ashleigh could always think clearer when her hands were occupied.

Janet continued. 'It was way too convenient that he just happened to choose the captain's boat at Dunkirk. Then to give Bill Symons some cock n' ball story about wanting to find you. It's just too far-fetched to swallow!' Milk was added to the coffees as Janet collected the biscuit barrel, she always planned better with a full stomach. Together they sat at the kitchen table.

'I could slip something into his dinner later m'lady. It would be quick and discreet?'

Olivia Ashleigh dunked her biscuit in her coffee. 'You're beginning to sound like Charlie. It is tempting Janet, but we can't take unnecessary chances. No, we need something that is quick and effective and doesn't leave a trail back to us.'

Janet laughed. 'Now you sound like Charlie m'lady.' They both laughed. 'We could always ask Charlie, he's had a lot of practice and he'd know how to do it without even the wind noticing?'

Olivia Ashleigh rolled the tip of her tongue between her lips. 'He's not getting any younger, but I admit Charlie would know what to do. However, if anything went tits-up I'd hate to think that you two had lost out on the chance of time together!' Janet tried not to look surprised as Lady Ashleigh continued to ponder over the problem.

'I had thought about sending Rakeesh back to France with Bill Symons where they could be conveniently lose him somewhere desolate and

173

miles from the nearest town or village. His taking photographs of the house and having a mobile phone has somewhat changed things and I sense our Indian guest will be a thorn in our side if we don't deal with the problem and quickly.'

Thinking hard she picked up her mug, took another biscuit before pacing the kitchen. 'Lawrence used to say that the best way to resolve any problem was to let it come to you because the perpetrator would unwittingly bring the answer along with him.'

Janet frowned. 'I'm not sure that I follow m'lady?'

'Rakeesh had been playing each and every one of us for fools.' She caressed the skin of her chin. 'So far the only people who know that he exists is me and you, Charlie and Bill Symons and our three young musketeers.' She snapped her fingers together, 'and Barbara Jenkins. She saw Rakeesh down in the garden earlier.'

Janet sighed. 'Now that is a shame, I liked Barbara!'

Olivia Ashleigh laughed. 'We're not about to eliminate Barbara Jenkins, we just have to concoct the right story so that she isn't too overwhelmed or mystified with Rakeesh being around and then gone the next. Barbara cannot be relied upon to keep a secret.'

'I could deal with her, you just say the word m'lady.' Janet's eyes narrowed, friend or no friend, she did not intend taking a spell in a women's prison because of idle gossip and more importantly who would make Charlie his dinner.

'No, it's kind of you to offer Janet, but leave it with me. I'm going for a long soak in a hot bath soon. I'll mull it over with a glass of wine and candles.' She put down her coffee. 'Now about Bill coming tonight, what have you got planned for us, something nice?'

Janet showed her the pages that she had marked in her cook book. It all looked good even the dessert. She checked the time with the wall clock. 'Did Charlie manage to slip the bottles back on the supermarket shelves without being seen?'

'Yes m'lady. You know Charlie he could slip through a football crowd undetected.'

'Now all we have to do is wait and step in at the right moment. I do hope that the customers don't suffer too much!'

'They'll get over,' Janet replied. 'My granny used to feed me castor oil for gut rot. I'd sit on the pan for hours.'

'We could send Barbara Jenkins to the supermarket this afternoon to see if there has been any reaction to sales of the wine. Unconnected with our business she will be there innocently. She'd only need a few items on her shopping list, just something as an excuse to get her out of the house.'

Janet liked it. She'd had soft spot for the late Lord Lawrence but Lady Ashleigh was astute and her head for business was envied. Janet smiled to herself. Had old Lawrence been a bit sharper he might have ducked out of the way that fated morning when the bullet had come whistling his way ending his life prematurely.

Janet suggested that dinner that evening with Bill Symons would be better served in the conservatory rather than the dining room where romantically the sunset would add a delightful charm to the occasion. Come midnight Janet had a surprise of her arranged for Charlie Luft. It begun with a cold game sandwich and pickles down in the kitchen accompanied by some nice brandy which she hoped would help warm his cockles. After that she would let Charlie take her back to her room.

*****

Dead on seven Robert Perry and Samuel Byrne arrived having slept, showered and changed their clothes. 'Will we be going far,' Rakeesh asked anxiously. 'I have heard that the sun goes down here in England very fast and you have night birds called owls who come out looking for prey.'

Samuel noticed that the Asian's head wobble was worse. He wondered if Rakeesh realised that he had been rumbled.

'Once around the village should do it,' Samuel replied. 'We want you to remember your visit to Willow Beck.'

*****

'Is the lamb to your liking?' asked Olivia Ashleigh, dabbing the side of her mouth with the napkin not that it was necessary. Bill Symons looked up from his plate, the next slice dangling from the end of his fork. 'It's perfectly cooked and very tasty, thank you!'

The setting sun was as Janet had said an excellent backdrop to the evening and the meal. On the table there were two bottles of fine red with brandy glasses supplied for later.

'You look incredible this evening,' Bill said lifting his glass in a toast, 'and your hair up suits you!'

Fanning her hand delicately in front of her face she was not accustomed to compliments. The last time she recalled had been when Lawrence had taken her to join the Fox Hunt one Boxing Day back in the nineties.

'Thank you. I had hoped that you would approve.' She stopped fanning feeling the intoxication of the moment growing. 'My grandmother would say that a woman with her hair up resembled a Rhode Island Red strutting about the farmyard with nothing better to do than parade herself in front of the visiting cockerel. I do hope that I don't fit her description.'

He laughed. 'So would I be the visiting cockerel?'

Fanning quickly Olivia responded. 'Well a hen needs a mate.' She wondered if it had been the wine that replied as he topped up her glass. She didn't tell him, but something else that she recalled her grandmother saying was *'that to get laid in the hen house, you first had to entice the cockerel in.'*

Watching him eat his lamb was a pleasure and to see him enjoy it was a compliment to Janet's hard work. Putting his knife and fork to one side Bill used his napkin around his mouth.

'Was you and your late husband in India long?'

177

'Almost twenty years. Lawrence was well liked by the officials in the British Government. We only came back because he contracted a touch of Dengue Fever which left him with antibody deficiency.' It was hardly the subject that she had wanted to discuss at the dinner table or on their first date together. It was however best to get it out of the way.

'And this Rakeesh, he was a boy when you were there?'

'He was the son of a house servant. I would see him playing in the garden with the other children. A bright child and polite.' She paused. 'Although he seemed to have an over active eye for anything else that was occurring in and around the embassy. Lawrence would say that I was over cautious and that Rakeesh was just curious.'

Bill Symons sipped his wine, which he found palatably pleasant. 'Hmmm curious. That's interesting. I still can't get my head around how he just happened to be aboard after we pick up a consignment of wine and cheese. Coincidence can sometimes be a dirty word.' She offered in turn to fill his glass again. He put his hand politely over hers. 'Too much of that stuff and I will be incapable of walking back home.'

Olivia Ashleigh put the bottle back down leaving her own glass half full. It was important to keep a clear head for what she had planned later. 'So what do you think we should do with our mystery guest?' she asked.

Bill Symons reached across and held her hand his expression one of confidence to match his smile. 'How about letting destiny be the downfall of his fate.' She liked the reply finding it reassuring.

The subject having been raised Bill was fired up.

'Having retired I thought that I was ready for cosy nights beside the fire with my pipe and rum, but having sailed to France with the lads and doing the deal with Victor Dupont, it got me thinking again. I missed the excitement of an adventure.' He squeezed her hand. 'You, Janet and Charlie have made things buzz again. You're beautiful Olivia, whereas Charlie is dark and mysterious and Janet, well let's say that she cooks some of the best lamb hereabouts.'

Olivia Ashleigh felt the blood rising up her cheeks *'beautiful'* it was a word rarely used these days. She wanted to fan her face, but not only were her cheeks burning, so was her neck and cleavage. Bill could feel her pulse racing beneath his hand.

'I like you being part of the team Bill and yes, this is very exciting times.'

Suddenly he was out of his chair. He pulled her from hers and into him finding her mouth where he kissed her passionately. The seconds passed before he allowed her to breathe again. When he did he was grinning like a Cheshire cat. *'And my grandmother used to tell me that there were plenty of fish in the sea, but to hook the right one you had to make sure that it looked and tasted better than all the rest!'* He kissed her again before she could reply.

Olivia Ashleigh had her hand around his back so that he couldn't break free. Next to the fabric of his shirt her bosom was heaving up and down like the pistons of a tugboat engine.

'Shall we take dessert here or upstairs?' she whispered.

With the ease of a much younger man he swept her up into his arms, lifting her clean up from the floor.

'I would suggest that we work up an appetite first before we think about dessert. I hope Janet prepared a cold dish!'

Janet heard her mistress giggling as Bill Symons carried Olivia Ashleigh up the stairs to the floor above where she heard the bedroom door click shut. Looking up at the kitchen clock she hoped that Charlie would return soon. 'I suppose I might as well clear away the conservatory table.' Janet mumbled to herself. Overhead laughter filled the bedroom as Bill Symons chased Lady Ashleigh around the bed.

Collecting the used plates and cutlery and unused vegetables she searched around for the bottles and glasses, but all she found was a single empty bottle. The other had been taken by Olivia Ashleigh to the bedroom.

Janet wrapped the rest of the cooked lamb in foil where she would keep it back for sandwiches the next day and make sure that Charlie had some with his tea in the garden. It was essential to keep up his strength. Older and wiser he might be, but beneath that toughened exterior a lion was waiting to escape.

She was still clearing the table when the reflection of the bedroom light above went out leaving only the stars through the conservatory glass roof. Janet smiled. It had been a long time since she had seen her mistress so happy.

A Rabbit in the Headlights

Taking their route home down the darkened country lane they could see the manor house and church in the distance. The moon was dancing between the clouds and every so often the stars made an appearance to let everyone know below that they were there.

Adding to the walk was a late summer mist which was hanging hauntingly around the tops of the tops of the evergreen shrubs that lined the lane beyond which were a scattering of various trees. Oaks, elms and birch. In the distance they could hear an owl calling.

Rakeesh scanned the sides cautiously hearing the odd creature scurry back into the undergrowth as they walked on past. When they passed the graveyard he thought of the dead hoping that their eternal sleep kept them from saying hello.

'Willow Beck has a lot of dead people,' he said, 'almost as many as the Ganges sees every day!'

Samuel winked at Robert. 'The black death claimed a lot.'

Rakeesh was suspicious of their good natured benevolence. 'This black death, it was at night yes?' he asked, watching for a reaction.

Samuel coughed as mist droplets invaded the back of his throat. 'I suppose. Although death don't have any agenda. It just happens when it happens!'

Having sampled some of the local beer which he found bitter Rakeesh had sensed a foreboding in their companionship. At the river he had refused to climb the lock gate to the other side so they had to come home via the country lanes adding another mile to their journey. He was surprised when Samuel disappeared into the bushes.

'Is something wrong?' he asked.

'No,' replied Robert, 'probably too much beer.' With Rakeesh peering into the bushes he missed Robert looking down the lane. A moment later Robert joined Samuel. 'That's the problem with some ales, they go straight through.' Rakeesh didn't know if he did or did not, but the bushes beyond the side of the road looked very dark.

When the owl hooted for a second time it had come a lot closer. Rakeesh pricked his ears searching for signs of movement, but everything was unusually quiet, too quiet. He felt very alone. *'Don't be too long,'* he asked, *'only Lady Ashleigh, she will want me back home soon!'*

When the motorbike started up the headlight instantly flooded the lane with a white glaring light illuminating Rakeesh in its path. As the revs of the engine increased the Asian prayed to Vishnu. With a spray of loose gravel and earth the motorbike came fast.

'You pirate bastards,' Rakeesh cried, realising that the evening had been a ploy to get him out into the open.

The motorbike was almost upon him when suddenly from out of nowhere appeared the biggest rabbit that Rakeesh had ever seen. Caught in the glare of the white light the rabbit went rigid mesmerised and unable to move. Rakeesh saw his window of opportunity as he dived into the bushes leaving the rabbit to make its own escape.

Charlie saw the customs agent dive for cover, saw the large rabbit. He tried to swerve missing the rabbit and hit Rakeesh but the slippery Asian was nimble and up and running into the trees. Changing gear the motorbike went into a skid, hitting the unfortunate rabbit. Charlie saw the agents legs scurry away. *'Oh fuck,'* cried Charlie as a tree was about to halt his skid.

'Fuck this,' announced Rakeesh, as he ran past Samuel and Robert who could only watch, their zips undone and their hands occupied. Charlie felt the impact as the motorbike careered into the elm.

'Where'd he go?' Samuel asked as he secured his zip.

'I don't know, he was here one moment and gone the next. I think he knows he's been rumbled.'

'Get the bastard and be quick about it.' Cried a dazed Charlie.

The pair ran into the wood, but Rakeesh was faster than a hare. Ten minutes later they returned to find Charlie struggling to free himself from the tangled motorbike and tree.

'Where is he?' he asked, the urgency in his voice suggesting that if they didn't find him all hell would rain down upon them.

'He's gone,' said Robert as he knelt to help Charlie pull his leg clear. He saw Samuel pick up the dead rabbit.

'Don't worry about me or a bloody rabbit get after him you silly buggers,' cried Charlie. *'We missed our opportunity and he knows it. The Asian will go to ground and bring the police and the customs to our door. He has to be found!'* Samuel and Robert re-entered the bushes knowing that in the mist and dark it would be futile, but their lives depended upon them finding the lucky agent.

Half an hour passed before they returned.

'He's gone Charlie, scarpered. We wouldn't find a scarecrow in this mist.' Robert helped Charlie get to his feet. He was unsteady.

'I think I've twisted it,' said Charlie. He looked at the motorbike which had a bent front fork. 'We'll leave the bike here. I can arrange for it to be collected in the morning.' He sighed long and hard. 'We'd best get back to the manor house and warn the others.'

With the dead rabbit in his free hand, Samuel and Robert supported Charlie back. In the vicarage nearby the light from the upper bedroom had been switched on illuminating the lawn below. A black silhouette came to the window to see what had caused the sudden noise.

Charlie noticed Samuel carrying the rabbit. 'He's a big bugger. He near bloody killed me. To think I survived the whole of the war and almost got snuffed out by a giant bug's bunny. Janet will piss herself laughing.'

It was almost midnight when helped by Robert and Samuel they got back to the manor house. Janet was shocked to see Charlie injured.

184

Ignoring the fact that she had on her sexiest nightdress and matching dressing gown she rushed to his aid. Samuel got an eyeful of Janet's chest as it swung loosely from side to side. He winked at Robert who thought they reminded him of the melon shoot they'd attended at last year's summer fete.

'*Help me get Charlie to the chair,*' she ordered. Having made sure that he was comfortable she went to the freezer returning with a bag of unopened frozen peas. Easing his boot form his foot she placed the peas over the swelling and his sock.

'*Jesus Christ,*' screamed Charlie, his eyes opening wide. '*That's bloody cold!*' Janet felt her expectations slump seeing her night of feasting and passion fly out of the window. She watched Samuel drop the rabbit on the worktop.

'What's that?' she asked.

Samuel held up the dead rabbit. 'An assassin in disguise.'

Charlie muttered something offensive under his breathe. 'Bloody rabbit scuppered a good plan and nearly got me killed into the bargain.' Janet was moving the bag of peas about the swelling when the door to the kitchen opened.

'Where's Rakeesh?' Olivia Ashleigh asked, concerned to see that Charlie was injured. Samuel nudged Roberts arm. They were dressed, but her ladyship's hair was a mess and the captain had appeared without his socks.

185

Charlie looked up, remorseful and embarrassed. 'I am sorry to say m'lady that he got away!'

Gretna Green or Die

The underground passage was much longer than Mary Nelson had originally thought and indeed darker. Following the beam of the torch she forged on apprehensively seeing two largish mounds ahead. Coming close she thought that the shapes looked human although at first glance it wasn't easy to tell. Training her beam on their motionless bodies she called out, feeling stupid as it was plainly obvious that they were dead and had been for some time.

Going even closer, she put a clenched fist of shock to her mouth. *'Oh my goodness,'* she whispered. *'May you both rest in peace.'*

Before her lay the skeletal remains of a man and woman. They were clothed in what they had been wearing the day that they had died, but like their owners the clothes had become dusty rags. There was no telling what had devoured human flesh. Mary felt her shoulders sag when she noticed the remnants of a vicar's collar about the skeletal neck of the man.

She recalled the conversation that she'd had with the Bishop when he had told her some of the history surrounding St Ridley's and how before Victor Higginbottom the previous man to hold the post had mysteriously disappeared. A mystery according to the police that was still unresolved.

Looking down at what was left Mary was sad. Montgomery Saul had been a young man of spiritual calling who according to the Bishop had found love in the arms of a parishioner named Elizabeth Dunn. Saul had asked for permission to marry the divorcee, but John Steele had refused. The day that they disappeared it was rumoured that they had run away to Gretna Green to get married.

Putting her fears aside Mary tentatively pulled aside the dead vicars clothing looking for signs of a violent struggle. A fractured bone or deep scratch would suggest a puncture wound or perhaps foul play. She found none. What she could tell was that they had died cuddling one another. Checking the vicars jacket pocket she found a prayer card. Written top left was the name Montgomery Saul.

Closing her eyes she offered a short prayer. *'May they find eternal peace with one another in heaven lord and grant them dignity. Their love was not wrong, the judgement was... Amen.'*

Leaving her find behind Mary made her way beyond to the end of the passage where she could see a door. On the wall beside the door she found an old iron hook and on the hook was a key. She tried it, turning the lock. Mary wondered if Victor Higginbottom or John Steele had known about the secret passage.

Applying a firm heave with as much strength as she could muster Mary forced the door open. The door swung free of the framework coming to rest the other side of the passage.

Holding her breath where the echo of the door landing against the stone wall had bounced loudly in all directions she listened for signs of movement wondering if anybody would come to investigate.

Relieved that she was alone she moved her beam first to the left then the right. To the left was another door. It looked solid. To the right was also a set of doors, four in all and three had a grilled front. She chose to go right.

The door immediately to her left was locked as were the others although they appeared more interesting. Using the beam from the torch she detected a stack of boxes, containing wine, shelves of waxed cheeses and crates of brandy and rum, port and sherry. The smells wafting through the grilled doors was inviting. 'That's an awful lot of alcohol and cheese,' she muttered to herself as she flashed the beam left then right. Most of the labels on the boxes were in French. She was about to check the next door when something at her feet scurried away. It made Mary jump and cry out.

Running away from where she stood watching was a small brown field mouse no bigger than the length of her thumb. 'You little bugger,' she laughed, 'you've come to check out the cheese. I can't blame you. It does look good.' Moments later the mouse vanished from sight. Checking the slow gradient that the passage took all the way up to the solid door at the end she deduced that the other side of the door would lead out into the grounds of the estate house.

Putting her ear to the locked door on the left she thought that she could hear muffled voices, belonging to at least three or more adults.

When a door handle being turned echoed down turned followed by a series of heavy footfalls descending a stone staircase Mary ran back as fast as she could the way that she had come. Pulling hard on the metal door she tried to heave it free of the stone wall but years of damp and dust had rusted the old hinges. Stubbornly the door refused to budge.

When the locked door at where she had listened opened she ducked out of sight.

Feeling the last of her courage vanish she turned and leaping ungraciously over the two skeletal corpses she reached the bottom of the stairs leading up to the rectory study. With her heart thumping like a drum she pushed the study wall panel shut.

Mary went straight to the window to look across at the Manor house she saw somebody looking back, but moments later the figure had disappeared.

Sitting at the desk to help regain her composure it had been an eventful first morning and not one that she had expected. *'Talk about ghosts in the closet, I've got them in the basement.'* She was grateful not to have found Grace waiting for her.

Placing her hands on her temples Mary closed her eyes. It was time to meditate and call upon her gift once again. Maybe somebody on the other side could provide her with the answers she sought.

A Roll in the Hay

Olivia Ashleigh wasn't particularly concerned with how she looked or the fact that she had appeared alongside Bill Symons. Her immediate thoughts were for Charlie and the missing customs agent. 'Did anybody check the cellar earlier?' she asked.

Janet looked up having replaced the bag of frozen peas and wincing when Charlie winced.

'I went down there just before lunch m'lady and everything was locked up tighter than a drum skin. That slime ball Asian wouldn't have known about the cellar.'

Olivia Ashleigh felt the tension leave her face. She walked over to where Charlie had the weight of his ankle supported by a velvet cushion and chair. 'Can you move it?' she asked.

Charlie wiggled his toes biting down on his clenched teeth. 'I'm okay m'lady and I've had worse!'

Olivia Ashleigh sensed Bill come alongside. 'I don't think it's broken, but you've a bad sprain. If needs be we can get the doctor in the village to have a look in the morning. In the meantime you'd best get yourself up to bed and have Janet make you a hot drink.'

Suddenly the light of hope shone in Janet's eyes. Tucking him in with cocoa wasn't exactly as she had planned, but it was coming a close second best. 'What about Rakeesh?' Charlie asked as Janet slid her arm around his back to help lift him from the chair.

'Don't you worry about him none,' Olivia Ashleigh replied. 'We can still take care of that little problem.' She looked outside at the garden beyond. 'It's dark outside and there's a summer mist about. If my memory serves me well Rakeesh was never keen on the dark. We have a few hours left before sunrise. We have the night in our favour.' With a wry smile creasing her cheeks Janet helped Charlie upstairs. One way or another she was determined to have him notice her nightie and what was underneath.

Bill Symons had a determined look on his face. 'Right, I think the three of us need to go out hunting. A fox doesn't return to its lair until daylight. Will you stay here?' he asked Olivia Ashleigh.

'Yes, somebody has to answer the door should Rakeesh be foolish enough to return to the house.' Bill knew that she had her hunting rifle should she need to defend herself. She looked down suggesting he put on his socks while she made a pot of coffee. 'You'll need something warm as the night air will chill you through to the bone. That is something else Rakeesh doesn't like and that's the cold climate.' Bill left to retrieve his socks.

As soon as Bill left she turned to face Robert and Samuel.

'Rakeesh being on board the Saucy Belle was a planned sting the same as conveniently having a photograph of me and my late husband in his shirt pocket. I don't like being played for the fool.'

'Nor me m'lady,' replied Samuel feeling betrayed. 'He got a lucky break because of that rabbit, but he won't get another, that's for sure!'

Olivia Ashleigh smiled back. 'That's the spirit Samuel.' She looked at Robert. 'You don't have to be party to this Robert considering your connections.'

Robert nodded. 'Thank you m'lady, but I am involved. What we started out to do, we finish.' She was proud of them both. They would do well in the diplomatic corp. She stirred a sugar into her coffee, thinking.

'The port official at Dunkirk, was he with the harbour or customs?'

'We don't know m'lady. Bill spoke to him, while we stayed below deck.'

She ran her fingers through her hair styling the loose strands remembering how Bill had done the same earlier.

'Our main concern is how much customs know. I suppose time will tell.'

'I'm sure Charlie would know how to extract the truth when we catch up with Rakeesh.'

Olivia Ashleigh nodded. I don't deny it. We need to know either way.'

Although he didn't want to say it Samuel felt that he had to ask. 'And the captain m'lady, can he be trusted?'

Olivia Ashleigh wasn't fazed by the question. She felt Samuel had the right to ask. Having spent the evening with Bill she replied with confidence. 'Yes, I've no doubts there Samuel and it was Robert's suggestion that we ask the captain to come on board, not the other way round. He appears rough around the edges, but I assure you that the captain's heart and loyalty is unquestionable.' She discreetly rubbed the soft part of her posterior where he had playfully smacked her chasing her around the bedroom. 'Bill Symon's is a hundred percent trustworthy. We've only the one traitor in our midst.'

'Who's a traitor,' asked Bill as he entered the kitchen, his hair combed and wearing socks.

'Rakeesh,' Robert was quick to reply, 'm'lady was questioning how long he's been tailing us back and forth to the continent.'

Bill took his place next to Olivia Ashleigh. 'That's the trouble with this world nowadays, you're stumped with who you can trust.'

Swallowing the last of his coffee Samuel had watched to see if the kitchen door opened again. 'Janet didn't make Charlie that hot drink!' Robert dug him sharply in the ribs.

Bill Symons helped out.

'Charlie's in good hands lad. Now we need to get our hands on that slimy bugger before he gains too much of an advantage and stumbles across Robert's dad.'

'Oh that won't happen,' Robert replied,' he's on a course at the moment up in Leicestershire something to do with protecting the wildlife.'

Bill rubbed his hands together. 'Perfect. Right let's go bag us a rat.'

194

They left Olivia Ashleigh alone in the kitchen with Bill Symons promising that he would be back. With the door shut she caught sight of her reflection in the glass pane. *'I'm wish I could say that I was sorry Lawrence,'* she muttered, *'but I'm not and a woman has needs and I needed a man tonight. As much as Janet needs Charlie.'*

She took the empty mugs over to the sink running hot water to rinse them clean.

Staring out into the darkness beyond the window she had let her hair down with Bill. She had done things that she had never done with Lawrence. Not even on their wedding night, anniversaries, birthdays or high days.

She could still feel the warm glow of intimacy inside. Holding herself she didn't want to let go. Hearing the owl hoot nearby probably in the belfry she hoped that they caught up with Rakeesh and soon. Having found the retired tug boat captain, she didn't want to lose Bill.

*****

'I thought they would never leave,' Janet murmured, as she lay next to Charlie her nightdress recklessly slung over the post at the end of the bed.

'I hope they catch the slippery bugger. I'd like a second pop at skinning him alive!' Charlie replied. But Janet who was comfortable nestled in the crook of his shoulder wasn't interested in him having a go at anybody except her.

'Calm down,' she cooed softly, 'and help me warm the bits that are going cold.'

'We'll have to change places,' he asked, 'only it nigh on killed the moment with my ankle bent at a funny angle.'

Pushing her bare breasts together Janet climbed on top before letting go again. As she bent forward to kiss his mouth her voluptuous mounds hit Charlie in the ribs. He wheezed as the air exploded from his lungs, *'take it easy old girl, I'm black and blue as it is…'* Janet laughed.

Their actions became more frantic as Janet sensed the passion rising throughout her body. Clamping her lips over his mouth she wiggled her hips until satisfied that he was where she wanted him to be. When she grabbed the headboard for extra support her breasts hung temptingly where Charlie could apply his tongue.

'Be gentle,' he cried, as she pushed down hard, *'you'll suffocate me.'* Charlie could feel the weight on his lungs as Janet rocked back and forth the strong desire escaping with each thrust. Charlie suddenly felt the effort straining on his heart. The plea for Janet to be merciful left his lips as no more than a weak whisper, *'you're sucking the life out of me, at both ends!'*

But Janet Simpson was all fired up and ready to go at it at full throttle. She was beyond the point of no return, needing and wanting her man again. With the blood pumping, beating like a native drum in each ear she failed to hear his wheezy response. Instead she added even more momentum, rocking her body back and forth like the piston of a Mustang in flight. Beneath Charlie the bed springs were at full stretch.

Charlie Luft didn't know what hurt most, his ankle, his groin or his heart. Both legs were going numb with the starvation of fresh blood. Like a limpet clamped on tight Janet was insatiable.

'Please Janet,' he pleaded once again, 'I need you to get a move on.'

Like a happy dolphin flapping its flippers her breasts were here, there and everywhere. 'I'm going as fast as I can Charlie,' she replied. Janet didn't want to disappoint, hoping that after a rest there would be more.

Charlie felt first his head begin to spin as flashing lights appeared before his eyes. He tried to talk, but no words left his mouth. As the seconds went by faster than the speed of light he saw flashbacks, good and bad moments of his life. He saw Mimi's beautiful face looking back at him as she smiled squeezing his arm tight with hers. Then from nowhere there appeared a huge rabbit caught in the beam of his motorbike headlights.

Charlie howled just the once as a mysterious glowing hand reached through the mist inviting him to join them. 'Who, where?' he asked, but the hand kept on beckoning as the light behind the dead rabbit began to fade.

Janet heard his cry mistaking it for the height of his passion. With one final last push she gave the moment her all. Reaching for the headboard again she gasped, **'they're yours Charlie, take me NOW!'** Seconds later Charlie Luft took his last breath as Janet felt herself explode.

Rolling clear of her lover she pulled him in close, real close. 'You were amazing Charlie, truly amazing.' She kissed his forehead and smiled seeing that his eyes were already closed. 'That's it my love,' she whispered affectionately. 'You sleep and in the morning I will bring you up the best breakfast that you've ever had.'

A Shot in the Dark

When the reverberation of the bed springs from the room at the top of the manor house had stopped rocking the floorboards Olivia Ashleigh saw the way clear to visit her secret dressing room. With only the moonlight illuminating the room she changed into shooting trousers and boots, adding a warm hunting jacket and leather gloves.

It had been an hour since Bill Symons, Robert Perry and Samuel Byrne had left the house going out to look for Rakeesh and there had been no word from them. It was time that she took control of the situation.

Next she visited the games room where Lawrence had had erected a snooker table and drinks cabinet. Reaching under the table she unclipped two clamps and retrieved her favourite hunting rifle, the one with a telescopic night sight. The last time that she had needed to use it was to eliminate a problem where a rogue fox had been stealing from their brood of chickens. The missing egg count had begun to affect Janet's recipes. Not even Charlie knew that the rifle existed.

Slipping a sufficient quantity of bullets into her pocket Olivia Ashleigh made sure that the night sight was correctly calibrated. Throwing open the turret window the owl called out from an oak tree nearby. Using the night sight she saw the owls head turn her way, its big inquisitive eyes staring back. *'Where is he?'* she asked the owl as it blinked. Making a minor adjustment to the sight she could clearly see the feathers of the owl's plumage. Satisfied that the range and sight was set right she made her way down to the garden below.

From her vantage point hidden by a thicket of bushes the light in Charlie's bedroom had been extinguished. With an approving smile Olivia Ashleigh bade them both goodnight as she settled herself. The hairs on her neck were bristling.

A stag dashing clear of the trees from the wood between the vicarage and the estate garden was a sign that something had startled the animal. A moment later the owl flew from the oak back to the wood to investigate.

Kneeling with the rifle butt pressed into her shoulder she scanned the sight picking up the spot where Charlie had told her that he had crashed the motorbike. Something definitely had the stag spooked. Scanning left then right she caught sight of three figures walking the perimeter of the grassy meadow at the back of the estate. Evenly spaced she recognised Bill, Robert and Samuel. *'I think you're searching in the wrong place,'* she whispered as she watched the stag turn and look back.

She noticed that there was a light on in the vicarage. When the new occupant arrived she would invite the vicar over to tea one afternoon, before any of the rumour squad got their claws into Mary Nelson first. Privilege and living in a big estate house did not always sit well with some in the village and over the years there had been spates of malicious gossip. The last concerning the unsolved death of her late husband.

Smiling to herself as she continued to scan the countryside Barbara Jenkins had been a useful asset. Unable to contain the merest snippet of gossip morning coffee around eleven had become a regular feature. Wondering who was burning the middle oil at the vicarage she shuddered thinking about the previous vicar. Victor Higginbottom had been a despicable man and had used his position in the community to feather his own nest.

She was trying to banish his memory from her thoughts when the stag's head shot up from where it had been feeding on fresh grass. She followed the sight of where the stag was staring, its magnificent head and body frozen in time, every muscle tense ready to run. She thought about getting closer to give Rakeesh a sporting chance. Perhaps call out and give him the opportunity to give himself up, but she doubted that he would do the same. His mother had hated Lawrence and looked down on Olivia Ashleigh. Slotting her forefinger through the trigger guard she depressed the trigger lever using the barest of pressure. In an instant the rifle could be fired.

When the does joined the stag she knew something was wrong. This time she did move, going fast and low. Crouched behind a holly bush she waited. This was like the tiger shoot that Lawrence had insisted upon her going, only the tiger to her relief had detected the scent of his aftershave and run off in the opposite direction. With a snap of a twig underfoot the tiger was coming her way.

Closer to the trees where the shadows were thick and misshapen she saw a movement, then another as the figure passed between the trees.

It was as she readied herself that she remembered Rakeesh had suffered from a nervous clack in his throat when faced with an anxious moment. The seconds passed as she waited and then she heard it. Like a suckling piglet greedy for more of its mother's milk she heard his clacking. Rakeesh was only metres away.

Not only shrewd she was a skilled shot. Gently, without the hint of any movement she released the pressure on the trigger lever. First Olivia Ashleigh wanted to see why Rakeesh had stayed so close to the house when by rights he should have been miles away. Crouched low she watched him pass.

Pensive and afraid of the unnerving silence, the undercover customs agent stood on the edge of the tree line peering across the expansive grass lawn and shrubs. His eyes furtively went ahead, left and right, but not behind. Confident that he had only the deer to worry about Rakeesh inhaled deep.

He had seen the captain of the boat and the other two looking for him, but they were on the far side of the field and too far away to come running back in time. He just needed to know where the door to the side of the garden went and then his job was done. Flipping open the lid of his mobile case he saw that the battery had died. Had he been back before the motorbike incident he would have had ample opportunity to charge some life back into the battery, enough at least to make that one vital call. He slipped the mobile in his pocket, looked one more time then ran towards the door.

Half a dozen trees back Olivia Ashleigh watched him cross the lawn heading straight for the cellar door. Once again she put her forefinger on the trigger lever. *'I thought that's why you'd come back,'* she muttered. With her free hand she pushed a potato that she had fetched from the kitchen over the end of the rifle barrel. *'You should have stayed working at the embassy Rakeesh, like your father.'*

Rakeesh checked the door chasing the framework, looking for a flaw in the design or where the English weather had rotted the wood. He was tugging on the padlock when the suppressed gases erupted discharging a single bullet leaving the barrel with a dull thud. Another trick that Lawrence had taught her in India when tracking tigers.

Like the mould of a jelly the Asian's head wobbled just the once then no more. Rakeesh lay on the grass dead with a single head wound. The Stag nearby heard the muffled shot, but it was too far away to concern him or the herd. Walking through the long grass they slowly made their way towards the church grounds.

Having collected the wheelbarrow that Charlie kept beside the compost heap Rakeesh was much lighter than she had thought he would be, as she hauled and dumped his corpse into the metal barrow. Transporting him to where the septic tank was deep underground she used the spade from the garden shed to prise open and prop up the metal lid. Pushing the wheelbarrow sideways Rakeesh fell to the sea of slurry below landing a sickly plop. He went under instantly. Olivia Ashleigh chuckled as she closed the lid. 'I bet you a pound to a penny of poop that your mobile won't work down there Rakeesh.'

It would be another couple of months before the waste disposal company was due and by then the natural microorganisms would have gorged themselves on his flesh helping get rid of any evidence. By the time that the tank was emptied Rakeesh would be nothing but slurry himself. A fitting end to shit. 'If by any chance you are discovered at the water treatment centre, it'll be difficult knowing from which tank you were sucked up. There are so many farms hereabouts who use the same company.' Picking up her hunting rifle she dusted herself down congratulating herself on a job well done.

An hour later Bill Symons returned to the manor house alone. It was almost one thirty and he was exhausted. 'We searched everywhere, but we couldn't find any sign of him.'

Having taken a refreshing shower and changed back into the clothes that he had seen her wearing earlier Olivia Ashleigh helped remove his jacket. 'No matter. It's dark outside and to continue searching would be like taking a shot in the dark.' Waiting on the side of the worktop was a brandy bottle and two glasses. 'We never did chance to enjoy dessert.'

'Do you think that he had the chance to contact anybody?' asked Bill chinking the side of his glass with hers. 'No, I doubt it. The signal reception in this area is dreadfully awful. My phone is always dying on me.' Like the mobile in the septic soil tank, she thought. 'Shall we take these drinks upstairs?'

The Gardener's Bible

Try as hard as she could Mary was unable to get any help form the other side. Something, although she wasn't sure what was clouding her channel of communication. 'It could be the spirits of the unfortunate souls down in the underground passage,' she thought. Mary knew that they would be restless having been found and would not move on unless the mystery was resolved.

Feeling disappointed and needing an injection of fresh air she decided to go for a walk instead in the woods nearby where she had noticed a herd of deer grazing in the grassy glade. Willow Beck was everything that she had dreamt about. Peaceful, it was like she had arrived at the Garden of Eden and St Ridley's was her own little patch.

Sitting on a broken bough beneath the trees that surround her on three sides Mary was happy to close her eyes absorbing the rich abundance of woodland smells and birdsong. She hoped that the souls of Montgomery Saul and Elizabeth Dunn were sitting beside her.

Listening to the birds talking to one another she pondered over the problem. Should she call the police, the bishop or say nothing. Willow Beck was a place where secrets were probably rife and what good would it do exposing something so awful. Looking skyward she placed her faith in God knowing he would provide the answer.

In a flash a thought appeared. 'Perhaps first before I do anything, I should see who owns the manor house.' The bird chatter ceased. 'Maybe they don't know that the bodies are there!' It was feasible.

The bird chatter recommenced. For five hundred years priest holes or secret passages as they later became known had hidden both the living and the dead. Entombed, starved to death without a means of escape victims had unwittingly taken the secrets surrounding their demise to their dusty, dark graves.

Her thoughts were interrupted by a dog walker, a middle aged woman who waved but had no intention of stopping to talk. Mary watched the antics of the dog as it spotted a young buck amongst the trees. Inca frantic pursuit the buck lead the chase, followed by the Jack Russell, followed by the woman who had no chance of catching up. Mary knew that she was going to enjoy living at Willow Beck.

She was still smiling to herself when a red breasted robin suddenly landed on the branch next to where she was sat. Chirping away she dare not move as it delivered its message. When it did fly to another perch Mary stood, looked up at the clouds and whispered *'thank you.'*

Walking back to the house she heard the dog as it continued barking. It was irritatingly annoying above the birdsong but suddenly ceased with a painful yelp. Mary guessed the animal had taken one chance to many with the young stag. It most certainly wouldn't chase another. Her time spent alone under the trees had been peaceful, thought provoking and fruitful.

It wasn't until later that night when Mary was sat up in bed reading she thought she heard a motorbike engine start up, roar into life and then nothing. Somewhere an owl screeched then seconds later nothing. Going to the window to look out Mary pulled her dressing gown across her front. 'Probably only youngsters messing about', she said pulling down the sash window where the mist over the fields nearby had chilled the evening air. It was long after midnight that she turned out the light and went to sleep.

Taking an early breakfast she was reading the pages of the local when a scream pierced the silence. Mary recognised that it could have only come from one place, the manor house. Rushing to the kitchen door she pulled it open and looked. Seconds later Grace appeared.

'What was that…?' Grace asked, pulling long strands of hair up into a bun.

Mary could see no sign of any movement from the adjacent house. 'I don't know, but it sounded extremely urgent, painful.'

Grace kept her bun in place with a long pin. 'It was probably Janet or Lady Ashleigh, the house is alive with mice. Do you fancy another coffee?'

Mary nodded. 'Yes please. Maybe when I'm dressed I'll go introduce myself.'

*****

Olivia Ashleigh and Bill Symons burst into the bedroom to find Janet standing over a naked Charlie. Distracted by the circumstances Janet had grabbed her nightie from the bedpost. She wore nothing else. Bill did his best to avert his eyes elsewhere, but not before he had seen the blue butterfly tattooed on Janet left buttock. Having faded it looked like the insect had been trying to escape. Olivia Ashleigh see him turn away reading his thoughts, but now was not the time for laughter.

Janet turned to see them arrive. She knelt and pointed. *'My Charlie… my poor Charlie,'* she cried agonisingly, *'he's gone. He's been cruelly taken from me during the night!'*

Bill checked. There nothing pulsing in the neck and Charlie looked too peaceful to be sleeping. He was also very cold. He shook his head at Olivia Ashleigh who was helping Janet into her dressing gown.

'He passed as he would have wanted Janet, with you by his side. You made Charlie a happy man!'

'He made me happy m'lady. Charlie was always smiling,' she said between sobs. 'It's just that it took the silly bugger ages to know how I felt about him.'

Gently patting her back Olivia Ashleigh searched for the right words.

'Men are at times too reticent to admit their feelings. Charlie loved you Janet, he was just shy, perhaps reserved.'

In between sobs Janet sniffed hard to reply. 'He fought in the last war. Went on dangerous missions. He wasn't shy m'lady. I think he was saving himself for me. In the end he gave me his all.' Bill raised his eyebrows, but Olivia frowned back.

Pulling up the bed sheet Bill stopped before covering Charlie's face. 'From his expression he died a contented man Janet.'

'Do you think so Bill?' she took one last look before raised the sheet.

208

'Take it from one man to another. He did!' Olivia smiled. Even Janet attempted a weak smile. 'He didn't have any family you know. That's why they picked him for the Special Operations Executive during the last war. Men without responsibilities back home could concentrate better. My Charlie was such a brave man all his life.'

Olivia Ashleigh agreed.

'We are all better for having known a man like Charlie. Often the silent heroes are the ones never mentioned, but God knows how they did their bit for King and country. Charlie will rightly take his place in the Garden of Eden.'

'He'll like that, tending to the gardens up in heaven. I hope they've got a vegetable patch.'

Olivia Ashleigh took Janet down to the kitchen where she would make them all a strong hot coffee, maybe laced with a little brandy. Bill elected to stay behind and help make the bedroom presentable for when the doctor and funeral director arrived.

Searching around Bill made sure that there was nothing incriminating left lying about. He was arranging the effects atop of Charlie's chest of drawers when his hand fell upon a bible. It fell open at a particular page. The print was also in French. Bill read where Charlie had marked the margin with a pencil.

Peter 4:8. 'Above all, love each other deeply, because love covers a multitude of sins.'

Also within the pages was a black and white photograph of a rather beautiful young woman. Bill studied the image and from her fashion assumed she was French. Turning the photo over on the back was inscribed *Mimi 1944.*

He replaced the photograph and closed the bible. He would take it back to Olivia's room where Janet wouldn't see the verse, inscription or Mimi. Bill would give undertaker instruction to have the bible buried alongside Charlie. Some secrets were meant to go to the grave. Whoever Mimi was she had reserved a very special for herself in Charlie's heart.

Bill took one last look around then satisfied he went to the bedroom door. Saluting the old soldier lying on the bed, Bill was pleased to have known Charlie Luft.

'We've both had out fill of exciting times Charlie, but whatever your secrets lad, you reveal them to nobody you hear. And if Mimi is waiting at the gate for you to arrive, tell her that her involvement is safe and buried forever. Be happy Charlie. I'll look after Janet and Olivia, I promise.'

The bedroom door clicked shut and the only sound left behind was the whistle of the breeze blowing in through the crack in the open window. The soul belonging to Charlie Luft was already airborne and about to begin another chapter, elsewhere.

*****

It was unusual for the telephone to ring so early in the vicarage normally meaning the vicar was required at somebody's bedside to offer spiritual comfort in times of need. Mary got to the phone first.

'The scream belonged to the cook at the manor house. It wasn't because of a mouse, but the gardener.'

'Charlie Luft, he's legendary. He was a war hero.' Replied Grace as she washed the breakfast crocks. 'Is everything alright?'

'Not exactly. The gardener died in the arms of the cook sometime during the night.'

Grace stopped cleaning the inside of a coffee mug. Circumstances as just described was normally found amongst the pages of a romantic novel, not in real life. Neither saw any humour in the tragedy.

'I know them both, Charlie and Janet. A lot in the village thought they'd get together one day.' Grace turned down the volume on the radio.

'They've asked that I go across and say a prayer.' Said Mary.

'Your first official engagement vicar. I thought it might have been taking evensong.'

Mary picked up the dishcloth to help with the dishes. 'So did I. The lord moves in mysterious ways sometimes Grace. I had best get dressed.'

Shocking Revelations

It seemed like an eternity before Arnold Greaves and Son, the funeral directors arrived to collect the body of Charlie Luft. Olivia Ashleigh kept Janet busy making breakfast and talking about happier times. When Arnold gave Bill the word that they were coming downstairs, he made sure that the kitchen door was pulled shut. What Bill didn't know was that Janet was in the study with Mary Nelson.

Wringing her fingers around the ends of her apron Janet had wondered what good would come seeing the vicar when all she wanted was Charlie back. However, the woman sat opposite her had a nice friendly smile. Janet thought she was too young to be in charge of a church and large vicarage.

'You're different. Much younger than any of the others,' Janet said as she invited the vicar to another cup of tea.

Wondering where the underground passage would emerge in the house Mary Nelson brought her thoughts back into the room and away from Montgomery Saul and Elizabeth Dunn.

'Makeup works wonders. It helps hide the cracks that you don't see,' replied Mary. She stirred the spoon around her tea cup adding a spoonful of sugar plus another smile. 'Please Janet, tell me about Charlie. Tell me the special bits that brought you together.

For the next quarter of an hour Janet spoke non-stop. She recalled moments, events that had taken place and his rugged smile. Every word was a catalogue of love and affection. Armed with a damp tissue Janet tried hard to keep back the tears between sentences. She felt it was her duty to tell Charlie's story.

'My goodness,' exclaimed Mary, when the room fell silent and Janet had finished. 'What a brave man. Dignified and yet distinguished by his love for all things to do with the estate. I should many in the village looked upon Charlie as a hero.'

'That was Charlie all over,' replied Janet. 'He was tall, handsome, strong and unassuming. A perfect gentleman and a fantastic...' Janet stopped short mindful of the vicar.

'Lover...' Mary replied ending the sentiment. 'Never be ashamed to say what you feel Janet. Physical love is all around. Jesus would spread his love amongst those that he walked amongst every day.' Ignoring the fact that Charlie knew how to kill, had killed, she saw Charlie in a long white robe doing much the same. Janet looked back at Mary Nelson the surprise in her eyes evident.

'But, you're a vicar!'

Mary grinned. 'That doesn't mean that I don't think about men Janet. When I feel the temptation is strong I kneel at the altar and pray. I have God instead. I feel his physical presence near.'

'I bet he don't rock the bed springs like my Charlie did!' The words spilled forth from Janet before she could stop herself. Her face lost its

213

smile as the memory of their lovemaking faded. 'Somebody upstairs decided however that it was time to cut short Charlie in his prime. I feel cheated vicar. A bit like Juliet when she woke to find Romeo dead beside her.

'God floats my boat in other ways Janet, only in the spiritual sense. Death is never easy to comprehend. There is no clock, no calendar or warning. I think of our being here as a journey and in this lifetime we're passing through onto the next. The good lord is the only one who knows all.'

Janet was a little embarrassed that she had spoken out of turn.

'Of course he does. I am sorry vicar and I never meant to imply that you was over the side. Are you married?'

Mary laughed. There would be a time she felt when they were closer as friends that she would explain about her past. 'Not yet, although there is always hope. My mission at present is to unite Willow Beck and help spread the word of God. I look upon marriage as a door of opportunity. If I don't arrive in time and it shuts before I take hold of the handle. It wasn't meant to be.'

Janet remembered how many times she had wanted to pull down Charlie's bedroom door handle and sneak in during the night.

'Did Charlie have any wishes regarding burial or cremation?' Mary asked.

The question brought Janet back from her memory. 'Burial,' she replied adamantly, 'and he wanted me to be buried alongside him when my time comes.' Janet felt it was better out in the open and now who deny her.

They ended the discussion with a prayer for Charlie, sending his soul on its way to heaven. Mary said that nearer the time she would visit again and discuss the funeral arrangements for the church service. Leaving Mary in the study Janet went to find Lady Ashleigh.

Mary was looking out of the study window when she noticed Bill Symons in the garden outside. He was walking towards the shed carrying a spade and hoe.

In need of oil on the hinges Olivia Ashleigh entered the study closing the door after her. She smiled and placed a wooden box on the piano lid before reaching out to take Mary's hand.

'Thank you for coming so promptly, I could think of nobody else who would console Janet in her hour of need. It would have been much nicer to have met on a less sad occasion.'

Mary Nelson smiled back. 'When heaven has St Peter open the gate and the calling descends, I would imagine that it's difficult to refuse.'

Olivia Ashleigh had never looked at death that way before. She wondered if Rakeesh would have seen his final moments the same. Buried beneath a ton of shit it might be difficult, if not spiritually impossible.

'Janet wants Charlie to be buried. St Ridley's is happy to make the arrangements.' Mary announced. She hoped it would help alleviate any anxiety felt throughout the household.

'Whatever the cost. I will cover them,' Olivia Ashleigh offered. 'Charlie was a loyal friend besides an excellent gardener. He will be greatly missed.'

Mary nodded. 'Janet was understandably extremely upset. From our brief chat it's obvious that the two of them were close.' Mary was discreet, not knowing how much was known of the relationship between the gardener and cook.

Olivia Ashleigh suggested that they sat down. 'I know about them being together last night and I helped Janet dress this morning. Charlie was a remarkable man and well liked throughout Willow Beck, he was a war hero you know and there will be many who will want to pay their respects.'

'I know, Janet told me. What did you have in mind?'

'Arnold Greaves and Son will do the honours. Janet has asked for an afternoon where people can come and pay their respects. Would you be available to say prayers Mary should any wish to participate?'

It was a rare request as relatives of the dead rarely requested an open viewing. 'It would be my honour to be there.' It would also please the Bishop.

'Thank you.' Olivia Ashleigh walked across to the piano to retrieve the wooden box. 'I had intended on coming over to the vicarage this morning, but events here precluded that from happening. Please accept this small token as our opportunity to welcome you into the parish of Willow Beck and I hope you will be very happy here.' Inside the box was a bottle of fine brandy from the Luberon Valley, Mary gratefully accepted the gift. 'Of course, if you don't drink you can keep it for medicinal purposes and the parishioners.'

Mary thanked the lady of the house for the gift. She lay the box down beside her chair.

'I have a confession to make Lady Ashleigh.' Mary saw the expression change on the face of the woman sitting opposite. 'I went exploring yesterday. The vicarage is a big house. In the study I found a secret door.'

'Which had a staircase to an underground passage,' interrupted Olivia Ashleigh.

Mary nodded. 'Yes, that's right. However, what I found below ground was quite shocking. I sleep well, but last night I was restless thinking about it.'

'Please, if we're to become friends Mary call me Olivia.' Having been married to a diplomat she thought it best to see what Mary had discovered.

'The passage from the vicarage went a long way and eventually emerged beneath your house.'

'That's right. Both doors are old priest holes from the time of the reformation. Men of the church needed a place to bolt too or hide when Henry's men were out searching.'

Mary nodded again. 'I had to tell someone Olivia. What I found chilled my bones.'

Olivia Ashleigh chuckled shaking her head. It was turning into a morning of surprises, first Charlie, then the underground passages and wine cellar. 'You mean you found my wine, spirits and cheese store.'

Mary grinned. 'Oh that, yes I did, but I wasn't referring to your private stocks. I found something much more macabre.'

Olivia Ashleigh was instantly curious. 'Like what exactly?'

'The skeletal remains of a man and woman. I believe that they are Montgomery Saul and the woman was his intended bride, Elizabeth Dunn.'

Olivia Ashleigh was clearly shocked. 'I had heard that they'd run away to Gretna Green to get married.'

'That's exactly what the bishop told me, over afternoon tea.' Olivia Ashleigh went over to the drinks cabinet where she returned with two brandies, she gave one to Mary. 'This has been an interesting morning.' She said sipping at her brandy. 'Not to cure any morbid curiosity. But would we go down under ground and look. It's not that I don't believe you Mary, but in a way I feel oddly responsible.' She felt the chill pass through her bones knowing why.

'There's not a lot to see, just skeletal remains. I think the man is Montgomery Saul because he is still wearing his clerical dog collar and there was a prayer card in his pocket with his name written at the top.'

'This might account for some of the strange sightings that Janet and my late husband claimed to have seen. They would sneak down to the kitchen when they thought I was asleep. Making cheese sandwiches with pickles, they get slowly pickled on port. Whenever they mentioned seeing ghost I dismissed their ramblings blaming an over indulgence of cheese and port. They were probably telling the truth.'

'I'd like you to see them,' replied Mary. 'At least then I can say that it wasn't only me who knew about the unfortunate souls. And you'll see for yourself.'

'See what?' asked Olivia Ashleigh.

'I suspect foul play or something as sinister. I checked, but there are no obvious injury scars. I'm no expert, but lovers don't go down to a cellar to die, not when they want to get married.'

'They were poisoned?'

'That was my first thought.' Mary agreed. 'I wonder why?'

Olivia Ashleigh went back over to the drinks cabinet bringing back the decanter. She topped up their brandy glasses.

'You'll need this,' she said as she sat back down, 'mainly because of what I'm about to tell you.'

The brandy was warming as it slipped down Mary's throat on its way to her stomach via her liver. 'I'm ready,' said Mary, 'fire away.'

'I'll begin by saying that it's common knowledge that there was a terrible quarrel between John Steel and Montgomery Saul over Elizabeth Dunn. Montgomery did his best to vehemently defend his lady's honour, but the stubborn John Steele was having none of it. Witnesses who overheard their raised voices stated the Bishop called Elizabeth Dunn all sorts of terrible names, a harlot without a heart. He added that she had serviced many men in the village. Of course there was no truth to his wild accusations.

'Montgomery Saul however was an upright man. A well respected resident throughout Willow Beck. He had no enemies. He didn't believe a word that had been said. When he threatened to inform the general synod of the Bishop's interest with his then young housekeeper, Saul had unwittingly made a dangerous adversary of John Steele.'

Mary Nelson felt a dagger pierce her own heart. 'You mean John Steele killed or had them both killed, and dumped down in the old priest hole.'

Olivia Ashleigh continued sipping her brandy. 'That's why I thought we would need a second glass. Nothing of course could be proven regarding their sudden disappearance and many thought that the pair had run away to be married. You finding them in the passages beneath the estate grounds clears up a dark mystery. People day that big houses have skeletons in their closets. Ours regrettably went underground. What an awful way to die.'

Mary finished the rest of her brandy gulping down the last mouthful appreciating the second glass.

'Bishop John Steele has always been a creepy guy and the other women on the course felt the same as me.'

'You're not the first to voice that opinion.' Olivia Ashleigh stood up, putting her glass down on the coffee table. 'Shall we go take a look and then we'll decide what to do when we return.'

She showed Mary the secret door via the pantry much to Janet's surprise.

Kneading the dough for fresh lunchtime rolls Janet thumped, rolled and punched again and again the ball of dough, bedding in another nail into Rakeesh's coffin. When she eventually caught up with the slimy Asian he would suffer badly. Had Charlie not skidded on the motorbike, the shock of the accident might not have weakened his heart. Picking up the sticky dough she slammed it down aggressively on the kitchen table sending a cloud of fine flour granules everywhere. *'You wait you slimy bastard,'* she muttered to herself picking it back up again, *'I'll wring your scrawny fucking neck and then I'll bury you alive!'*

Descending the stone staircase to the cellar below they both heard the cook's rancorous, hateful threats and mutterings. 'Is Janet alright,' asked Mary, 'I thought my talk might have helped settle some of her agony?'

'That's just Janet letting off steam, she'll be okay,' replied Olivia Ashleigh. 'Janet works through troubles by baking bread. It makes for interesting meals. You must come over and join us Mary, and sample one soon!'

They stood solemnly either side of the skeletal corpses. Olivia Ashleigh was visibly upset to see how the lovers had been dumped unceremoniously alongside one another. 'Somehow, we'll solve this mystery Mary. I am so angry inside.'

Mary put her hand on Olivia's arm. 'As am I Olivia, but where there's a way, there's a will and God will help.' She knelt and straightened the hem

221

of Elizabeth Dunn's dress. 'By enticing him out into open where the church cannot protect him!'

'You'll stay for lunch please?' asked Olivia Ashleigh, hoping that the vicar would agree. Having lost a good friend, a confidante in Charlie, she had suddenly found another in Mary Nelson. 'You can sample some of Janet's homemade meat pie!'

Two for the Price of One

The cashier at the checkout called the manager down from his office because she was unable to placate the customer no matter how hard she tried, and the middle-aged woman was determined to get satisfaction, whatever the cost, or indeed who heard.

Wilfred Tummings weaved a path through and between the trolleys as he entered the main hub of the supermarket floor. It had already been a long day with a big delivery from head office, and uncommonly this was his sixth complaint already. He hoped it wasn't about the wine again. Passing several whispered conversations, other customers had already started gathering to watch and listen.

Smiling confidently he went and stood Gladys Bartlett demonstrating his moral support. Like a drawbridge the metal counter and long grocery belt offered a means of protection from any physical attack. Verbal abuse was nothing unusual but Wilfred was used to receiving an ear bashing, even at home from a long suffering wife.

He lost his smile realising that it had been a mistake. Hanging menacingly, held by a bunched hand the female customer had her handbag ready. Why did women always use a handbag as a weapon thought Wilfred.

'Good day madam and what seems to be the problem?' he asked.

'It's not what seems to be the problem it's what is the bloody problem. My poor Ernie hasn't been able to get off the bog for almost two days. He looks like he's pissing vinegar when he takes a leak.' She held up the bottle for all to see. 'This wine that we purchased here last week is rancid. It's gone off, it's bad!' Stood behind her the rumblings started up. The revolutionaries had all decided to shop at the same time.

Wilfred Tummings stretched out his hand to take the bottle, but Gwen Parsons was shrewd. She knew all the tricks used by large commercial grocery outlets. She pulled the bottle back, pointing at Wilfred with her free hand. 'Yeah right, what'd you think I was born yesterday? I give you the bottle and you deny that it was rightly mine in the first place?' More mutterings from behind supported her stand.

Wilfred noticed that even Gladys on the till was concurring with the woman. 'I was merely going to smell the contents madam. The bottle remains your property until I refund the money or give you an alternative product.'

Narrowing her eyes suspiciously the bottle was reluctantly handed over. Several other females had their handbags at the ready, just in case. Wilfred took a sniff, quickly pushing the offending bottle away from under his nose. He agreed, it was bad. 'I am terribly sorry about this madam,' he said, placing the bottle on the counter, 'and you were right to return the wine. Would two bottles of another brand, plus a five pound grocery voucher compensate your husband's distress?'

'Make it two bottles, plus a tenner to cover the extra loo paper that I've had to buy today and we'll call it quits!' The look of victory puffed up her rosy red cheeks.

Wilfred nodded and the crowd cheered. With the sixth complaint in the bag all remaining stock of the wine was removed from the shelves and placed back in the warehouse. So far the petty cash tin was down by forty five pounds of grocery vouchers and several bottles of more expensive wine or spirits. Emerging from where he had been watching Bill Symons was smiling although he had to admire the way that Wilfred had effectively and calmly handled the situation.

'You had your work cut out there mate,' he said, offering a friendly hand which Wilfred was grateful to take.

'That's the sixth complaint today, it must have been a bad consignment.'

Bill launched straight in with his offer.

'I'm in the import business and have a good quality wine that could help replace your deficit. In fact only this week I've taken possession of a very good red, grown and sourced from the Alsace region.' He saw Wilfred's eyes light up. 'The taste is rather exceptional and the cost is extremely competitive.' Bill could almost hear Wilfred's cogs ticking over. 'It would help balance your books. You would recover some of that lost profit margin.'

Wilfred Tummings was easily appeased. He hadn't relished telephoning head office and speaking to the buyer. 'I would need to try a sample first and as long as the price is right, we might have a deal.'

Bill raised a forefinger. 'I've got some bottles in the boot of the car. I was just on my way to another customer, but seeing as you're in a pickle I'll help you instead. I can go back for the other order.'

Bill returned from the carpark armed with two bottles of the best red. He gave them to Wilfred free suggesting that Wilfred should take one home to share with the wife later that evening. The other they should uncork and sample there and then. Wilfred invited Bill through to the warehouse out back where the shop had a small canteen for staff. Finding two clean glasses and a cork screw he set about opening the bottle.

'This very good,' he said. He took another mouthful. 'In fact it's one of the best that I've ever sampled. How much per bottle?'

'This particular line retails at twelve pound a bottle.' Bill mused rubbing his chin thoughtfully. 'Tell you what Wilfred. I could let you have a case of twelve for a hundred and twenty all in. You'd save twenty pounds on each deal.'

'Make it ninety and we can shake on it?' offered Wilfred sticking out his hand.

Bill grinned grabbing Wilfred's hand. The shop manager felt the power in the old sea captains hands. 'Take a dozen cases and make it ninety five per case and we can shake on it. Think about it Wilfred effectively you'll be getting two bottles free for every case. Charge twelve to fifteen in the shop and you'd have a tidy profit. Head office wouldn't need to know about our deal and we could keep the supply rolling in every six weeks.'

Wilfred saw a good deal and an opportunity. He shook Bill's hand enthusiastically. 'With a wine this good, a hundred and forty four bottles wouldn't last very long, not if the brand becomes popular!'

Bill rubbed his chin again and played his trump card. 'I can supply as many twelve cases as fast as you can sell them.'

Wilfred had forgotten all about Ernie's wife. 'That sounds perfect. You say that you're in the business, do you have any other products?'

Bill placed his hand on Wilfred's shoulder. 'It so happens we do an extremely good line in whiskey and brandy, and only this week we have invested in French cheese.' He looked at the aisle selling dairy products. 'Nothing like the packaged brands that you have on the shelf. This cheese is the real McCoy.

'McCoy,' Wilfred repeated. 'How come?'

'The vineyard grow some of the best grass in the whole region and probably throughout France. The cows cannot get enough of it. Trust me Wilfred, the taste of cheese will linger on the palate and have the customers craving for more. With a good bottle of wine they will complement one another and you'll have the customers queuing up outside the shop entrance.'

Wilfred agreed the price of the cheese. Along with the free bottle of wine, Bill offered a gratis bottle of brandy and whiskey, plus a generous cut of cheese, enough for Wilfred and his wife to sample that evening at supper.

'Think about the promotion drive you could have Wilfred. Cheese and a bottle of wine as a *'two for the price of one'* deal, you'd knock any competitor for six.' Wilfred was also a cricketing man. With young Sandra from the delicatessen counter having the ideal physical attributes she could run the promotion stand. She was bound to attract the male customers and Wilfred would be on hand to dish out samples of the wine. Wilfred rubbed his hands together gleefully. 'You've a fine head for business Bill. Providence shines on those that dare!'

Waving goodbye as Bill left Wilfred saw a way to cream a little off the top for himself. Having worked his way up to management from that of a Saturday warehouse boy, he considered it was time that he saw some of the benefits coming his way.

One Last Mission Charlie

'You managed to do what!' Olivia Ashleigh shrieked, overjoyed that Bill Symons had secured the deal with the local supermarket.

'We might need to cut across to France again and sooner than planned,' Bill added, 'especially if Wilfred's *special's* promotion takes off.'

'Can I come too?' she asked.

'Across to France?'

Olivia Ashleigh smiled. 'Yes why not. I'd find out if I have sea legs and I'm overdue an adventure Bill.' She came in close. 'I would very much like to share one with you!'

He laughed at the same time smiling. 'And what happened last night, was that not the start of an adventure?'

She kissed his cheek. 'What happened last night was a new chapter for us both and exciting. Taking a trip over to France however will put another stamp my passport, get us some more stock and adds a memory we can share together in years to come.'

He pulled her in even closer. Olivia Ashleigh felt her heart begin to pound inside her chest. Every moment with Bill Symons was the start of an adventure.

'Did you arranged the funeral for Charlie?' he asked.

'Yes, Arnold Greaves is making the arrangements and Mary Nelson the vicar is doing the service. Why do you ask?'

'I'm just making sure that our trip doesn't clash with Charlie's funeral.'

'So am I going or not?'

'Of course. I was going to ask you irrespective of Charlie passing on.' Bill took the pocket bible from his own pocket to show Olivia. 'This belonged to Charlie. I tried to slip it to Arnold earlier, but Janet was always in the bloody way. I get it to him later.'

Looking through the bible Olivia saw the picture of Mimi. Bill nodded at her. 'A long lost love I would say.' Olivia nodded back. She read the verse where it had been marked.

They saw Janet wandering outside in the garden.

'When I was at sea I dreamt of owning a patch like that,' said Bill, 'somewhere where I could put up my feet after sowing in the vegetables. After I lost the boat, I did think about giving up and buying a small holding.'

'You lost your boat?' she repeated.

'We hit a big squall and immediately began taking on water. By the time I got in sight of Great Yarmouth the boat was already lost. The lifeboat came to our rescue. I never did know if the boat was scuppered or just a freak accident. It was a wakeup call Olivia. Sitting on the deck of the lifeboat, I made a conscious decision there and then to retire. The insurance paid up without asking too many questions. I managed to pick up the *Saucy Belle* dirt cheap.'

Back to the bible. She watched Janet pick flowers. 'Charlie was in some ways a dark horse. I guess we've each a few skeletons in our cupboard. What did you expect Arnold to do with it Bill?'

'Put it in with Charlie without Janet knowing. Some secrets have to go to the grave Olivia.'

She nodded thinking about the day that her late husband had died.

They watched Janet place the flowers beside the shed door then sit and wipe her eyes. *'Don't you worry my darling. When I catch up with that slimy toad, I'll cut off his knackers and bury him alive. He'll pay dearly for taking you away from me. I will avenge your death Charlie and one day we'll be together again!'*

*****

The weeks that followed were hectic, as the three of them sorted the deliveries to the supermarket. They cut and wrapped the cheese using parchment paper, boxing each consignment for Wilfred and Sandra to sell on their promotion counter. Soon the money tin was brimming.

As Bill had predicted the two for one was an instant hit and big draw with Wilfred's customers and stock in the manor house cellar was dwindling faster than expected.

A few days before Charlie's funeral was due to take place Olivia Ashleigh attended another private service accompanying Mary Nelson to the grounds of the church. There they stood alongside two specially crafted coffins that had been discreetly delivered by Arnold Greaves and his son, Gerald.

Dressed smart, but casual, so not to draw attention to what they were doing the two women stood beside the open grave. They watched as the coffins were gently lowered down into the hole below. Mary conducted a short service after which they sought the shade of a tree nearby to watch the gardeners fill the grave with earth.

'They're together at last and for all eternity,' said Mary to Arnold. 'And available if ever the police want to investigate.' Arnold lowered his head in respect. 'I think they've suffered enough already in the name of love. Let's hope they can now rest in peace.' Mary added amen.

Olivia Ashleigh nodded her respects. 'Love can be a very powerful weapon. Controlled by the thoughts of an evil man, it can be a dangerous outcome.'

Mary didn't need to look, knowing to whom Olivia was directing her comments. Arnold went to join his son. 'Evil beyond acceptable practice,' she replied. 'I've been giving the matter some serious thought these past few days. I'm going to confront John Steele. I want to see his reaction about the whole sad affair.'

Olivia Ashleigh placed her hand over Mary's wrist. 'Don't be too hasty Mary. There's are other ways to skin a rabbit. To trap and catch a murderer, you must first employ cunning. Second you need to be as subversive. Treachery wears two faces, deceit and a confidence that they can get away with almost anything including murder. As an ambassador's wife, I witnessed both. To catch a mouse, first you need to have bait and a trap.'

Mary was interested. 'What have you in mind?'

'Most politicians employ blackmail to achieve an aim. They use others to do their dirty work. My plan would be to send John Steele the photographs of the skeletons in the cellar, anonymously of course. We dangle the carrot enough to have him worry who else knows. We accompany the photos with a short hand written note telling the Bishop that if he doesn't play ball we will send everything to the Chief Constable. We say we know who killed the couple, why and that new evidence has recently come to light. There's no need to point the finger of suspicion, let his conscience prick deep. We'll give the bishop the opportunity to pay us hush money to keep it quiet.'

'Do you think he'd fall for it,' Mary asked. 'I might not like him, but John Steel is no fool?'

Olivia Ashleigh smiled confidently.

'Curiosity and conscience will get the better of him. He'll undoubtedly ask for a meeting with the author of the letter where he would hope to silence them forever. He will act accordingly depending on the circumstances. He needs to bury this awful secret once and for all.'

'It's risky,' Mary was apprehensive. 'What if he had an accomplice?'

Olivia watched Arnold and Gerald talking to the gravediggers. 'My guess is that he did. But he's dead. You took his place.'

'Victor Higginbottom!'

Olivia nodded. 'Higginbottom and Steele were as thick as thieves. The Bishop needed Victor to be close and what better than at St Ridley's.'

Mary felt a cold shiver invade her body. 'We might never know who killed poor Montgomery Saul and Elizabeth Dunn.'

Olivia agreed. 'We'll cross that bridge when and if it comes to that. Let's see how blackmail strikes home first. At least the church might raise some needy cash to help the poor.' She placed her hand over Mary's. 'And that old church roof won't last forever.'

'How much was you thinking of asking for to buy our silence?'

Olivia Ashleigh did the sums in her head. 'Fifty thousand is a nice round sum. Not too greedy, not to less. I know that John Steele has a healthy bank balance. Lawrence and the Bishop belonged to the same Masons lodge.'

Mary looked surprised. 'John Steele, a Mason.'

Olivia was surprised that Mary was surprised.

'How many of the church elders are not Mary. How do you think they get promoted so quickly? It's not spouting the scriptures from the pulpit every Sunday and marketing Jesus. Nowadays, it's all about you scratch my back and I'll scratch yours. The old boy's network is as active as it has always been. It's how Lawrence went places in the diplomatic service.'

Mary gave a shake of her head. 'There's an awful lot to the church that I have yet to uncover.'

With the backs of their spades the gravediggers patted down the last of the sods atop of the grave. They left the shade of the tree going across to show their gratitude.

Olivia Ashleigh gave Arnold Graves a white envelope, inside was loose cash. 'Please share this amongst yourselves. You gentlemen have done us a great service this morning.'

Wiping the sweat from his brow with a large handkerchief Arnold nodded at them respectfully. 'This isn't necessary Lady Ashleigh, really. Montgomery Saul was a very good friend of mine. A kind and gentle soul who never harmed a fly. Gerald and I feel honoured that you took us into your confidence. Not one word will ever pass from our lips about what took place here today.'

'Thank you Arnold, thank you Gerald. ' Mary said a short prayer to protect the men present before they parted company.

'Coffee at the vicarage,' Mary asked. 'I know that I could certainly do with one?'

*****

There was only a few days left before the funeral of Charlie Luft. Arnold and Gerald had washed and shaved Charlie, brushed his hair, well at least what was left of it and dressed him in his finest clothes. Each item having been meticulously pressed by Janet Symons.

By prior arrangement Janet was permitted the first viewing which she wanted held in the old timber workshop where Charlie had spent many a

235

happy hour whittling into shape small ornaments or toys for the arts and craft fayre that was held annually in the vicarage grounds.

'He looks so peaceful,' she said wiping the tear from her eye. 'Just like when I saw him last.' She gently pushed the wisp of hair across his forehead. 'He's still sleeping.'

Arnold Greaves lowered his head. Nobody had told him that it was Janet who had found Charlie.

'Do you think he knows?' she asked.

Arnold looked up. 'Knows what Janet?'

'That I've come to see him.'

Arnold gently placed a reassuring hand upon her forearm. 'Charlie will always be around in spirit I am sure.'

She ran her fingers down the inside of his jacket lapel. 'He looks really nice. A real gent. I never ever saw Charlie dressed like this. He was always wearing his old work clothes, even when he drove the Rolls. I wonder what he would have worn, had we got married.'

'His finest suit,' Arnold replied. 'Charlie had style despite his gruff exterior. People here will flock to see him today. Charlie was a hero and they have a great respect for what he did during the war. Some never forget.'

Janet caressed the lapel lovingly. 'He was very brave Arnold. Charlie would tell me about the missions that he went on. His jumping from a plane in the middle of the night over France. I would have been too scared to have gone up in the first place, let alone launched myself out into the darkness below.'

'As you rightly say,' repeated Arnold, 'a brave man to his last breath!'

The procession of people seemed to be endless that day. Men, women even children came. They wanted to see the hero and gardener for the last time. Standing at the side of the workshop Samuel, Tommy and Robert found it difficult to comprehend that Charlie had actually gone.

Leaning over Tommy had something to add to the occasion. *'My aunt said Janet shagged the poor old bugger to death.'*

The other two looked at him aghast. *'That's disrespectful Tommy. It was his heart which gave out!'* Robert quickly replied.

Samuel grinned wryly. 'It's no bloody wonder he snuffed it with Janet Simmons sitting on top of him.' He shivered. 'Can you image her running at you stark naked.'

They saw Janet look across from where she was standing alongside Arnold Greaves. They each gave her a wave and an encouraging smile.

'They're such nice boys,' she whispered to Arnold. 'A bit cheeky at times, but they're young and they have their whole life ahead of them. I envy them.'

Arnold was pleased to see that the three young men had dressed sensibly for the occasion.

Tommy blew out between his lips. 'Her chest is like the melon stall at the market, stacked proud, round and...' he took another look, 'and can you image her thighs. They could crush like a vice. Old Charlie must have been a strong bugger for his age.'

'Give it a rest,' warned Robert, 'somebody will hear you two.'

'Hear what exactly?' asked Bill Symons as he came alongside without warning.

They looked at him, their eyes opening wide and their brains thinking fast. Samuel saved the day.

'We were just discussing the next trip Bill and how well trade is going at the local supermarket.'

'Yes, it is, but keep that under your hat. When you're done here we need to discuss our next trip to Dunkirk. Wilfred Tummings called me to say that stocks are getting low.'

Samuel felt the relief wash through him. Using the various social media sites he had managed to find Chantelle's mobile number. They had been texting one another back and forth. 'When are we sailing captain?' he asked.

'As soon as we get Charlie's funeral out of the way.' Bill looked around the workshop expecting to see Olivia Ashleigh, but she was nowhere to be seen. 'Remember, we need to make plans.' He nodded at the body in the coffin then made an excuse to leave.

Samuel watched him leave. 'He's got a lively spring in his step today,' he whispered, 'only last week Bill was complaining of a stiff hip.'

Tommy glared at Robert. 'It's all the exercise he's getting. He's shagging her ladyship day and night.'

Incomprehensibly Robert could not believe his friends. 'Something else your aunt knows, I suppose!'

Tommy grinned back. 'She cleans the bedrooms, enough said.'

Robert wasn't amused. 'One day Tommy Jenkins, delving into other's private business will be the undoing of you.' Tommy looked at Robert and began laughing. Samuel and Robert dragged him out from the workshop to find Bill Symons.

With respects paid the queue dwindled until there was only Arnold Greaves and Olivia Ashleigh alone in the workshop. Wearing a sombre outfit she wore a thin veil. She was carrying a long slender object covered over by a blanket. Laying it down on the workbench she joined Arnold.

'It's been a very good turn out,' she said.

Arnold agreed.

'I'll miss him,' she said. Looking down at Charlie he looked to be at peace. 'It's hard to find loyal friends and even harder when you lose them.'

'Would you like a few moments alone,' Arnold invited, 'I can step outside?'

Olivia Ashleigh smiled. 'Thank you Mr Greaves. That is very kind of you.'

As soon as Arnold stepped beyond the door of the workshop Olivia Ashleigh pulled open the blanket and unzipped the bag within. She removed the hunting rifle, went across to the coffin where she raised the lower half. Placing the rifle between the corpses leg she gently lowered the lid. Spinning the brass bolts into place she secured the lower half.

'I'm sorry Charlie, but I know you'd understand. You always did suspect me of shooting Lawrence so please consider this is your last mission. Protect my innocence and take the rifle with you.'

Wedged between his arm and chest she saw the bible containing the photograph of Mimi. She smiled knowing Bill had protected not only Charlie's memory, but Janet as well. She left it another five minutes before she called Arnold Greaves back inside.

'Can we close and lock down the upper lid as well,' she asked. 'I think Janet would prefer that Charlie was left to rest in peace now!' She watched Arnold spin the wingnuts tight.

Placing her hand on the long polished casket, Olivia Ashleigh spoke very softly. *'Goodbye Charlie, sleep peacefully old friend.'*

Lumps, Bumps and the Mumps

Bill Symons informed them of the time that they would be sailing. He added that Lady Ashleigh would be joining them on the next trip. It was amusing as much as surprising.

'Is that so she can check out Madame Charron?' asked Samuel cheekily.

Bill Symons frowned back.

'Barking up the wrong tree can be risky indictment young man.' Bill grinned which was even more menacing, 'and don't forget the North Sea can be an unpredictable place!'

Samuel zipped his lips together.

Robert changed the subject. 'It's strange that we've not heard anything of Rakeesh since the motorbike incident. I thought we would have had customs crawling all over us by now!'

Bill shrugged his shoulders. He agreed with Robert.

'I'd like to know where he is too. I guess we'll know if made contact when we arrive back in Dunkirk. Anton Martine and the troops will be waiting.'

'And if they're not Bill, what then?' Tommy asked.

Bill smiled. 'Then we go ahead as planned. We collect the van and head for Saint Cambrae toot de suite. Just remember to watch your *p's and q's* around Lady Ashleigh and keep the jokes clean lads. Whatever you think she is a lady.'

They were going over last minute details when Samuel received an unexpected text. He walked to where he could read it in private. It was from Chantelle.

'Sammy when are you coming here again? I think that I am late. We need to talk.'

He read the message twice over before hitting the dial button. Annoyingly the call went straight to voicemail. Bill Symons called across. 'Is there something wrong Samuel?'

'No, nothing that cannot be sorted,' he replied. His expression was less convincing.

'Good. First the funeral, then we can get around to your love life.' Bill had his suspicions as to why the colour had suddenly faded from Samuel cheeks.

Slipping the phone back into his pocket he had only one word whirring about inside his head *'late, late... late'*. Suddenly his life was flashing before him.

Come the day of the funeral St Ridley's church was packed without a space to be found amongst the aisle seats and late mourners stood at the back. Willow Beck had turned out in force as did neighbouring villages to pay their last respects to Charlie. Amongst the mourners were Benjamin

Chapple and Antoine Vincenzi. The Italian was accompanied by his wife. Sitting alongside Janet, Olivia Ashleigh was armed with a supply of tissues.

'You see,' she whispered looking around. *'I told you Charlie was a much loved man. Now perhaps you'll stop doubting just how much he loved you!'* Janet couldn't see the connection. She was more concerned why some of the other women in the church also had big tears running down their faces.

Supported by two strong wooden trestles the coffin looked resplendent. The many flowers and wreaths were everywhere. Olivia caught Janet looking up at vaulted ceiling.

'I reckon the old bugger is up there right now and watching us all weeping and a wailing for him. He would have found that irritating.'

Olivia Ashleigh didn't bother looking up. Instead she lowered her head to smile. *'I reckon if Charlie had half the chance again, he would use the rifle that I put between his legs and take out one or two sitting in the pews here. They might have liked him, but he certainly didn't like some of them.'*

Squeezing Janet's hand she sniffed. 'I am sure that he wouldn't have missed today. Charlie liked a good party.' She replied.

Janet Simpson responded with a smile. She wished she was with Charlie dead or alive. She was trying hard but the tears kept on falling. Thankfully Bill Symons who was on her other side was also on hand with an additional supplies of tissues. Sat in the last pew next to the door was Robert, Tommy and Samuel.

'What's wrong with you,' muttered Tommy, sitting next to Samuel. 'You've had a face like a slapped arse since receiving that text?'

'It's Chantelle, she reckons she's late. I'm depressed.'

'Late for what?'

Samuel stared at Tommy. 'Well, I'll give you a naffing clue. It rhymes with a train climbing a steep hill, going chuff fucking chuff...'

Robert gave them both a stern look.

'I don't know,' whispered Tommy, scratching his head, 'something running out of steam.'

Robert sighed and whispered in Tommy's ear. 'Chantelle thinks she's up the duff, pregnant!'

The laughter caused everybody to turn. Tommy quickly raised his hand and apologised.

'I'm sorry vicar, please carry on. It was just a funny thought about Charlie. I was only thinking out loud!' The mourners around where they sat let the interruption pass. At the altar Mary Nelson was about to begin the service with a prayer.

'You'd best pray that she's not Samuel,' whispered Robert. 'Bill will keelhaul you all the way back to France. I dare not think what Lady Ashleigh will do, if she finds out.'

'Bugger them,' replied Samuel leaning across Tommy, 'what will my mum and dad say?'

'Forget them, what will Chantelle's dad say?' added Tommy. He was struggling suppressing another laugh. They all went forward kneeling on the pew cushion to pray.

'He's already out looking for the father. So far Chantelle has refused to tell him who she's been with.'

Tommy was really struggling. 'Christ, how many blokes has she been with?'

Samuel was pale discussing his prospects of being an expectant father. 'How the fuck do I know. I did it with her the once and in the back of the van while you, Bill and Robert were sampling grapes and eating cheese. Chantelle is in the pudding club and the recipe could involve a mix of ingredients.'

Tommy sniffed rather than hoot, blaming the dust between the wooden pews.

'You'll have to have one of those tests where they prick your dick. Some dishy bird in a tight uniform takes a biopsy of your old man and then she makes a match with Chantelle and her fanny.'

Samuels's eyes bulged. He'd seen the documentaries on TV and watched the bull have a similar examination performed by the veterinary down on the farm.

'Nobody's pricking my dick. I'd rather just own up and be done with it!' It was more vocal than expected.

Covering his mouth with a clenched fist Tommy got up crossed his chest twice then left the church going outside to explode. Bill Symons watched him go. 'The service must be getting to the lad,' he explained to Olivia Ashleigh. 'When we all go outside I'll give him a snifter of brandy.'

Later that day Robert Perry, Samuel Byrne and Tommy Jenkins arrived at the manor house. Settling in the back of the Rolls, Olivia Ashleigh sat up front in the passenger seat with Bill driving. In under an hour they arrived to where the boat was moored. They were about to cast off when Olivia Ashleigh raised a hand of caution to Bill Symons.

'Hold fast there captain,' she cried. She walked over to where Samuel had hold of his casting line. Pulling down the front of his sweat shirt she examined his neck and chest, before checking his back. Placing the engine on idle Bill stepped away from the boat controls.

'What's wrong?' he asked. Samuel had confusion in his eyes. She pushed up the young man's chin and pulled down the front of the sweatshirt again. She pointed.

'There, look. I might be wrong, but I think young Samuel has the mumps!'

Samuel felt the glands around his throat, feeling the swelling.

'No wonder my balls have been aching the last couple of hours. It must have been that snotty nosed little shit that was stood behind me in the church. He kept sneezing every time we sung a hymn.'

Bill checked Samuel's neck and agreed it definitely looked like the mumps. 'Sorry lad, but you're to stay ashore for this trip young man.' He checked the time with his watch, counting down the minutes to the tide.

'WHAT… you're joking Bill,' Samuel cried. *'I've got to go… trust me my life depends on it!'*

'I bet it does,' replied the old sea salt. Bill looked at Tommy Jenkins who had his line stowed. 'Sorry lad, but you'll have to drive the Rolls and take Samuel back home. He'll need to be in isolation for at least a week.'

'A week, that's impossible. I can't be bed ridden… not now!' Replied Samuel. He was down on his knees begging Bill Symons to let him go, but the captain was adamant.

'I'm sorry lad. We can't risk us all getting the mumps. Don't you worry. We'll get everything sorted the other end, I promise!'

The three of them cast off watched by Tommy sitting behind the driver's wheel of the Rolls with Samuel sitting dejectedly in the back. He didn't feel privileged. Looking in the rear view mirror Tommy could see Samuel glaring back at him.

'Don't say a fucking word Jenkins, otherwise I will not be responsible for my actions.'

Bill let Robert steer the boat towards the harbour entrance going below deck where Olivia Ashleigh was making them coffee.

'What exactly do you need to sort Bill,' she asked. 'You were very masterful talking to Samuel before he reluctantly agreed to stay behind?'

247

The captain didn't like breaking a confidence, but seeing as he and Olivia had become close he felt compelled to tell her the truth. That and she would be meeting Chantelle and her family soon. He told her everything that had happened on the previous excursion, emphasising that it could be a false alarm and end up as nothing but a storm in a teacup. She handed him his coffee.

He was surprised to see her looking so pensive.

'I would like to have found myself in Chantelle's shoes Bill. At least once in my life, but Lawrence didn't want children. He said that they were socially embarrassing, an awful bind and nothing but trouble.'

Bill went and sat alongside. 'He made children sound worse than having pets.'

Olivia Ashleigh sighed ruefully.

'Oh no, we had a pet cat, Missy. Lawrence adored her and the cat could do anything she wanted. There were times when I would look at Missy padding up the stairs last thing in the evening, thinking that she should have been a little boy or girl. I so wanted a child that I could bath and brush their hair before putting them to bed, before I read them a story. Over time the subject and lack of children drove a wedge between us. It was more noticeable when we came back to England where I had more spare time on my hand.' She laid her head on Bill Symons shoulder feeling the tears of regret begin to dampen her cheek. 'Whatever Chantelle's circumstances, we'll sort it.'

He kissed the top of her head. 'Strangely enough, I half expected you to say that.'

Steering the boat towards the open sea Robert Perry had overheard the conversation taking place in the cabin below. He smiled to himself, the captain and his lady were well suited to one another and Samuel Byrne was lucky to have them on his side.

Leaving the safety of the harbour behind Robert set the course for Dunkirk cutting through the swell of the waves, watching the bow rise and then drop. The sea had more to offer than the last trip and the waves were higher. They were already a mile out when he sensed somebody standing behind him, he turned to see Bill Symons.

'You've done really well lad.' He congratulated Robert patting him on the back. 'The sea is a bit lumpy tonight, but we'll soon reach Dunkirk safely.'

Robert held the bow straight heading into the next wave. 'You got the gist Bill that Chantelle might be pregnant?'

'Aye lad, replied Bill. 'He's a damn fool, especially if it was just a roll in the hay with the lass and it meant nothing else.'

Robert kept his concentration on the sea ahead. He glanced sideways at Bill Symons who rarely missed anything going on around him. Smiling to himself the old sea salt watched Robert steer the bow through the waves. The boy was a natural, a gifted sailor. He acknowledged that the *Saucy Belle* was in good hands.

Napoleon's Code

With the lights of land mere small dots the middle of the North Sea had suddenly and mysteriously calmed making for a better sailing. Olivia Ashleigh had come up on deck to relieve Robert so that he could get some rest. Standing by in case she needed help Bill watched her take charge of the Broom Admiral. Overhead the late evening clouds were blanketing the sky like a gloved hand.

'Is it always this dark?' she asked.

'Only when there are no stars present or a storm might be due.'

She wished she hadn't asked.

'Don't worry,' said Bill. 'I checked before we left and there's no bad weather due for a couple of days.'

'How do they know,' Olivia asked. 'I always thought that the weather more or less did what it liked at sea?'

Bill laughed. 'That's true at times although we've more sophisticated weather buoys nowadays and then there's satellites flying about working twenty four seven. We can pinpoint problems and avoid incoming bad weather.'

The *Saucy Belle* suddenly rolled to the side caught out by a rogue wave. Olivia Ashleigh went with the roll, but she was skilfully caught before she fell by Robert Perry.

'Are you alright m'lady, it can do that out here. Often without warning.' Bill looked on. He was in admiration of Robert's knowledge of everything nautical and his delicate handling of Lady Ashleigh.

'I'm fine, thank you Robert. It might however have been a different story had you not been there. I thought that you'd gone below to rest?'

He grinned. 'I like the night crossing too much to miss out.' He pointed suddenly peering ahead. 'Land ahoy captain!'

'Aye lad, we've made good time. Another couple of hours and we'll beat the tides along the French coast.'

Olivia Ashleigh had her hands clamped tightly around the spoke handles of the wheel determined that the rudder wouldn't catch her out again. Bill Symons placed his hands over hers. 'She's just like a lady, you hold her gently and she'll react to your touch I assure you.'

Under his guidance she mastered the feel of the rudder sailing successfully into the busy marina at Dunkirk. Securing the stern quarter lines so that they could load their cargo that much quicker, Bill Symons kept a watchful eye out for any unsuspecting harbour officials, especially Anton Martine. He was relieved to see that their arrival had gone unnoticed.

'Are we safe captain?' Robert asked, making sure that the buffers were set proud to prevent other boats from damaging the sides of the boat.

'We are so far lad,' he replied.

'Then we can assume Rakeesh couldn't have made contact?' Bill Symons shook his head and Olivia Ashleigh remained silent.

'Aye, that's right. Don't ask me how, but I've a feeling that we've seen the last of him!' Bill looked at Olivia, but she was looking elsewhere. Making sure that the lines were secure they used the dark shadows of the backstreets to relocate the Citroen van. Olivia Ashleigh looked on astonished unsure whether to laugh or cry.

'Does it even work?' she chose laughter.

Bill tapped the bonnet. 'It runs like a dream. The interior is a bit rudimentary, but it serves our purpose. It once belonged to the baker.'

'I'm not surprised. It reminds me of an Indian tuk tuk only this has four wheels instead of three.'

Bill Symons dusted the passenger seat with the back of his hand as Robert settled himself down in the back of the van using the cushions that had been stacked from their last visit.

'Will you be comfortable enough?' Olivia asked concerned.

'It's better m'lady without the other two tagging along and I have all the cushions to myself.'

Driving clear of the rear yard of the restaurant Bill left a note pinned to the back door to let Madame Charron know that they were back in Dunkirk. He added a postscript to say that they would dine at the restaurant on their return journey.

Olivia wanted her passenger window open smelling the harbour air. 'I've only ever been to Paris the once and that was when Lawrence was invited by the French Ambassador.'

'Staying at some posh hotel no doubt?' Bill added.

Olivia seemed embarrassed. 'George the Fifth. It wasn't by choice although it was memorable to have the Champs des Elysses so close. I would have been just as happy with a hotel in Montmartre alongside the artists.'

'Wow,' Robert said impressed. 'The only George the Fifth that I know is the pub over at Tenchyard south of Holkam. '

Olivia Ashleigh laughed. 'Posh hotels are mostly grand on top surface Robert, but beneath the surface the poor staff run around like headless chickens to please the guests. I much preferred the real Paris, but my visit was brief.'

'Where did you meet?' asked Bill Symons, taking the road to Lille.

'At the time I was working for the foreign office. It was nothing glamourous and I was merely an overseas administrator. My main responsibility was arranging visas and ticket reservations. Renewing passports, booking accommodation, catering and hiring chauffeurs. I was known as a fixer. In other words a general dogs body for the diplomats so that they didn't have to concern themselves with the mundane trivialities of life. Lawrence was amongst their number.'

'A bit like a tug boat captain. I'd haul someone's arse end in and out of the port making them look good.'

Olivia smiled hearing Robert snigger. 'That about sums it up. One day Lawrence walked into my office to check on his itinerary. We got talking and he asked me out to dinner. One thing led to another and before I knew it I was married. The title came later.'

'And Willow Manor where did that fit in?' Bill asked.

'The house and estate belonged to his great grandfather. A hand me down. With no children to inherit everything the blood line ceases to exist. It's legally mine.'

Bill nodded as he concentrated on the early morning traffic. 'That's why me and the *Saucy Belle* get along so well. She's my mistress and in a way I'm her master. We sail together, ride the storms out and emerge the other side still smiling. In a way we're like an old married couple.'

Robert chuckled to himself thinking again how they suited one another. Talking that had almost forgotten that he was in the back. Olivia Ashleigh changed the subject and her expression. 'When we arrive at Saint Cambrae, do you think the reception might be less cordial than your last visit?'

Bill sucked in air through his teeth.

'That depends. The Dupont's are typically honourable and French. It depends on what Chantelle, the daughter has said. They're a tight-knit family.'

'And Chantelle,' she pushed. 'Is she easy going?'

'She's beautiful,' Robert added.

Bill checked the rear view mirror and Olivia Ashleigh raised her eyebrows. Robert lowered his eyes.

'We'll just play it by ear.' Bill advised. He checked the signage at the side of the road for Reims getting ready to change lanes.

Olivia Ashleigh was optimistic.

'Let's hope that the circumstances hasn't soured the taste of the wine or cheese. We're flourishing well at home. It would be a pity for something seemingly trivial to mar the arrangement. A solution can be found to any problem.'

Robert piped up once again. 'Samuel's never been any different m'lady. He goes in head first without considering the consequences. He road crashes common sense for fun.'

Bill and Olivia glanced at one another. It was an unexpected outburst from Robert, and charged with emotion. Bill nodded although it was hardly noticeable. Did Robert have underlying feelings for the winemaker's daughter? He saw complications arising as they took the junction. Small talk covered a lot of subjects for the remainder of the journey. An hour later Bill turned the steering wheel left and pulled up alongside the old barn.

Letting the bedroom curtain drop back into place Chantelle Dupont felt her heart rate anxiously increase. She ran down the stairs and was through the front door of the house before her mother could stop her. She came to a halt when Bill, a woman she didn't know and Robert stood beside the van.

'*Sammy, where is Sammy?*' she cried, her tone racked with desperation.

Bill explained. 'He couldn't make the trip over Chantelle. He's sorry, he's got the mumps… oreillons!'

'*Oreillons… no,*' she screamed agonisingly, '*I need Sammy here. We need to talk urgently. Time it marches on!*'

Olivia saw a woman come to the door of the house.

Robert surprised them all taking control of the situation. He walked over to Chantelle, produced a handkerchief and suggested that they went for a walk where they could be alone. Chantelle agreed as her mother watched Robert place his arm around her daughter's shoulders.

Bill felt Olivia's hand slip into his. 'He has a very attentive and caring nature that lad. If he was my son, I would be very proud of him.'

Olivia Ashleigh agreed. 'He'll make somebody a fine husband one day, Robert is sensitive to people's needs.'

A cry of welcome emerged suddenly from behind, coming from the wine store. 'Bienvenue mes amies.'

'Victor Dupont,' Bill told Olivia.

Olivia Ashleigh smiled back, pleased the welcome was jovial. 'At least he seems happy to have us back,' she whispered.

Bill stuck out his hand to greet the wine producer. 'Hello Victor, it's good to be back. Please let me introduce Lady Ashleigh.'

Victor shook Bill's hand, then promptly kissed both of Olivia's cheeks. 'Such beauty, no wonder the sun is shining today!' Olivia Ashleigh graced the moment with an engaging smile.

'The pleasure is entirely mine Monsieur Dupont and please call me Olivia. I only married into the title.'

Victor placed his hands over his chest. 'But such an honoured guest and you being here. It will almost certainly bring prestige to our door, qui?'

'Well, that aside Victor,' interrupted the captain, 'how's the wine doing?'

The wine producer kissed the gathered tips of his fingers. 'Magnificent my friend and we have your order all boxed and ready as instructed. However you must be tired, and hungry and thirsty after your long journey. I will have Adele prepare a continental style breakfast.'

Victor had expected to see Tommy, Robert and Samuel emerge from the side of the van. 'Have the others gone to stretch their legs?' he asked, his brow creasing into a frown.

'Only Robert came back today. He's taking a walk with Chantelle.' Replied Bill.

Victor's right eyebrow went up on one side. He checked the house for signs of Adele before leaning in close. *'My wife, she is very upset only not as much as her husband. Somebody has been inappropriate with my young daughter. Adele, she thinks that Chantelle might be pregnant.'*

'A local lad?' asked Bill, his fingers crossed behind his back.

Victor was somewhat reticent with his reply.

'Quite possibly my friend. I have already questioned several of the suspects locally, but my young daughter she is stubborn like her grandmother and she refuses to tell me anything.' Victor promptly threw his hands into air. 'She has no shame that girl. How you say in England, 'she has had a roll in the hay and is now with a pudding in the oven, qui?'

Olivia Ashleigh stepped in believing that a woman's touch with such a delicate subject might help quell emotions. 'It must be quite a worry Victor, but there is always a solution to be found somewhere.'

Victor ran his fingers worryingly through his hair, exhaling loudly, but he did save a smile for Olivia.

'Her mother and father have sleepless nights, but we are Dupont and we are strong. Like Napoleon, we have honour in defeat. As head of my family it is my duty to protect them at all times. They must come before the wine even.' He sighed again. 'Napoleon, he lost the battle at Waterloo because he did not have the right strategy in place, whereas I... Victor Dupont have a list of possible sutors.'

Bill grinned. 'A cobble, shoemaker. I think you mean suitors old chap.'

'Qui, qui... and if she is up the duff, heaven help the suitor!'

'Is it a long list Victor?' Olivia inquired.

From his back pocket Victor produced a scrap of paper where there were written ten names, some with a black line already ruled through.

Both Bill and Olivia saw that one was ringed, that of Samuel Byrne. Victor pointed to the name.

'As I recall, he was unwell on your last visit from mal de mar!'

'He suffers from bad sea legs,' Bill replied knowing his explanation was weak.

Victor insisted on tapping at the name with the end of his finger. 'And why has he not come this time?'

'Oreillons!' replied Bill weakly.

At last Victor could see some humour in the moment. *'Ah, oreillons, good it will affect his oomph, qui?'*

Bill shrugged. 'There's no telling what the mumps can do to a man Victor, young or old.'

They watched Chantelle and Robert walk back into the yard. Bill expected Victor to launch an attack on Robert, but instead he walked over and held out his hand in greeting. 'I am sorry to hear about your friend Samuel, but it is good that you are here.'

Chantelle suddenly turned running to the open door of the house.

Again Victor raised his arms. 'Like her mother, always emotional.'

Adele was pleased to meet Olivia Ashleigh and they talked when the men talked business. After a while though Adele made her excuses to go attend to her daughter realising that she had been absent and not eaten.

Victor helped load the van with the boxes of wine, spirits and a good quantity of mature cheese. They promised to return again and soon to which he promised the same supplies would be available.

Shaking their hands as they were about to leave Victor kissed the back of Lady Ashleigh's hand. *'Bien sur, cela pourrait etre juste une tempete dans une tasse de the et un voeu pieux des jeunes filles.'*

Checking the lane before they turned back the way that they had come Robert looked up at the bedroom window where he saw Chantelle and her mother looking out. Chantelle was smiling at him. She waved and he waved back. It was a moment not missed by Bill and Olivia.

'What was that all about with Victor?' Bill asked heading for the high street that ran through the centre of the village.

Olivia waved at Adele and Chantelle.

'Victor was just telling me that it could be just a storm in a teacup and the fanciful wishful thinking of a young girl who thinks she is in love.'

In the back of the van Robert was left smiling to himself.

The walk with Chantelle had been on his mind ever since they had left England. He wondered if she would consent to walking and talking to him, but he needed to find out for himself how she felt about Samuel and the baby.

Robert knew, what the other's did not.

Skeletons in the Closet

Mary peeled away the kitchen gloves from her hands, throwing them in the bin having folded and placed the letter in the envelope along with copies of the photographs. She added a first class stamp having sealed the gummed strip. Staring blankly at the envelope on the kitchen table, it went against all of her morals and religious principles, but then so did murder.

It was very late and dark when she went across to the church where kneeling before the altar with a single candle flame to keep her company she prayed. Mixed feelings were playing havoc with her thoughts, she hoped God would not abandon her.

'Forgive me for my sins lord. What I do, I do in the memory and name of a good, honest and just man and his lady love. They were two gentle lost souls, abandoned without mercy or kindness of thought. The action that I take is to see justice served. I ask, is the bishop's part in this terrible tragedy not a greater sin than that of my own. You can punish me lord when we eventually meet, but with luck that might not be for a few more years to come. Amen.

Mary wondered if her prayer would be heard. She was still kneeling when a sudden breeze made the flame of the candle dance erratically. Turning around she saw a dark shadowy figure approaching. Mary stood looking for a weapon by which to defend herself. A moment later she was relieved to recognise the face.

'Goodness Olivia you made my stomach turn. I thought you might have been the Bishop.'

'I'm sorry, I didn't mean to startle you. I was at the bedroom window when I saw the flicker of light from the church. I did try calling the vicarage, but there was no reply.'

No, you wouldn't. Least not tonight. Grace's has every Thursday night off.' Mary held her beating heart hoping the pace would slow. 'I had this sudden urge to come and pray. I don't like giving prayer in the vicarage knowing what might have taken place before I arrived. That together with what went on in the passage below the study. I thought the candle would give out the minimum illumination and not attract attention.'

Olivia Ashleigh sat on the pew beside Mary Nelson.

'I overheard your prayer. I take it that you've written to the bishop?'

'Yes, that's partly why I am here.' Olivia saw Mary wring her hands. 'I had to wear kitchen gloves to write the note and put the contents in the envelope. My writing is quite bad, awful in fact and my hand wouldn't stop shaking. I left the envelope on the kitchen table.'

Olivia fisted the air before her. 'That's perfect don't you see. The shakier the writing, the better. It means John Steele won't be able to identify who wrote or sent the letter. Did you add the amount that we agreed?'

Mary looked at the altar. It looked quite beautiful in the candlelight. 'Fifty thousand pounds. Strange but it didn't seem a lot for the price of two people's lives.'

'Look upon it as a thousand a piece for every year that the perpetrator should have served in prison for their murders.'

Mary still wasn't convinced. 'We've no real evidence to suggest that it was the bishop who killed them!'

Unmoved Olivia Ashleigh looked on somewhat sternly. 'John Steele has always considered himself above the law and if truth known, above God. It's about time that the pompous ass was brought down to earth with a bump and answerable for his sins. Fifty thousand isn't to be sniffed at Mary and it would save you having to go down on bended knee, pleading in a year or two for permission to begin a restoration fund.'

Mary accepted that Olivia was right. She extinguished the candle and together they walked to the door of the church.

'Was it a good trip over to France?'

Olivia Ashleigh laughed. 'It was good is as much as it was entertaining, enlightening and exciting.'

'I'll take that as a yes.' Mary replied.

'Well it certainly wasn't boring.' Olivia looped her arm through Mary's. 'Come on. I brought you back some wine and a chunk of cheese. Let's celebrate your restoration fun by cracking open a bottle.'

*****

'Well how did she look?' Samuel was eager to know. He sat down on a wooden bench as Robert perched himself atop of a hay bale.

'Much like she did the last time that we were there.'

Samuel exploded his fingers out front of his stomach to emphasise a swelling. 'That don't tell me a lot. You know what I mean Perry. Did she look bigger out front?'

Robert dismissed his gesture. 'Victor Dupont has you top of his hit list, and the likeliest offender!'

Samuel hung his head low. *'Fuck'.*

'Well, what do expect,' Robert retaliated. 'You have no self-control. The first time we visit Saint Cambrae you decide to shag the owner's daughter. What kind of signal does that send out?'

Samuel looked up, shocked. 'I've got the bloody mumps. That means I could lose my sex appeal, my ability.'

The laugh was loud and without sympathy. 'Think of all the girls in Willow Beck would cheer, who would be saved.'

Samuel made himself more comfortable on the bench. 'It's not funny.' He looked serious. 'I might never get it up again.'

Robert was almost beside himself with laughter. 'The way Victor Dupont was describing what he would do with the father when he caught up with him, I think getting it up again would be the least of your worries. When we left he was sharpening the castration knife that he uses on his bulls.'

Samuel crossed his legs at the thought. 'What am I going to do Rob?' he asked, the saliva catching at the back of his throat.

'You could try calling Chantelle and talking. You've not made contact since Bill, Lady Ashleigh and myself left for Saint Cambrae.'

Samuel had his head low. 'I don't know what to say to her. I've never been in this position before.'

'And neither has Chantelle.' The words left his lips with venom attached.

Samuel looked up, the frown was set deep. 'How would you know that?' he asked.

'Because when we arrived I took Chantelle for a long walk. We talked. She told me things. She was upset that you weren't there with us.'

'That doesn't answer the *fucking* question and how you know.'

'Because I asked the question and I trust the reply that she gave me.' There was anger in both their eyes. One mistrusting, the other protective.

'Then you're naïve Perry. Chantelle had already had half of the boys in Saint Cambrae long before I arrived on the scene.'

Robert came back fighting defending Chantelle's honour. 'That's pure speculation and hope on your behalf.'

'And what makes you so sure and such a bloody expert all of a sudden?'

'Life Samuel. I meet my problems head on. I don't walk around wearing or looking through rose coloured glasses, unlike you!'

Samuel turned the conversation around getting away from his failings. 'You like her don't you?'

'Sure I do. Chantelle's a really nice girl and who in their right mind wouldn't.'

Samuel Byrne relaxed realising that the sides of his neck felt very swollen. 'So this cosy little walk that you had, what else did you talk about?'

'Nothing important. Most of it was about you and what her father would do if he caught up with you!'

Samuel sensed a conspiracy. He could see the look of victory in Robert Perry's eyes. On his shoulder sat a little red devil holding a sharpened pitchfork.

'Well, I've made up my mind and I ain't going back!'

Robert looked shocked, stunned. '**YOU WHAT**… What are you talking about not going back? What about the arrangement that we have with Lady Ashleigh? What about the wine, the spirits and cheese. Bill's got things sorted and then there's Lady Ashleigh. It's not something that you just give up Samuel like you do a naffing paper round.'

Samuel however was determined. 'Getting the mumps has made me think a lot. It's time that I settled down and went to work with my old man on the farm. He could do with me around full-time rather than have me keep flitting off abroad every six weeks.'

'And Chantelle,' Robert came back angrily. 'What about Chantelle and the baby?'

Samuel shrugged. 'Girls find themselves pregnant all the time. They survive and get by. Chantelle will find some other mug to shag and be logical. She's never going to struggle. Her old man is loaded. Christ he owns a successful vineyard. She'll be well cared for and looked after.'

Robert slid down from the bale. 'You shallow contemptible bastard Byrne. You live your life without any scruples or moral principles. You really don't give a fuck about anybody but yourself. One day the skeletons in your closet will come back to haunt you. Mark my words!'

Samuel sat upright pushing against the bench back, his mouth and eyes were open shocked by his friend's outburst. Robert Perry rarely swore unless he was really mad.

'Oh come on Rob,' he pleaded. 'We've been friends for so long. Since school. We don't argue over girls and certainly not when they live so far away. Christ Chantelle is six hundred and twenty miles away and the North Sea is enough of a barrier to keep anybody at bay, even her old man.' His brain and thoughts were working overtime to salvage the friendship. 'In time Chantelle Dupont will forget me and move onto the next bloke.'

Robert Perry felt the indignation prick him hard. Samuel's indifference was unbelievable. He looked at the man who he thought was a friend.

267

Samuel Byrne, the farmer's son however, was nothing more than an ignorant slimy slug who crawled from beneath his hiding place to nibble upon anything that looked juicy. Once tasted, devoured, he would crawl onto the next vegetable without so much as a thought as to the pain or suffering he left behind. A slug fitted perfect.

Hearing Samuel's ringtone announce that he had a call Robert decided it was his cue to leave. Ruefully Samuel watched Robert go as he answered the call.

'Oh hi Chantelle, I've been meaning to call you!'

Robert Perry gave a shake of his head, muttered under his breath and didn't look back. Later that evening he would call Chantelle. There were things that they had discussed on the walk, things that needed some clarity.

*****

John Steele heard the postman push the mail through the letterbox. Ordinarily Martha would collect it and bring it to his study, but the Bishop had been expecting a communication from the church synod regarding another post deep seated in the Yorkshire Dales where the scenery was more picturesque and the demands less problematic than that of Trumpington Salle. It was a secret that he had applied and so far he had discussed the matter with Martha for fear that she would not want to go.

Eagerly he flicked through and sorted the mail putting side the adverts, bills and other non-urgent communications when he recognised the envelope with the symbol used by the synod top left corner. John Steele sighed. At last he thought. He looked skyward, God favoured those who worked hard in his name. He was about to open the letter from the synod when another caught his eye. From the style of the writing it looked like a child had written the envelope.

Using the blade of the envelope opener, he slit the top apart. What fell out had him stand back aghast and clutch his mouth with his hand, his free hand reaching for his heart

'*Noooo not now,*' he cried.

He bent to pick up the photographs. Feeling his mouth go dry he went from one to the other, each image a tainted memory that he thought had long disappeared. Not wanting to, but realising that unless he did the unknowing would crucify him, he pulled open the fold of the note that accompanied the photographs.

'*The sins of the past have come back to haunt you John Steele. Did you honestly believe that you could cover your tracks without the spirits of Montgomery Saul and Elizabeth Dunn seeking answers as why they should have died? Love is never a sin, not between two consenting lovers.*

'*The sins of your past will cost you fifty thousand pounds or else the next letter sent plus copies of the photographs will be to the police. Nothing escapes the public condemnation like that of a senior church elder who has wronged his cloth. Disgrace is an awful burden to carry into hell.*

'*The money should be delivered in used bank notes, bagged and left at the war memorial in the middle of Willow Beck at midnight tomorrow night. You'll see that the memorial is being renovated and surrounded by a dust proof tent. Place the bag with the money inside the tent and leave, or suffer the indignation of your downfall. If you try to deceive me or fail to turn up, I promise the wrath of hell with fall upon you so fast that you will beg for mercy. If you leave Trumpington Salle without honouring this arrangement, I will seek you out. You have been warned!'*

John Steele felt physically sick. He placed both note and photographs on the desk top.

'Who would know?' he muttered. He racked his memory for faces and names. 'It had to be somebody who had known both of the deceased, and him.' His thoughts were so mixed, jumbled that he couldn't think straight. When the knock came on the study door he cried out making Martha Matthews bolt into the room almost spilling her tray.

'Are you unwell bishop?' she asked, 'your cry sounded painful.' She put down the tray of baked croissants and hot coffee.

John Steele released his grip from the edge of the desk. He looked up at the housekeeper his eyes damp.

'Occasionally Martha, the path that we follow in life is difficult, not respected. The dead do not stay dead and they deem it necessary to rise from the grave to make one's life a living hell.' He puffed up his chest, his mind made up. 'Have you ever been to Scotland?' he asked.

'Not for a long time Bishop although I did once have a distant cousin who lived up that way. Every summer I would go for two weeks and spend my days at a little village just outside of Glencoe exploring the Cairngorms

National Park. The walks there are amazing. Enough space to yourself, to clear your head of negativity and fill your lungs full of clean fresh air.'

He saw her chest expand as she breathed in. 'Would you like to go again, walking I mean?'

'With you Bishop?' She was honoured that he had asked.

'Indeed with me Martha. We might not however come back this way again for several years!'

Martha saw the fear that haunted his eyes. Whatever had frightened him, had him running scared. 'This troubling worry that has you so agitated, is it something that I can help you sort?' she asked.

John Steele responded with a wry laugh.

'The irony Martha, is my dear lady, if only that were possible. Alas however, not on this occasion. Wicked, sinful accusations have already condemned me without a fair trial. Instead it is best if I disappear from public life and hide, rather than shame the church. In time I will emerge forgotten and forgiven, a different man.'

Martha was angry. 'There are so many gossips here. It is disgraceful that they seek to destroy a man so dedicated to the welfare of others.

'Alas,' replied John Steele, 'such is life, and death.'

Martha smiled feeling her bosom swell with admiration for her lover, she went to him. 'Then I know just the place John, a place where not even the devil would find us.'

The Bishop steepled his fingers together.

'Let us pray now Martha. We should give grateful thanks to the good lord that I have you to watch out for me.' He saw the tray. 'After which we'll share the coffee and the croissants. Later I need to make a small trip to the bank.'

They agreed to pack as much as they could in the car for the long journey ahead. Martha insisted upon packing her sexiest nighties and underwear, making additional space down the side of the suitcase for her leather whip and thigh high boots.

'When we get there John, I promise to make all your troubles disappear.'

John Steele sighed wantonly in anticipation of their arrival. Slipping the envelope with the photographs into his desk drawer he would burn the evidence before they left for Scotland.

Revelations

Standing in the shadows the pair watched the Bishop arrive. Leave his car and deposit the bag with the money inside the protective tent surrounding the war memorial. Although neither could not see the face of the woman sitting in the passenger seat Olivia Ashleigh was convinced that it was none other than Martha Matthews.

Taking one last look around before he returned to the vehicle John Steel shook his head remorsefully. Sliding into the driver's seat he exhaled loudly

'What was that which you left?' asked Martha. She had her eyes peeled for signs of life, but everywhere was still and silent.

'An expensive parting gift,' he replied.

Mary Nelson and Olivia Ashleigh watched the Bishop drive away. They left it ten minutes in case he decided to return before they deemed it safe to collect the bag.

'You stay and keep watch. If you see car lights approaching or hear the faintest of sounds you whistle.'

'I'm not a stronger whistler,' Mary replied, 'do you have any other suggestions?'

Olivia looked at the whites of Mary eyes. 'No, just make a sound that sounds like a whistle!' Mary agreed she would.

Mary went to the edge of the shop doorway where she could see in all directions. Olivia Ashleigh stepped out from the shadows. 'It's better that I get caught than you,' she smiled. 'I still have some friends in high places that could help. You on the other hand would have a tough time facing John Steele in court.'

A minute later she put her hand through the gap in the protective tent pulling back out the bag. It was heavy. A quick check, a smile and a thumbs up to Mary meant that their plan had worked. They left the memorial taking a back alley that Olivia knew between the shops which would bring them out near the recreational ground.

'You're very resourceful,' said Mary admiringly.

'I learn fast. Lawrence always had a shady deal going somewhere. That's how diplomats work. It's a game of tit-for-tat. I looked upon my opportunities as I had the tits so why not use them to my advantage.' She pushed Mary's jaw shut. 'In this world Mary, woman have the brains and the beauty, men the brawn and balls. Therein lies the problem. The distance between is greater so the message gets lost in translation. Women however are more closely attuned and we can think faster. You should try it sometime.'

Mary was aghast. 'With who exactly. I am the vicar.'

Olivia smiled. 'What about that dopey man David Gambitt.'

'The verger?'

274

'Yes, him. He's always fiddling with his balls.'

They laughed. Fifty thousand pound richer and nobody was any the wiser. Most certainly not the Bishop, John Steele.

*****

Switching off the television Reg Perry stood and stretched his arms high. It had been a long day and he was glad that his bed was calling. Cutting the power to the living room light he ascended the stairs to the bathroom above. He was about to enter when he noticed the narrow shaft of light beneath his son's bedroom door. Reg pondered, it had been almost a week since their paths had crossed. Tapping gently on the panel of the bedroom door he heard a voice from inside say that it was okay to enter.

'Hello son, how's tricks?'

'Okay, thanks dad.' Robert replied, although Reg noticed that the usual chirpy tone was missing from his son's voice. Pushing the bedroom door shut he went across and sat himself down on the edge of the bed.

'It doesn't sound like it son. Has your mother been on at you again to find yourself a job?'

'No, she's fine dad. It's just that I have things on my mind!'

Reg Perry stifled a yawn.

'You know, I remember that as a young boy you'd come and find me in the village to ask for help when you had a problem. Times change Robert and so do we as individuals, but I'm still here son. Older now maybe than when you were little and probably not any wiser, but I can still help. What's ailing you?'

'A girl.'

Reg grinned raising his forefinger. 'A conundrum to be sure for any young adventurer venturing out into the world.' Reg shook his head. 'Trust me Robert, the problem don't improve when they get older.'

Robert grinned back. 'No dad, this girl is different. I've not got any girl into trouble. Well not that I know about... but...'

Reg kept his finger raised interrupting. 'Sowing your wild oats is what it's all about Robert. I never could find the book on the birds and the bees so I went to the cinema instead.'

Robert frowned. 'To see what?'

'A Swedish movie. That was my education and it was better than any book I can tell you.'

'I don't need any extra tuition dad. I think I'm in love.' Since calling Chantelle, Robert had felt different inside. His heart felt different, the fluttering and his thoughts jumbled.

Reg's finger changed to a whole hand as it dropped fast to his knee. 'Is that all that's worry you. Christ Robert when I was your age I was falling in and out of love every month with different girls in and around Willow Beck, only pick them close to home. Neighbouring village's means you have to walk back after seeing them home. That walk can be a killer if you've been at it all evening.' Reg rubbed the bristles on his chin. 'I still see one or two that I courted when I'm out on patrol. Believe me falling in then out of love with them was a godsend. Cupid needed a new set of arrows by the time I was marrying your mother.'

Robert was astonished that his father was being so free with his past. One thing was sure and that was that his father and Samuel Byrne had both attended the same charm school. Had chivalry died along with decent music from the early eighties he wondered.

'No. I really do think that I am in love with this girl. I feel it here.' He touched his chest.

'Oh really,' replied Reg. He breathed in hard through his nose. 'Then that adds a different complexity to the matter. Is she pretty?'

Robert smiled. 'Yes, very.'

Reg nodded. 'Good, that helps.' He cupped his hands under his chest. 'And stacked well?'

'Yes that as well,' added Robert.

Reg winked before the expression on his face changed. 'Is she a local lass?' He was concerned it could be the daughter of an old-flame.

'Not as close as you'd think dad.'

Reg was relieved. He noticed the muscle bulge beneath his son's tee-shirt.

'That's a bonus. If you're serious finding one outside the village can work in your favour. If you've a girl too close to home your mother would be like an owl with extra-long ears. Why do you think I got her that pair of rabbits last year? It was to keep her busy when I wasn't at home and out of my hair when I was.'

'Dad, she lives in Alsace in France.'

Reg felt his jaw drop. *'Fuck me. Your mother will need a small holding if you fly the nest!'* Reg held his head between his hands. The problem had just got serious.

'What do you think then dad?'

Reg Perry sat up straight allowing the blood to flow around his brain quicker and help him think. 'France has a lot to offer son and in some ways they're better off than we are over here. It's just the distance involved. My ear would be bent from the time we got in the car until we arrived. Where's Alsace anyway, anywhere near the coast?'

'On the French, German border.'

Reg nodded. He could already envisage the problems that lay ahead.

'It's your life Robert. My advice is make the most of it. I made my bed, so here I am lying in it.' he paused. 'If you really love this girl and she feels the same about you then you're halfway across the Channel already. We just have to think about how, when and where to deliver the bombshell to your mother. As our only son, she will demand new outfits to visit and most probably needs a new passport as well.'

'Why the outfits?' Robert asked frowning.

'Women always want new clothes whatever the excuse son. Remember that. If they say we've been invited to a wedding or a christening, it's a good reason to be buying a complete new outfit including accessories.'

Accessories?'

'A handbag, same colour as the shoes. Take a look in your mothers' wardrobe, it's full of empty bloody handbags and shoes. And yet go anywhere and she can tip out virtually everything bar the kitchen sink. Christ, I have trouble remembering the number for my bank card in my wallet. And there's never any loose cash in the money sleeve.'

'I would have to find a job out there, is that hard?'

Reg Perry shrugged. 'I doubt it son. Least not with Lady Ashleigh's connexions. I'm sure that she knows somebody, who knows somebody that could help.'

Robert looked surprised. 'Why would I involve Lady Ashleigh?'

Reg grinned. 'I'm not half as daft as you think I am Robert. I don't suppose you remember, but some years back I passed my sergeants exam, but I turned down promotion because it would have meant leaving Willow Beck.' He tapped the side of his nose. 'I've known about your trips over to France during the past year. And a short while back an Asian purporting to be from Delhi and employed by customs and excise came to see me about the people living up at the manor house.'

Robert felt his eyes opening wide. 'Christ, what'd you tell him dad?'

Reg was pleased to be catching up with Robert again. It was like old times.

'Not a lot. Strange looking bloke and his eyes seemed too close together. Annoyingly his bloody head wouldn't stop wobbling about neither. It must be a hereditary condition or they suffer from arthritis very young.' Reg paused to gather the right words. 'Willow Beck has been my life, your life and that of your mother's. I took an oath to save life and limb, protect property and the people, and to uphold the law including any number of oddities that my cross my path. That didn't include sending my son or his friends to prison.' Reg lent closer. 'The smuggling, the wine. Does it make much?' he asked.

'Enough to keep us happy!'

Reg nodded approving of his son's adventures. 'Funny thing was that old Gunga Din just vanished into thin air. I've kept my eye out for him when I've been out on patrol, but he's never materialised again. I reckon he went back to Delhi.'

'I hope so. He could have scuppered our operation big time.'

'How'd he get here?' asked Reg.

'He just appeared like a genie, emerging from the cabin wardrobe.'

'A stowaway,' mused Reg. 'The crafty bugger. Had I known that I would have had him for being an illegal immigrant.'

Robert laughed, the thought amused him.

Reg put his finger to his lips. 'Not so loud you'll wake your mother. That was very unfortunate what happened to Charlie Luft. It must have left a big dent in the overseas operation?'

Robert nodded. 'Bill Symons stepped in just at the right time. He filled the gap left by Charlie.'

Reg nodded. 'I know. I was going to pay a visit to the manor house and introduce myself properly to Lady Ashleigh.'

Robert saw a red light appear before his eyes. 'Why?'

'Because you great lummox, I thought I might be able to offer my professional services.'

'But you're the village policeman dad!'

'That's right and who better to know what's going on. I could turn a blind eye and look out for you lot. I could help keep unwanted visitors like our friend from customs and excise away.'

Robert smiled, it could work.

'I've got to see Lady Ashleigh and Bill Symons in the morning. Did you want to come along with me?'

'Why not, it'll be fun just seeing the expressions on their faces. That and Janet Simpson.'

'So what about France, what do you think?'

'Why not sleep on it tonight Robert and when you wake decide then. Things always look better in the daylight, including your mother.'

When the laughter stopped Reg wished his son goodnight and went off to the bathroom to clean his teeth.

Peering out of the bedroom window at the night sky above Robert Perry pondered over his life in Willow Beck and what could be if he followed his own stars. Sliding his fingertip over the illuminated screen he sent a goodnight text to Chantelle Dupont. Moments later he received another back.

'Goodnight Robert. Perhaps next time you come visit we can go for another walk xx'

*****

Watching her struggle to pack her suitcase and bags Benjamin Chapple had offered to help, but Marge had refused scowling back.

'You've customer's downstairs to serve remember, why don't you attend to their needs.'

Pressing down with her elbows she clipped the lock into place. Inside her overnight bag it was stuffed full of lipstick, various powders for her face and hair dyes.

'And before you dare pass comment, I have not decided yet whether or indeed how much I'll be claiming from you to cover my maintenance costs. I will need something to live on!'

The pub landlord felt the euphoria rising slowly inside of him knowing that the day had finally arrived and Marge was moving out, leaving.

'Did you want me to save your mail and give it to Bert Tonks when he makes the next delivery?'

Through a thick layer of eye mascara Marge looked over. 'Don't be facetious Benjamin, it doesn't become you. Humour was never on of your strong points.'

Benjamin Chapple studied his wife. It amused him how her backside wobbled sideways as she took another garment from the wardrobe, bent over the suitcase carefully folding it down on top of others, each item neatly placed to gain maximum storage. Wearing a pink two piece she reminded him of Farmer Bryce's old sow.

'Okay, I'll sort it as it arrives.' Benjamin shuddered at the thought of making an advance on Marge, if only for old time's sake. He turned and walking the short landing went downstairs.

Marge sniffed contemptuously as the door at the bottom of the stairs clicked shut. 'You'd have thought he might have argued, fought for me to stay.' The tear that appeared in the corner of her was more out of anger than hurt. A minute later there was an almighty cheer from the bar below.

Somebody shouted out *'Yes'* loudly although Marge couldn't rightly tell who. Swearing under her breath she put her knee on the middle of the suitcase lid and pushed it shut.

Walking through a hushed but packed bar with bags protruding at different angles and her suitcase hanging limply down one side Marge had the tip of her nose raised heading for the door of the pub. One of the customers jumped from his chair and held the door open for her. 'Thank you,' was all she said. Outside the minicab driver had the boot already open.

She was about to take her seat in the back of the cab when she heard Benjamin announce that the next round was on the house. The cheers and applause echoed in her ears as she closed her eyes shutting the rear door. Holding herself together as best she could she gave the driver the address.

'It looks like a nice pub,' said the driver as he engaged gear in readiness to pull away.

'It was,' Marge replied, 'it went downhill when my husband had it decorated after my mother died.'

*****

Robert was almost unconscious on his pillow when his mobile beside the bed shook him from his semi-slumber state. He reached out grabbing the phone hoping his mother hadn't heard it ringing. His heart raced when he saw it was Chantelle calling. Alsace was an hour ahead of England which made it even later. Outside the sky was very dark.

'Are you okay,' he asked, *'you're not hurt or unwell?'*

'Je suis huereux Robert, tres huereux!'

Although his French was rusty he did remember two words - *tres huereux* from his school days. *'So what's made you so happy Chantelle?'*

Her reply was no more than an excited whisper. *'I am no longer pregnant Robert!'*

'That makes me tres huereux.' he replied fisting the air triumphantly.

'How do you know?'

284

Chantelle laughed. *'Trust me Robert I just know. I had to ring and tell you. You're not angry at me I hope for phoning? I know it is very late?'*

'No… I was hoping that you would.'

'I spoke to Sammy earlier and he couldn't care less, it was very hurtful.'

He didn't tell her that he had been there when she had called.

'He's not the friend that I thought he was Chantelle. We had a disagreement, a falling out – une brouille. I'm unhappy and perhaps a little sad although I can't say that I like Samuel very much anymore.'

'Me neither.' She replied.

There followed a brief moments silence as Robert closed his eyes seeing Chantelle standing in front of him. He held onto his beating heart with his free hand hoping it wouldn't burst.

'Chantelle, if I moved to France, could I be your boyfriend?'

'Do you mean you would come visit again Robert?'

'No, I mean to live and work in Alsace. To find a place where I can be close to you.'

Her moments silence was longer than his. The seconds went by agonisingly. Finally she breathed down the connection. *'Where would you live and work?'* she asked.

'Somewhere not far away. Somewhere where I could see you every day. I'd do anything for work, just as long as I could be near you!'

'You are so different Robert and so caring. Tell me please, would you still have asked to be my girlfriend had I been pregnant?'

'Yes, qui, qui.'

'When are you thinking of coming?'

'As soon as I can. I've got to talk to my mother, Lady Ashleigh and Bill. I've an idea that might favour their future as well.'

Chantelle breathed heavily down the phone. 'My father, he likes you Robert and he told me that you were thoughtful to have taken me for a walk. He's a little old fashioned my father, but he loves me very much.'

'I think I love you too Chantelle.' The words came out before the thought had finished forming inside his mind. Robert sat up in bed.

'Yes,' she replied.

'Yes what?' he asked, his fingers crossed.

'Yes, I would like very much to be your girlfriend and have you live here in Alsace.'

'I would need to talk to your mother and father before I come over.'

'No. Let me talk to ma mere et mon pere. They are old fashioned, but they only want what is best for me.' Again the silence was excruciatingly long albeit only seconds. 'And Sammy, what would you tell him?'

'He already knows how I feel about you and how angry I am about the way that he has treated you.'

'You will call me and let me know when you are coming over.'

'You'll be the first to know, I promise.' A thought suddenly hit Robert. 'Your mother and father, do they know that you're not pregnant?'

'Non, pas encore. I will tell them in the morning, but I had to call you first.'

'And Samuel, does he know?'

'Certainement pas, laissez-le mijoter un peu plus lentemps, le cochon.'

'You lost me there in translation Chantelle?'

She laughed. 'I said definitely not, let him stew a little longer, the pig!'

Robert joined in her laughter. 'Good idea and you got that right, he has turned out to be an insensitive swine!'

'Robert,' Chantelle whispered.

'What?'

'I love you too!'

Hearing his son happy Reg Perry turned away having been woken by a phone ringing in the house. Reg smiled to himself. His son, the little boy that he remembered had become a man. Reg was proud of Robert and he envied his ambition, his adventure. Slipping back into the bedroom he promptly shoved his wife in the back interrupting her sleep.

'What's wrong Reg?' she asked dozily.

Slipping his hand beneath her nightdress coming to rest on her breast she complained.

'*Your bloody hand's freezing Perry, bugger off!*'

'Well come over here and warm me up then. I imagine that this is the first night of our honeymoon all over again.'

Emma Perry was suddenly wide awake. 'If I thought that you would be sleeping downstairs Reg Perry with the dog.'

Reg laughed, his eyes twinkling with lust. 'Alright then, what about the last night of our honeymoon!'

Watching him undo the front buttons of her nightdress, her thoughts were travelling in reverse, going back in time.

'*Here, that was just as bad as the first night!*' she remembered.

'That's right,' said Reg, as he sat up to admire his wife's voluptuous body.

The moment of passion was reaching forgotten heights and climbing higher still when the phone beside their bed shrilled into life.

Instinctively Emma Perry pulled together her nightie forgetting that the caller couldn't see that she naked. Reaching across to pick up the receiver Reg felt the soft edge of the mattress give way under his weight. He toppled ungraciously forward unable to prevent the wood side of the bed from striking his manhood which was still stood proud. Reg landed on the carpeted floor, fortunately landing on his side.

Unable to contain herself Emma was still laughing when she picked up the receiver.

'Oh hello Sergeant. Would you mind holding on a moment please, Reg is just arranging himself.'

She was passing across the receiver when Robert came rushing in through the bedroom door. 'I heard an almighty crash. I thought somebody had crashed a car through the lounge wall downstairs.'

Reg tried in vain to cover his modesty as his wife and Robert's mother buried her head in the pillow desperate to stifle her laughter.

Robert saw the colour drain from his father's face as Reg listened to the message from the control room sergeant. He said nothing in reply other than to say *thank you* and *goodbye*. Replacing the receiver he totally forgot about his nudity standing clear of the bed.

'John Steele and Martha Matthews were both killed in a head-on traffic collision tonight just shy of Goslington in Lincolnshire. I suppose I had better tell the vicar.'

Robert sat on the edge of the bed handing his father his trousers.

'Do you want me to come with you?'

Reg shook his head as he slipped into his underwear then his trousers.

'No Robert. You stay with your mother son and tell her about Chantelle.'

Emma Perry slipped from the other side of the bed discretely buttoning the rest of her nightdress.

'And just who might this Chantelle be?' she asked.

Robert suggested that they went downstairs leaving Reg to put on the remainder of his uniform. At the sink Robert filled the kettle.

'You'll really like Chantelle mum, she's a lovely girl. She's French!'

Both Sides of the Law

Janet was clearing away the last of the breakfast dishes when a knocking at the kitchen door sounded urgent. Without waiting to be invited in, Mary Nelson entered. She was as pale as a ghost.

'Christ vicar you look like you could do with a brandy followed by a coffee.'

Hearing Mary's voice Olivia Ashleigh came in from the study.

'Whatever's happened Mary?' she asked. 'You look awful, like you have the weight of the world on your shoulders?'

'The Bishop and Martha Matthews, they were killed last night in a head-on collision.'

Janet felt the coffee jar slip from her fingers, but after a frantic juggling act she prevented it from falling to the floor.

'Where exactly?' asked Olivia, seeing Janet put the jar on the worktop.

'Just outside of Goslington in Lincolnshire. Witnesses told the police that they were travelling at speed when the Bishop lost control of the wheel careering across the carriageway into the unavoidable approach of an oncoming van. Both were killed instantly. Fortunately, the van driver mercifully survived with only a few bruises. I thought you would have heard, only it's all over the local news this morning.'

'No,' replied Olivia, as Janet went over and switched on the radio, but they had just missed the hourly report by a few minutes. 'We'll catch the half past bulletin.' Said Janet.

'Who told you?' Olivia asked.

'Constable Perry came to see me around one this morning. They wanted somebody who knew the Bishop to make a formal identification.'

Janet refilled the kettle. Getting bad news was always upsetting, but Mary having to make sure that the dead were John Steele and Martha Matthews was even more horrifying. She put out three mugs. Watching the hot water boil Janet felt compelled to say something. 'I hope Martha had on clean knickers, if any at all.'

Both women looked at the cook, their mouths open.

'Well...' Janet explained. 'She was always leaving her knickers in places that she ought not to when she was at school. She was known throughout the years, old and young as *'Magnet Martha'* because she would turn up for girls PE without any underwear. She would immediately attract the attention of the older boys.'

Mary tried hard not to laugh as Olivia Ashleigh looked on incredulously. Since Charlie's death there had been a significant change in Janet's outlook. She was suddenly more daring. Mary thought it best to try and help Janet.

'I know nothing about Martha because I had never met her, although I was told that she had reputation.' She breathed in deep. 'Not that that matters now. She had been decapitated in the accident. Luckily, I wasn't asked to identify her. The police said they would make a match using her dental records.'

Janet handed around the coffees going to the larder to fetch the biscuit barrel.

'Here help yourself to a chocolate ginger nut vicar, you need to put some colour back in your cheeks. I find ginger nuts have got one hell of a kick and the ginger itself will help calm your jangled nerves. I went through packets after losing Charlie.' Olivia nodded, she had noticed. Not sure that ginger was what she really needed Mary took a biscuit if only to be polite.

Smiling to herself Olivia Ashleigh saw a problem disappear. Now there was no way that the fifty thousand pounds would ever be traced. They were sipping their coffee and nibbling ginger nuts when there was another knock at the door and in walked Bill Symons.

'It looks like I've just arrived in time,' he said. Janet was about to get another mug when Bill put his hand on her shoulder. 'It's okay Janet, you sit and enjoy your coffee. I'll make mine.'

'Have you heard about the Bishop and his housekeeper?' Janet asked.

Stirring in a cube of brown sugar, Bill Symons grinned. 'No. Is this one of those knock, knock, who's there jokes?'

Mary saw Olivia head drop as she tried not to smile back at Bill. Mary liked being with Olivia, Janet and Bill where life had a different meaning. Together they made traumas seem trivial.

'Your innocence will see you in heaven one day Bill!' she replied. Olivia Ashleigh quickly intervened to help save Bill Symons blushes.

'The Bishop and his housekeeper were killed last night in a tragic car accident.'

Bill Symons stopped stirring the spoon around the inside of the mug. He felt bad offering an apology.

'I am really sorry that was in such bad taste.' He directed his apology to Mary as well. 'I am sorry Mary, I meant no offence. I never really knew John Steele. I knew of him, but we'd never met. I do remember Martha from when I was at school.'

Olivia Ashleigh turned her head sharply in the direction of the retired tugboat captain. 'Just how well did you know her?' she asked.

Bill shrugged. 'Not that well. Why do you ask?'

'Martha Matthews apparently had an unsavoury reputation. It was one that followed her around throughout her school life and perhaps beyond the gates after school.'

Bill clicked his forefinger and thumb together. 'Oh, you mean *'Magnet Martha'*. Why every boy in the school knew about Martha, as did some of the younger male teachers. I remember one particular term when there was a bet going around to see who could collect as many pairs of her knickers as they could possibly get their hands on.'

Unable to prevent the grin form appearing Olivia felt fiendishly that she had the right to ask. 'And how many did you collect?'

'Me, why none. Goodness no. Martha was never that attractive.' Olivia Ashleigh grinned smugly at Janet knowing what she was thinking. 'Besides that…' Bill continued. 'I'd been sacked from my paper round the week before so I didn't have the ready cash to join in the wager!'

Janet spluttered her coffee landing all over the table before her and Mary could no longer contain herself and she burst into laughter, followed by Olivia. They were still laughing when there was another knock on the kitchen door.

'Are we expecting anybody?' asked Olivia looking inquisitively across at Janet. The cook gave a shake of her head. Olivia Ashleigh got up and went to the kitchen door. She was surprised to see Robert standing there accompanied by his father.

'Good morning, would you mind if we come in?' asked Reg Perry.

'Why no please do, the more the merrier,' invited Lady Ashleigh, standing aside. Seeing the policeman standing in the doorway Janet held her chest feeling that the coffee, the laughter and shock of the car accident was only the beginning of the day.

Reg acknowledged the presence of the other's sat around the table.

'I hope we're not interrupting,' Reg said, catching sight of the open biscuit tin.

'Not at all constable, you're always welcome.' Replied Olivia Ashleigh. Janet started to splutter again only this time Bill helped by slapping her hard on the back.

'Thank you Lady Ashleigh.' Reg turned to Mary. 'I hope you're feeling better vicar. That was a nasty shock you had last night.'

'I feel much better. Thank you officer, thank you for asking.'

Olivia Ashleigh offered that they sit at the table while somebody made them a coffee. Mary offered to do the honours as Bill was still attending to clearing Janet's obstruction.

Robert launched into why he was there with his father.

'I invited my dad along this morning because we've something to tell you.'

Bill Symons offered the biscuit barrel. 'I think I know what you're going to say lad,' said Bill.

Olivia Ashleigh, Janet and Mary looked at Bill, then Reg and Robert.

'How's that?' Olivia asked.

'Call it intuition and male hormones,' winked Bill. 'Firstly, Chantelle's not pregnant and secondly, you're thinking about moving to France.' Bill reached across closing Janet's mouth. He saw Reg smile. 'Young Robert here is indeed a rarity. A gentleman he acted out of chivalry.' He tapped the side of his nose for Janet's sake. 'Robert hasn't made any girl pregnant, but somebody else instead thought he had. Robert is the knight in shining armour in our midst.'

Munching on his biscuit Reg nodded appreciatively. 'Could not have put it any better myself captain. Thank you.'

Robert smiled at Olivia Ashleigh. 'What Bill say's is right. Yes, I do intend going to Saint Cambrae and as soon as I can.' Olivia Ashleigh looked round the table. All eyes were on Robert. 'That's why, I brought my dad along this morning.'

Nobody spoke as Reg Perry asked if he could have another biscuit. Dunking it in his coffee, he explained why he was there.

'I've lived and served in Willow Beck long enough to know about all the comings and goings. The ups and downs of families and the strange oddities that take place in and around the village and perhaps those slightly further afield. Many think of me as plain old daft Reg Perry riding around on my bike, but I hear and I see all, missing very little. Quite a few years back I took an oath to uphold the law, but there are as many crooks in the police and senior management as there are out on the streets. A couple of years back I did something to blot my copy book and since then I changed my approach. Nowadays I tend to turn a blind eye and let folk get on with life. Anything that makes them happy.' Robert nodded and smiled.

Olivia Ashleigh liked Reg's honesty.

'However,' Reg concluded. 'I've no wish to see my son or indeed any of you end up in the dock and facing a possible prison sentence.' Janet enthusiastically pushed across the biscuit barrel again quickly. Not going to prison was worth another chocolate ginger nut, maybe two. 'I could help fill the gap left by Robert going?' offered Reg.

Olivia Ashleigh looked at Bill who looked at Janet, then Mary before it came back to her. 'How exactly would that be constable? This is smuggling after all that we're talking about?'

Reg grinned. 'Consider it a business arrangement m'lady, rather than giving it any romantic title!' Olivia Ashleigh liked that option better.

Again looking around the table at the people taking coffee, she saw a cook, a retired tugboat captain, a newly ordained minister of the church, a policeman and his son, and finally herself, a titled lady. It was an odd collection and Reg was right in what he had said, Willow Beck did have a long and at times undocumented history.

'You would be willing to take Robert's place and turn a blind eye to everything else?' asked Bill. 'That would be pretty risky Reg, considering your position in the village?'

'Why not, my records already tarnished. I'm not likely to be getting a gold watch at the end of my time. If you agree, I would look upon the venture as helping and giving back something to the community. A bit like you do vicar.'

Mary returned the smile wondering if Reg Perry had seen what went on just prior to midnight at the war memorial. 'My calling demands that I answer to God, what about you constable?' she asked.

Reg chortled looking at Robert. 'I respect your calling and faith vicar. I have to answer to my wife and hell hath no fury like a woman's wrath.'

'Here, here...' Bill voiced. Lowering his eyes so that he didn't have to look at Olivia Ashleigh.

'And you can vouch that this is not some police sting operation to catch us red-handed? Asked Janet.

Janet had known Reg Perry for a long time, as had Bill Symons. The captain watched the policeman, looking for any signs of deception, but Reg was undaunted by the question.

'Had that been my motive Janet, why I would have made arrests a long time ago. As for trusting me, only time will be the judge of my worth. I do however have one question of my own though.'

'And what would that be constable?' asked Olivia Ashleigh.

'Does anybody here know what happened to a certain Asian bloke that I saw wandering around the village the same night that some poor bugger crashed his motorbike? The strange thing was that the motorbike had no registration plate or engine number so my enquiries hit a dead end. I went back the next morning to take some extra details, but low and behold if the bike hadn't disappeared too, just like that mysterious Asian. He had a wobbly head.'

Everybody present except Mary Nelson gave a resounding shake of their head.

'I thought that I saw somebody prowling about the church late at night,' Mary began, 'and I did hear a motorbike rev its engine, but I didn't realise that it had been involved in a crash. I do hope nobody was hurt.' She suddenly remembered something else. 'There was also a herd of deer about that night in the wood nearby, although I didn't think any more of it. A large deer could easily have been mistaken for a man walking about.'

Olivia Ashleigh felt her blood cooling as it ran down the length of her body. She watched Janet hoping that the cook kept her emotions together. Any sign of tears over Charlie would have Reg know that they were involved.

Reg saved the day holding up his hand.

'Not that it's of any real consequence. Our mystery man gave me some cock and bull story about a contraband operation taking place in the area.' He grinned, directing his mirth at Olivia Ashleigh. 'I told him that he was mistaken to which he told me that I was a fool. Serves him right if he fell into a deep ditch full of mire and hasn't been found!'

Everybody laughed, except Mary. She wanted to join in, but God would only forgive so many sins. Mary spoke instead. 'It's ironic that you should come here today Robert. Admirable too that you should want to go to a girl in need in France because she thought that she was pregnant. I have already had two young women this week visit the rectory needing my advice on a similar matter.'

'About what?' Janet asked.

'Finding themselves pregnant.'

'I can't see how that can be a surprise Mary?' questioned Olivia Ashleigh. 'It happens all the time and at times when you least expect it.'

'I agree. The only oddity was when tested, both said their estrogen level was much higher than expected.'

Bill looked across at Robert. 'Do you remember Victor Dupont telling us that to help flavour the wine they would add a small amount of resveratrol?' Robert nodded. 'That's right Bill and that it also had health benefits protecting against age related diseases. Chantelle likes her dad's wine.'

Janet looked on anxiously at Olivia and Bill. 'The wine m'lady, what about the batch that we gave Wilfred Tummings?' Reg cottoned on quick. He was unable to stop himself from laughing. 'Constance Tummings will have kittens, if she thinks that Wilfred is responsible for any of the local women getting pregnant.'

Testing the Waters

They all thought it best to leave it another couple of weeks to determine if it was just a mere coincidence about the women in the village getting pregnant or whether the expectant mothers had indulged in Wilfred' special offer deal of *two for one.*

Robert Perry had said goodbye to Tommy Jenkins, who thought his long standing friend was as mad as the constable. When Robert told Tommy that his father was taking his place in the smuggling operation Tommy himself disappeared overnight with his girlfriend Alice. They are both still on the missing persons register.

It was a tearful farewell at the railway station as Robert stepped onto the train armed with just his suitcase, but Reg had promised Emma that once their son was settled in France they would go visit.

A day before Robert left home he had heard through the grapevine that one of Samuel Byrne's old flames had gone to see him to say that she was pregnant. Her father was demanding that they be married as soon as possible before the baby was due. The news put the cherry on top of the icing for the start of Robert Perry's new adventure.

Bill Symons had, as agreed met Reg on deck of the *Saucy Belle* and explained how they intended running the operation without the three lads.

Whether coincidence or otherwise, Tommy's aunt Barbara Jenkins had also given in her notice to quit working at the manor house stating that she missed the atmosphere of the pub. Janet Simpson promised Olivia Ashleigh that she would test the waters to see what Barbara knew before they let her go.

That afternoon Olivia Ashleigh went out into the vegetable garden knowing that Barbara would be watching from the upstairs bedroom. Armed with another game rifle from Lawrence's collection she was determined to get in some target practice with the unfortunate pheasants.

At Saint Cambrae, Adele Dupont had welcomed Robert's arrival believing that he would bring with him a stability to their daughter's wayward life style. She helped find a cheap one bedroom apartment near to the vineyard, close enough for Chantelle to visit and Robert to come in the evenings to take Chantelle for a walk.

Having discussed the matter with her husband, Victor had agreed to take on Robert as an apprentice winegrower. This news was welcomed by Reg and Emma Perry, and Lady Ashleigh.

Robert had been working almost three weeks at the Saint Cambrae Vineyard where one evening he was enjoying an after work drink with Victor, while Chantelle was busy with her mother.

'Have you heard from Bill lately?' Victor asked.

'Yes, they're due Wednesday of next week.'

Victor nodded as he stroked the underside of his chin. 'That is good news because we need to sit down and talk.'

'Is there something wrong Monsieur Dupont?' Robert asked.

'I'm not sure my young friend. My wife was in the village today getting provisions. She overheard several of the women talking. They were discussing some young women who had found themselves pregnant, when no pregnancy was expected!'

Robert remembered the conversation with Mary Nelson in the kitchen.

'Did you not tell Bill and myself, that adding a small amount of resveratrol, would not only flavour the wine, but has health benefits and that it could affect a woman's estrogen level?'

Victor stopped sipping his wine. 'Qui, qui... I did. You were listening.' Victor got up and began pacing. The problem is Robert. This afternoon I had the water tested and the levels are still rising.'

Robert looked through his glass at the wine which he had been drinking, it looked clear enough. 'There were similar cases back in my village before I left Mr Dupont. Do you suspect that it has something to do with the wine?'

Typically French, Victor Dupont was instantly non-committal and guarded. 'You know yourself, our grapes are some of the best in France. However if it is not the grape at fault, then it has to be the water!'

'I thought that the water hereabouts originated from a natural spring both north and south of the region.'

Victor Dupont smiled at Robert, he was pleased with his protégé. 'This is good and you are learning fast Robert. Yes, indeed you are right. The spring water also supplies the beer industry in the region. I know somebody connected with a beer producing factory. I called them after the test and they say that the water content levels are perfectly normal.'

Robert sipped his wine, waved at Chantelle who was watching from the kitchen window where she was busy preparing the evening meal. There had to be another reason he thought.

Adele Dupont shook the excess water from the salad leaves that she had just washed.

'Robert has settled in nicely. He appears to like it here.'

'Qui mama. He is happy and it makes me happy that he is here!' replied Chantelle.

Adele Dupont had seen a sudden change in her daughter since Robert's arrival. It was a pleasing change that suggested that at last the rebellion of her youth might have left and been replaced by a young woman, with a different outlook.

'And you like him?' Adele probed.

'Qui mama. Robert is not like the other young men in the village. He is kind and very thoughtful. We talk about the future and Robert tells me about his plans.'

Adele Dupont wiped her hands dry. 'Plans are good. They express a maturity that is sometimes missing in your generation.'

Chantelle sighed, although only slightly. 'Oh mama, you say that about all my friends.

'And Robert, is he just a friend to you?'

Chantelle lowered her head so that her mother could not fully see what secrets lie hidden behind her eyes. 'He is not my lover mama if that is what you mean. Robert is old fashioned and is how the English say, saving himself for the right girl.'

'And are you not the right girl Chantelle Dupont?'

'Qui mama, I am. I am also happy to wait.'

Adele Dupont watched her husband discussing the wine industry with Robert. She recalled when Victor had started dating her. At first, all he ever talked about was the different variety of grapes and making wine. It had been she who made him see the other things in life besides grapes. During their courtship she had introduced the subject of living together, getting married and the possibility of a family.

'And these plans that Robert makes for the future,' she asked. 'Are you ready for the future Chantelle?'

'Qui mama, I am ready. Robert too.'

'I will need to talk to your father later you know.'

Chantelle clutched her chest. 'You will not make him send Robert home?'

Adele Dupont slipped her hands into gloves to check on the chicken breasts cooking in the oven. 'Send him home, don't be stupid Chantelle. I need to encourage your father and have him show Robert more of our business.'

Sending Chantelle out to begin laying the veranda table Adele Dupont smiled to herself remembering a similar conversation that she'd had with her own mother when Victor had been sitting drinking wine with her father. She watched Chantelle take care laying out the table mates, the cutlery and making everything look nice. Yes, her daughter was changing and becoming a young woman. When she did fall pregnant it would be for the right reason.

Robert was deep in thought as he watched Chantelle flit about. 'So... if it is not necessarily the water and definitely not the grape, then what I wonder?' he tapped the side of his head thinking.

Victor Dupont smiled. 'L'inspecteur des raisins, he believes the problem could be my barrels.'

Robert put down his wine glass.

'How can a barrel affect the wine and estrogen level?'

Victor Dupont grinned emphatically. 'The wood is seasoned Robert and the older the wood the better the wine production. A good barrel will enhance flavour and add a maturity to a wine. However, because the world climate is changing and last year was so very hot, the temperature was too hot and split some of my barrels. A combination of age with heat we were left with no alternative, but to change our most seasoned barrels.'

'Brand new oak barrels?' Robert pondered. 'A different wood?'

'Le charpentier, he is a skilled man who uses not just one oak, but three varieties sourced locally. It is this mix of wood and the bark that I believe which has caused us the problem.'

'Then the trees could have influenced the chemical imbalance?'

'Qui, qui mon jeune ami, you do have a good grasp of our little problem.'

'But, why not just change the barrels again?'

'Non, replacement is costly Robert. Claude has promised that he will look at the affected barrels. I've stored them in the back of the old barn until such time that he can fill the cracks. Our immediate concern is if an inspector arrives expectantly and makes some tests. We send our wines all over the world.'

Robert picked up the wine bottle and poured himself some more offering Victor a refill.

'Unless Claude talks out of place, I believe that you're in the clear Monsieur Dupont. Who would ever suspect the problem as coming from the Saint Cambrae Vineyard.'

Victor Dupont felt the weight of their discussion had helped halve the problem. Robert was a young man with a wise head on his shoulders. 'You think so Robert?' he asked.

'Monsieur, we're barking up the wrong tree if we blame ourselves. We should think instead that you are a pioneer. You help women who have trouble in getting pregnant. Doctors cannot always help. But buy a bottle of wine from the Saint Cambrae Vineyard and suddenly all your problems could end up as little ones. You could resolve a couple's problem and make their dreams of having a family come true!'

Victor's smile was huge. *'Mon dieu Robert, you are so right.'* He cried. Victor Dupont leapt from his chair with Chantelle watching on from the veranda. When she saw her father grab Robert, yank him from his chair and promptly kiss both cheeks, she laughed. *'Mon dieu, you are a genius!'*

Inside the kitchen Adele Dupont smiled too knowing that everything was going to be alright. Somehow the men had found a way around the problem.

A Sock on the Chandelier

As suggested by Olivia Ashleigh, Janet had enthusiastically taken herself off to the Anglers Arms to see Benjamin Chapple. She and the pub landlord had both lost somebody close recently and Olivia was of the opinion that they could support one another through an emotional crisis. Having noticed how Benjamin had kept on looking at Janet at Charlie's funeral, it did not take a rocket scientist to work out that he harboured an underlying interest in the house cook.

'And Janet didn't raise any objections to the idea?' asked Bill.

'Not in the least. In fact it only took her an hour to get ready.' She grinned mischievously. 'Janet's visit could help kill two birds with one stone. She could market our latest stock and perhaps bring back an order from the pub landlord, plus have some fun at the same time.

Bill laughed heartily. 'Always the business woman.'

'One must take risks and do what needs to be done in order to survive in this world.' She replied.

Bill was fast understanding how her mind worked. 'I thought the orders were coming in thick and fast, especially after our last shipment?'

'They are Bill, but this place has overheads that need to be met. This is a big old house and takes a lot to heat and then there's the ongoing maintenance. Charlie, did his very best, but his days were catching up with him.'

'The spirit was willing, just the body couldn't keep up!'

Olivia nodded. 'Something like that. I'll miss having a man about the house.'

Bill studiously studied the interior of the kitchen where Olivia was adding the final touches to a cold meat salad. She was right it was a big house. More lately, he'd been spending more time under its roof than at his own home.

'Would it help if I was to take on some of the responsibilities left by Charlie's absence?'

Olivia Ashleigh finished wiping the cutlery with a clean cloth. 'Do you mean like tending to the vegetable garden?'

'Well, I've not exactly got green fingers, but I'm willing to give it a go, if it would help.' He helped lay the table. 'I was really thinking about the internal needs like woodwork, a bit of painting here and there, and the odd plumbing problem.'

He saw her smile pondering over the offer.

'That would help immensely Bill, thank you. I've just remembered that one of the upstairs lavatory systems needs looking at. It's been playing up something awful lately. Only this morning Janet told me that she couldn't shift an offending obstruction.'

'I'll take a look after dinner.'

Olivia Ashleigh however had other ideas for after dinner. 'It can wait until another time. Janet and I have an en-suite each. I hate to say it but the obstruction is something quite unmentionable that was probably left behind by Barbara Jenkins before she left.'

'People do the oddest things,' he replied picking up his wine glass. 'By the way did you get a response from the advert that you posted on-line for a new cleaner?'

'Two actually, although I'm still somewhat undecided about either. The first applicant was a very nice young man named Alistair. He wiggled his hips a lot when I showed him around the place and rather irritatingly he would keep referring to every task as *'ooh how wonderful'*. I'm a bit unsure Bill only his wrist flicking and pushing aside the one curl over his brow could become annoying. The other whose name I cannot recall was a middle-aged woman, a widow from the village who told me that she needed the extra money as the social were always on her case. My concern is that she suffers from lumbago and finds climbing stairs difficult.'

Bill topped up her wine glass before adding more to his own.

'So really what you're looking for is a lively handy person who hits the ground around the middle. Somebody who can take the stairs two at a time carrying a mop and bucket. Flick a duster about without worrying as to how the energy expended will affect every joint in their body.'

Olivia Ashleigh laughed. 'Put like that, I should have employed Alistair.'

Bill inhaled through his nose sucking in courage. Now felt the right time to ask. 'About us Olivia, where exactly do you see this relationship going?'

Olivia Ashleigh was stunned into silence.

'I would have thought that was obvious Bill,' she replied. 'We've something special. Something that grows stronger each time we are together. Some that I want to hold onto. What about you?'

'I'm just curious. Are we heading towards a permanent relationship?'

Removing her hand from where it had been covering her heart she relaxed. 'Oh, I see what you mean.'

She moved in close.

'I was dubious to begin with. I mean who has a boat named the *Saucy Belle*. But having chased me around the bedroom and had your wicked way with me, I would have thought that by now you would have picked up on the subtle hints that I have been leaving about the place.'

'Subtle hints?' he repeated.

'Freshly laundered socks and an ironed shirt.' She put down her wine glass. 'Underneath the top surface is just a woman Bill. I am looking for something a little more tangible than just the odd trip over to France, a romp in the hay and a candlelit dinner. I want something permanent in my life.'

'Like marriage?' Bill asked. He watched for a reaction.

Olivia Ashleigh picked up her glass again. Her heart felt like it was on a spinning Wurlitzer.

'Is that something that you would like to consider?' she asked.

'Do you always turn about a question with another question?' Bill laughed cutting through the tension in the air. 'Yes, the idea has been bouncing back and forth since we went to France together. I've not raised the subject before, only I'm also mindful of how short a time it has been since your late husband had his accident.'

Olivia was quick to reply. 'Death is not a reason to stand still. As my husband found out.'

'How come?' Bill frowned.

'Had Lawrence been more agile that morning, the bullet might have missed him!'

Bill suddenly dropped down onto one knee. 'Olivia Ashleigh, will you marry me?'

'If I say yes, will you still be interested in clearing the obstruction in the toilet?'

He laughed, 'be serious!'

'I am and yes, of course I will.'

Leaving the salad which was cold anyway they went upstairs having the house entirely to themselves. Undressing as fast as they could Bill flicked off his socks enthusiastically flinging them away. One flew through the air coming to rest on the chandelier above. Lying naked on the bed Olivia looked up at the dangling sock. It looked like a used condom.

'Bill...' she asked, 'do you think that I'm too old to have children?'

Climbing on the bed beside her, he started nibbling working his way down from her neck, kissing her navel on the way. 'I always did think you had sensual child bearing hips Olivia, even before we got together!'

Sometime during the night the sock fell of its own accord. Probably blown down either by the breeze coming in through the open window or perhaps the ghost of Lord Lawrence Ashleigh.

Bumps in the Night

They were awake with a start to the sound of somebody or something bashing about downstairs.

'It's probably only Janet,' said Olivia as she looked at the time on the clock beside the bed. She noticed that only four fifteen and it was still dark outside.

'No. I don't think so only I heard Janet come back about half past midnight. You were sound asleep.' Bill strained to listen again. 'And that doesn't sound like Janet. She might be a little bit clumsy at times, but she's much more considerate than that. That sounds more like mice wearing hobnail boots.' He slipped from under the duvet and into his trousers, shirt and shoes.

'You stay here. Grab the poker from the fire. I'll go and investigate!'

Olivia Ashleigh wanted to go with him, but Bill insisted that she stay where it was safe. Clicking the door shut he crept along the landing. Olivia went to the bedroom fireplace picking up the poker before going to the window to peer at the garden below. She had only been there several seconds when she saw the shadow of a man emerge from behind the hedgerow. Slipping on her dressing gown, she went to the door armed with the poker.

Having descended the stairs Bill could hear muffled voices, there was at least two in the house. Collecting a wooden walking stick from the mandarin umbrella stand he made his way to the kitchen. He was almost at the door when from within came a plaintive cry of pain, followed immediately by an almighty crash as something cumbersome overturned one of the kitchen chairs. Bill rushed in to find Janet wielding a robust looking rolling pin. On the floor of the kitchen lay the bodies of two unconscious intruders.

Bill went to her side. 'Are you alright?' he asked.

Grinning from ear to ear, she had the rolling pin poised for another strike. 'I've never felt better Bill. It was just like the old days when we used to get the odd burglar chance his arm. Back then of course Charlie was around. Cor you should have seen the fight, the chase. Some battles we won, some they got away.' She looked down at the unconscious men. 'Whoever these culprits are, they definitely lost out tonight.'

One of the intruders moaned, attempted to get up groaning. Before Bill could stop her, Janet hit the burglar again and this time he stayed down.

Seconds later there was another groan only this time from the other side of the kitchen door.

'That came from the garden.' He said rushing to the door. He found Olivia outside brandishing the poker. Lying at her feet was another unconscious man.

'If there are any more, we might have to consider charging an entrance fee.'

Bill was relieved to see that she was unharmed. 'I wish that you'd stayed upstairs.' He pointed. 'This one could have been dangerous!'

'What and miss out on all the fun. Not bloody likely,' she replied. 'You'd best bring him inside and we'll give Reg Perry a call.'

Bill dragged the unconscious man into the kitchen where they found Janet searching through the pockets of the two intruders she had dealt with. She put silver ornaments and other items of value on the worktop. Coming across the wallet belonging to one of the men she removed the cash before putting it back.

'And that you bastard is one for the kitchen pot. Call it your contribution to our mid-morning coffee supplement.'

Bill looked on mildly amused. 'Biscuits,' he added, 'chocolate ginger?'

Janet smiled, nodding back. 'Too right and better than the stale variety that he and his compatriots will be getting in prison.'

With the help of four other officers all three detainees were handcuffed, arrested and taken away leaving Reg to take statements.

Bill watched Olivia put the poker on the worktop where it was available should she need to use it again. 'You pair make a formidable team,' he said, as Janet filled the kettle for coffee.

'In more ways than one we do,' replied Olivia Ashleigh.

Reg was at the manor house in minutes arriving with other officers who arrested and carted the offenders away to the nearest police station. He told his colleagues that he would follow on soon, but that he needed to get statements from the occupants at the house.

'I had a call from Robert earlier. Saint Cambrae has also seen a rise in the number of young women getting pregnant. Victor thinks that the wood used in the barrels is to blame.' He saw the wine bottles on the table that Olivia Ashleigh and Bill Symons had finished off that evening.

'Think of the marketing drive that Wilfred Tummings could exploit,' said Janet. 'We produce, where doctors have failed. Wilfred would sell out overnight!'

Bill was also looking at the empty bottles. Turning to Reg, he had a question.

'You say it's a natural chemical reaction produced by the bark that can increase the estrogen levels?'

Reg nodded confident of his facts. 'A wine with a special kick by all accounts!'

Olivia slapped her palm down enthusiastically on the kitchen table. 'A wine that produces miracles.' She envisaged more sales.

'I did think about buying some myself,' continued Reg, 'but Emma's already threatened that if I do, I'll be sleeping in Robert's old room.'

There was a knock on the kitchen door and in burst Mary Nelson.

'God preserve us,' she exclaimed, 'are you okay.' She was breathing hard, having run all the way from the vicarage. 'I saw the flashing blue lights and thought something terrible had happened.'

Janet went to the shelf tom retrieve another mug. 'Here, come and sit down vicar. A strong coffee with a couple of ginger nuts will help lower your heart rate.'

Mary spotted the poker, the wooden walking stick and the rolling pin lying on the worktop. 'This is like that game,' she said flicking her forefinger and thumb together trying to recall the name. Bill helped out by telling her.

'Yes, that's it.' She shrieked with excitement. 'Do you know, I really do know a Reverend called Green.'

After the laughter had died down Bill tapped the top of the table and called for a moment's silence.

'Not that we had planned to take coffee at five in the morning, but this seems like an ideal time to announce that I proposed to Olivia earlier and she has agreed to marry me.'

Janet went to the larder to retrieve a bottle of champagne. Even Mary was happy to have a glass despite the early hour. Taking Olivia to one side Mary asked if she could officiate. 'You'd be my first wedding.' She said.

'Bill and I wouldn't have anybody else Mary, but you.'

Looking at the empty wine bottles Olivia wondered if they would stay a couple or would there be little additions. Hearing Janet laugh, the excitement of having a man about the house again making everything right again. Olivia thought Janet would be even more delighted if she knew the lady of the house might be expecting.

Later that morning with Bill upstairs taking a shower Olivia Ashleigh was left in the kitchen alone with Janet where she was helping clear away the breakfast dishes where the five of them had feasted on a celebratory breakfast. Janet was aware that her mistress was unusually quiet.

'Do you have something on your mind m'lady,' said Janet. 'I've known you long enough to sense it!'

Olivia Ashleigh grinned, but it was only luke-warm. 'Perceptive as ever Janet. Yes, I do have something troubling me. Can we sit for a minute.' Facing one another she explained. 'I know how close you and Lawrence were before he died, so this might come as a bit of a surprise.'

Janet put her hand over the back of Olivia Ashleigh's. 'Not that close m'lady, I assure you. We would only meet up at midnight to share, bread and cheese, the odd onion or gherkins and a tot of port. We never had sex!'

Olivia Ashleigh felt the laugh explode from between her lips.

'I never ever thought that Janet, not that it would have mattered if you had. Lawrence however was very fond of you.'

'*Was he…*' Janet looked surprised.

Olivia Ashleigh inhaled deep. 'Very, but what I am trying to offload here Janet is that it was me who killed him.'

'*Oh shit!*' Janet's eyes grew wider.

'Yes,' replied Olivia Ashleigh. 'It had nothing to do with you or your midnight trysts, but something entirely different.'

Janet felt her heart racing beneath her massive bosom. 'Was it because of that tart from the riding stables?'

This time Olivia Ashleigh's eyes grew wider. 'You knew,' she muttered. 'You knew about the affair between Lawrence and Francesca Harrington-Bowles?'

Janet nodded.

'I did m'lady. It wasn't the master who told me, but what I had seen, heard and worked out for myself. It wasn't right that the master was going behind your back. If my Charlie had done that to me I would have killed him too!'

Olivia Ashleigh looked on, her mouth was slightly open. She quickly checked to see that they were alone and that Bill was not listening in. 'You said too. Does that implying that you've killed somebody as well?'

Janet nodded again. 'I have m'lady.' Janet's eyes were soft and without any shame. 'The day that the master was tragically killed, I went to the stable block later that evening where I found the owner alone. I had gone with the intention of talking to her, only she refused to discuss the matter with a lowly cook. She walked off in a huff going into the hay barn where I followed.

'Climbing to the upper level of the barn where they kept the spare saddles we argued. I got angry and accused her of interfering in your marriage. She shoved me away and so I pushed her back. It wasn't a hard push, but with enough force to make her realise that I wasn't going to leave until she heard me out. Unfortunately, she stumbled catching her heel in a loose bridle that lay on the wooden floor. She fell to the barn floor below before I could catch her. There was no scream m'lady. No astonished cry, just a bump in the night. When I looked down at Francesca Harrington-Bowles, she just lay there unmoving and dead. The fall had broken her neck.'

This time Olivia Ashleigh held Janet's hand. 'So what took place, occurred because you were looking out for me and not Lawrence?'

'Not your husband m'lady, just you!'

They both sighed. 'Thank you Janet, you've always been so loyal to me. I don't know what I'd do without you.'

'And Lord Ashleigh, m'lady,' Janet asked. 'Was that an accident?'

'No. I knew of the affair. Lawrence threatened to divorce me then move Francesca Harrington-Bowles into my home. I was livid Janet. Through thick and thin I had stuck by my husband and his diplomatic service. I was not about to have some scrawny, wild haired two-bit aristocrat take my place in the flick of a light switch. When Larry went shooting that morning, I was already concealed in the bushes in the wood.

When he took aim at a passing pheasant, I steadied myself, my finger on the trigger lever. When he fired, I fired. Those nearest Larry thought the recoil had knocked him backwards. It wasn't until they saw the bullet wound that they realised Lawrence had been shot. The rest you know.'

Together they held hands. 'Your secret is forever safe with me m'lady. I'll never tell, ever!'

Olivia Ashleigh smiled. 'And the accident in the stable block is safe with me too. There is however one thing that has always puzzled me. The police and the newspapers reported Francesca Harrington-Bowles as missing, never found. What did you do with the body?'

Janet sucked in. 'I contacted Charlie. He drove the Rolls to the door of the stable block where together we collected the body. Later that night we dumped her in the sceptic tank out back. It's due to be drained soon although I doubt very much that there'd be much left of that snotty nosed cow. As the saying goes m'lady, *'shit happens!'*

Olivia Ashleigh didn't know whether to laugh out loud, cry or hang her head in her hands. 'What's wrong m'lady, did we do wrong?' Janet asked, her heart racing faster than a charging bull.

'No, no Janet,' she replied laughing. 'It's just that the sceptic tank is where I dumped Rakeesh.'

Janet's chest started to wobble as the laughter emerged.

'Do you remember that wine run that the boys did m'lady where they got stopped by customs at Dover? Later that night we had to get rid of Bob Crutch. Charlie and me that is, we did it. Bob was the only witness to see the lads return to the village. We couldn't take the risk. Daft as a hairless brush Bob might have been, but we couldn't take the chance that he had a lucid moment and tell the police what he'd seen. Charlie told me old Bob never saw it coming.'

Olivia Ashleigh suddenly unravelled three fingers. 'So we have three bodies in the tank. Are there any others that I don't know about?' she asked.

Janet shrugged, shaking her head from side to side.

'Not unless my Charlie bumped off anybody in the night m'lady when we thought he was in bed. He did go out occasionally when he thought we had poachers about.'

Olivia Ashleigh closed her eyes. Three murders under one roof. It could make the Guinness Book of Records.

Janet leaned forward.

'You don't think they'll get stuck do you m'lady?' she asked.

Olivia Ashleigh shook her head confidently. 'No. That suction pipe is pretty big and extremely powerful.'

Saying Goodbye to Unwanted Problems

The telephone ringing in the entrance hall was answered by Bill who just happened to be passing. Having taken the message he found Janet and Olivia in the kitchen. They appeared startled.

'Was you expecting somebody else?' he asked.

'No, only you,' replied Olivia. 'Was that Mary on the phone?'

'No, it was some company called *Dump-it-Clean* who say that they'll be along tomorrow morning around eleven to drain the septic tank.'

Janet swallowed the saliva at the back of her throat as she looked at Olivia Ashleigh.

'What is it with you two,' he quizzed, 'you look like you've just seen a ghost?'

'We might need of some of your technical expertise.'

Bill gave a nod. 'The tools are in the boot of the car.'

Olivia patted the chair besides hers. 'It's what's in the sceptic tank that worries us more Bill.'

'That's way beyond my plumbing knowledge and *Dump-it-Clean* are the experts.' He watched their eyes knowing that there was more. 'What's going on?' He sat down next to Olivia.

They told him everything leaving out nothing. 'Would a coffee be appropriate?' asked Janet.

'A brandy would help,' he replied.

She supplied coffee the biscuit barrel collecting three glasses and the bottle of brandy.

'Are we still getting married?' asked Olivia Ashleigh, chewing on the ends of her finger nails.

'We are,' mumbled Bill. 'I am just thinking about how we can get around this little problem.'

Drumming his fingertips rhythmically on the table top he was deep in thought. The kitchen was silent as they watched and waited. When the drumming stopped he had the solution.

'Besides the chickens are there any other animals here on the estate?'

Olivia responded first. 'The deer. Other than the herd the nearest animals to that are the sheep, but they belong to Farmer Byrnes. You'd find them grazing normally the other side of the wood.'

Bill nodded thoughtfully. 'But like all sheep they tend to wander, right?'

Olivia Ashleigh shrugged. 'I suppose they do. Occasionally they've been found in the church graveyard or the back lane. Samuel's father can be a little remise at times ignoring that some stretches of his fence need repairing. Why?'

Bill slapped the table. 'Then that's the answer to our problem. We entice one of his ewes onto the estate. We kill it and dump it down the septic tank. I'll call *Dump-it-Clean* and put the collection back a month. Sheep have a tendency to be buoyant in water. By the time the tanker arrives to collect the waste the sheep will have become bloated. They'll have to arrange for a much larger and powerful truck with a better suction. If it can suck up a full grown ewe, it'll work wonders for three dead bodies.'

Olivia looked across at Janet whose cheeks were creasing into a smile. She liked Bill's plan. Olivia nodded agreeing. He had a devious mind, as corrupt as her own.

'I'll steer clear of any lamb dishes for the wedding breakfast menu m'lady.' suggested Janet.

'Purely out of interest,' Bill asked. 'How did Charlie get rid of Bob Crutch?'

'Charlie took Bob out early one morning hunting for rabbits. After his previous accident Bob was obviously reluctant to put his hands down any of the holes and tickle the burrow, but Charlie said he'd be on hand to help. East of the wood next to the church where the warrens are plentiful I was hid amongst trees. The plan was when Charlie and Bob arrived I would jump out naked as a jaybird, hoping the sight of me would cause old Bob to have a heart attack. Charlie had heard that a recent visit to the doctor's had confirmed that his heart was deteriorating.'

Bill could only imagine what Bob must have thought having seen Janet starkers. 'So did it work?'

'No. Charlie said seeing me naked gave old Bob a new lease of life. A sort of second wind.'

'But he's been missing weeks!'

'That's right,' Janet continued. 'Bob had a sister who lived up Cumbria way. The following afternoon I had a coffee break with Barbara Jenkins planting the seed that old Bob had gone to visit his sister. Before you knew it the whole village was convinced that Bob had left for Cumbria for good. If Barbara Jenkins is good at anything, it's spreading gossip.'

Bill topped up his brandy glass. 'But he ended up in the septic tank?'

'Yes, Charlie put him there. I saw him wiping his commando knife clean, but there was no need to ask why.'

They found the sheep grazing in the field just beyond the wood out of sight of the vicarage. Olivia hoped Mary wasn't anywhere around. Stealing sheep was not in the bible. Armed with a bag of kernel nuts Janet was poised nearest the broken fence where the gap was wide enough for a full grown ewe to squeeze through. Olivia and Bill were the other side.

'At least old Bob died with a smile on his face.' Said Bill.

'What do you mean?' whispered Olivia.

'We'll can you image what a shock it must have been when Janet jumped out naked. It's wonder she didn't spook the flock.'

To any dog walkers out walking the adjacent field the sight of Janet feeding the sheep would not have seemed out of place.

Janet was enticing a solitary ewe through the gap when another suddenly appeared deciding that it also wanted to join in the free meal. *'Bugger off,'* she told the latecomer. The smaller ewe however was having none of it. It let out a loud bleat and within seconds several more were heading Janet's way. Looking behind her Janet didn't know what to do, now that there were five ewes interested in her bag of nuts.

'Captain what should I do?' she cried.

Bill stood up. 'Throw some of your nuts over there by those holly bushes. Remember to entice only the one ewe through. We don't want the whole flock following.' Janet did as he suggested, but the smaller ewe insisted on following its larger companion.

'Don't worry about the smaller one,' Bill advised, 'keep heading our way Janet and I'll go around back and make sure that the others don't follow. We'll work out what to do with the small one later.'

Janet continued walking back spreading the kernel nuts as Olivia Ashleigh joined her. Together they enticed the two ewes towards the estate garden. 'We might be having lamb after all,' she said. Not far away was the walled vegetable garden.

'I couldn't kill a sheep m'lady. A human yes, but not an animal this big. Charlie would be the one to wring the neck of the turkey at Christmas.'

'Don't worry, I'm sure Bill can. The knife that he has on his boat isn't just for whittling.' Having distracted the other sheep Bill joined them. 'Did they follow you?' Olivia Ashleigh asked.

'Not really, I laid a trail of nuts back to Mary's church garden. They've been found there before, so it would make their wandering more plausible when Farmer Byrne goes to check on them later.' Ushering the two ewes through the gate they went immediately for where Charlie had been growing broccoli. Shutting the gate Bill noticed the long handled axe which had been left embedded in the bark of a fallen tree trunk.

'Should we wait until later or kill them both now?' asked Olivia.

'Now I suppose, Bill replied, the uncertainty having become a reality suddenly. 'You should have brought your rifle. Nobody takes any notice of gunfire, not in the country.'

Just then they heard car tyres screech, a whelp of pain and then silence as the vehicle came to a halt. Olivia ran to the back gate to find the driver, a young woman standing over a distressed dog which had been struck by the car. She asked if the driver was hurt.

'I'm fine, but this poor dog isn't.' The driver looked on anxiously. The dog just launched itself from the hedgerow and into the path of my car. I braked, skidded, but there was nothing I could do to avoid hitting the dog.'

Bill checked the dog which was in a bad way. Suddenly he saw an opportunity which had unusually presented itself. 'Why don't you go on your way and let us handle this...' he offered.

'Shouldn't I report the matter to the police,' the woman asked.

'Leave that to me. The village bobby is a good friend of ours. I'll give him a call and tell him what happened and you did everything possible. It's the dog's fault, not yours.'

'Would you,' she asked checking her watch, 'I'm running late already for an appointment.'

Olivia nodded putting her hand on the drivers shoulder. 'The dog is going to die very soon. There's a very nice wood nearby where we can give the animal a decent burial amongst the trees. We'll talk to the constable and make sure that you're not involved.'

'Are you sure. I feel awful putting you to so much trouble?' said the young woman.

'Absolutely not, now you go and make that appointment. Don't look back. Doing so never does anybody any good.'

They waved goodbye as the driver followed the lane around the next bend and from sight. Looking back down the dog was already dead.

'Right,' said Bill rubbing the dirt from his hands. 'We'll throw the two ewes out into the lane and let Farmer Byrne find them in his own time. Providence presented a solution to our problem and who would blame anybody from an inquisitive dog that accidentally fell in and died in the septic tank.'

Olivia and Janet were relieved. They were sad about the dog, but it was much better than killing a pair of innocent ewes.

'At least we can think about having lamb now at your wedding m'lady, and not chock on it, knowing where the meat came from.

Middle Names and Big Noses

Surprisingly the collection of the waste from the septic tank went much smoother than expected. The bio-organisms in the tank doing their job effectively. Except for the dog which was the most recent addition and that was easily explained by Bill. He told the driver that he had inadvertently left the lid open having been called away for an urgent phone call. It would be a further two months before one of the decomposed bodies caught in an upsurge of bubbling gases would rise to the surface. Wholly unrecognisable the deceased would be given a hasty burial service in an unmarked grave, miles from Willow Beck.

All in all everything had gone as planned, including the trip over to Saint Cambrae which included Reg and his wife Emma, although she knew nothing of Reg's involvement with Olivia Ashleigh, Bill Symons and Janet.

'Is it always this rough in the Channel?' she asked as Olivia Ashleigh held onto her arm with Emma perched perilously over the side of the boat. Her complexion the colour of the sea below.

'Only sometimes, other times it's really quite smooth like a millpond.'

Standing beside Bill Symons, Reg Perry was going over the finer details of the arrangements for when they arrived at Dunkirk.

'You will have to take Emma into one of those clothing shops to keep her distracted,' Bill advised. 'That way I can slip away and get the van. It's best that Emma doesn't know where we keep it.'

Reg tapped the side of his nose. 'That's wise Bill. Emma has eyes like a hawk and ears the envy of an elephant.'

Bill checked to see that Olivia and Emma were safe.

'The hotel in Saint Cambrae where we're staying,' asked Reg, 'is it far from the vineyard?'

'I don't think so,' replied Bill. 'The last time that I spoke with Victor he told me that it belonged to a family friend. I don't image it would be that far. Why?'

'I was just checking. Emma has really missed Robert. She been like an expectant hen all week wanting to know that he's all settled in at Saint Cambrae.'

Bill held the wheel as a wave made the boat lurch. He saw Olivia rubbing Emma's back. 'Has Emma been curious why you've been coming to the manor house a lot lately?'

'No. She never asks after what I'm doing or where I'm going. Emma's never been entirely overly happy being a policeman's wife and she's counting down the days until my retirement.'

Bill remembered what it was like when he took retirement leaving the tugboat for the last time. He thought that he would miss the life, but he had never looked back.

'Life throws up challenges all the time Reg, trust me, even in retirement. Look at me, I lost a tugboat, saved another from being scrapped. Got myself the *Saucy Belle* and now I'm getting married.' He made sure that Olivia wasn't listening. 'I thought I'd end my days, old and grey with my paint box and pipe to keep me company.'

Reg tapped Bill's shoulder confidently.

'You know Bill, I was the first on the scene when her late husband got shot. Strange incident though and it was never solved. The witnesses that day never heard the extra shot and none could tell me from where it originated. The Detective Inspector who took over the investigation reckons that it was either an accident from another shooting group nearby or a professional hitman seeking revenge. Lord Ashleigh must have made some enemies in his years in the diplomatic service.'

Bill grinned. 'Or perhaps Reg it was Lady Ashleigh and because her husband hadn't brought up her morning tea that day before he went out on the shoot.'

Reg laughed catching the attention of both women. 'Getaway,' he replied. 'Olivia wouldn't hurt a fly. Now there is a lady and there's not a vengeful bone in her body. You've done well Bill landing that catch.'

Bill looked over at Olivia Ashleigh and winked. She smiled back not knowing what had been said, but whatever it had amused the policeman.

Meanwhile Emma Perry found nothing amusing. Her stomach felt like it was involved in a raging battle with her head. Disgorging most of her breakfast over the side Olivia Ashleigh took Emma below deck so that she could have a short nap. Coming back to where she stood between the two men she had a suggestion. 'You might be flying back Reg. I don't think Emma could stomach another sea crossing.'

Reg felt his shoulders sink. The trip was beginning to turn out a costly excursion. Emma had insisted on getting two new outfits for the trip along with additional clothes for Robert. Adding in the cost of a flight home he was already out of pocket. At least the hotel had been paid for by Lady Ashleigh.

'I might just leave her with Robert,' he replied. He laughed to himself. 'No, that wouldn't be fair on the lad. He's just managed to escape her clutches whereas I signed on the dotted line.'

Olivia Ashleigh dared Bill Symons to comment, but he had the sense to stay silent.

Almost as soon as they landed at Dunkirk, Emma Perry felt better jumping up onto the wooden pontoon where Bill had moored the boat. Accompanied by Olivia Ashleigh and Reg, Emma was glad to be back on dry land and heading to the shops.

Having paid Madame Charron an additional two month's rent to keep the van around back of the restaurant Bill promised that they would call in on the way back to see her. The restaurant owner asked about the young men, Robert, Samuel and Tommy, wondering why they had not come on the trip. Bill told her that young women had come between them, turning both head and heart. It was possibly the case for at least Robert and Tommy, but almost certainly not for Samuel Byrne.

The hotel at Saint Cambrae was modest, although comfortable and Marcel Martin and his pretty wife Paulette were excellent hosts. Having seen Adele and Victor Dupont that afternoon, Olivia and Bill had left the Perry family to catch up introducing Charlotte to Emma.

'Why the wink on board the boat,' she asked flopping back on the mattress.

'Reg was adamant so many words that you couldn't hurt or kill anything, animal or human.'

Olivia grinned. 'That's reassuring to know. You'd best watch your step Bill Symons only now I've a cast iron alibi in the constable.'

Bill lay beside her placing his hands behind his head. 'Before we get to the altar have you a middle name?' he asked.

She turned to face him. 'I've two. Willow and Lachlan. My mother was originally from the West Coast of Scotland and when I was born she thought that I resembled the look of an owl. In some odd way she chose a name to fit each letter. Olivia Willow Lachlan. It was pure coincidence that I should end up living in a village with the name Willow. When I become Mrs Symons however, I will no longer be Lady Ashleigh, but known only as OWLS.'

He caressed his hand up from her abdomen to her chest, but she slapped his hand away playfully. And you, do you have any?'

'Andrew.'

'That's nice, I like that. You must have been christened William, why Bill?'

'I abbreviated the name William as soon as I could. Bill always made me sound more grown up. As captain of a boat it sounded better as well.' He kissed her forehead. 'So you don't mind losing the title?'

'Definitely not, I never did like it. Lady this and lady that, it was like a constant ball and chain around one's neck. It will be nice to be known simply as Mrs Symons, trust me.'

'And how do you think Janet will take to calling you Olivia?'

'Difficult I would assume. Janet will always call me m'lady, although it does make me sound like that awful doll dressed entirely in pink who had a chauffeur named Parker, with a big nose.'

Bill checked the shape of his own before laughing. 'At least my mother got something right!'

Slowing Down and Wedding Bells

As expected Emma and Reg did fly back to England rather than endure another crossing on the *Saucy Belle*. Having seen her only son, been introduced to Chantelle and her family, and walked the village of Saint Cambrae, Emma was already contemplating a life in France with Reg mulling over early retirement.

Events were changing fast. Perhaps faster than what Olivia Ashleigh had expected. She too had sat back and reflected, giving serious consideration to the past, present and future. Would she, she wondered still get the same buzz that she had from importing illicit wine, spirits and cheese. With Bill she saw a different future and like Emma Perry she liked France. Maybe she thought, it was time to slow down and cross over from the fast lane of life.

Mary Nelson who was now well established in Willow Beck had become the champion of many good causes in around the village, including setting up a counselling and support group for young women who found themselves inexplicably pregnant. One of the first to attend was Tracy Weathers, although not accompanied by Samuel Byrne. The farmer's son had asked for a DNA test to prove that the baby was his and that he was indeed the father. Of course with her father breathing heavily down his neck, he agreed that it possibly was.

Following the announcement of the wedding Mary had been working tirelessly with Olivia Ashleigh and Janet Simpson on plans for the big day. They had even checked with the London Weather Centre and received a long range forecast for the Saturday in question. Olivia wanted a two thirty afternoon ceremony giving guests the chance to arrive and a marquee would be set up on the manor house lawn to accommodate the event.

Bill Symons had very few family or friends upon which he could invite, so Olivia suggested that he ask the Duponts, Robert and Chantelle, plus Emma and Reg Perry to help bolster his side of the pews in the church. Bill added Madame Charron to the list of invites, keeping the balance of European trade and friendship equal.

Janet who for once had the day off, found herself aimlessly walking around the house and grounds feeling quite lost in her own surroundings.

She wanted to help, get stuck in, but she had strict instruction from Olivia to let the catering company deal with everything. Finding a corner of the tent where she could not be seen she watched Arnold Drummond the butcher unload and set up the spit for the evening hog roast. A wedding gift from Farmer Byrne for helping round up his lost sheep.

Come the Saturday it was both sunny and warm with a gentle hint of a breeze, the ideal conditions where hats wouldn't be blown around or indeed hairstyles destroyed.

Olivia Ashleigh had found time to have a coffee with Janet prior to the service explaining that once married she would no longer be Lady Olivia Ashleigh, but plain Mrs Symons. The news came as a welcome relief.

'I hadn't thought about that m'lady,' Janet replied, stirring her spoon randomly around the inside of her coffee cup. 'So Bill won't become Lord Bill then?'

Olivia Ashleigh laughed. 'Goodness no. Can you see Bill as a titled gent, I can't.'

Janet raised her eyebrows. 'I was just getting used to calling him the master.'

'What about captain.' She suggested. 'Although he rarely mentions the sea, I know there are times when he misses the challenge of the waves.'

Janet agreed, captain was good. 'Reg was telling me the other day that he and his wife were thinking about moving to Saint Cambrae on a permanent basis. Pretty much soon we'll have nobody to help with the wine run!'

Olivia Ashleigh looked pensive.

'That's something that I've been giving some consideration too lately. After the honeymoon I think the three of us, you, me and Bill should sit down and evaluate our options.' Janet's eyes had suddenly become moist.

'I'm sorry m'lady, it's just that with Charlie gone, the spark seems to be missing.'

'Did you invite Benjamin Chapple to the wedding?'

'Yes m'lady. He just needs to find somebody to look after the pub for the afternoon and evening.'

'I doubt that he would have much trouble finding volunteers.'

Janet responded with a smile that was hardly convincing. Olivia Ashleigh wasn't entirely convinced that Janet was holding it together well and she didn't want Charlie's ghost ruining her day, not her wedding day.

'He's asked Marge for a divorce,' Janet cried, blurting it out quickly as though saying it any slower would invoke trouble.

'Well that's a step in the right direction. Olivia Ashleigh nudged Janet's arm. 'Perhaps Benjamin's getting fired up for something romantic for the future!'

Janet looked aghast.

'What really worries me m'lady is that I am not as young as you and Bill. I feel that these past few months I've slowed down and I'm finding it difficult to find the motivation anymore.'

Olivia Ashleigh's expression changed from one of surprise to apprehension. 'Are you saying that you want to leave the manor house?' she asked.

'Goodness no m'lady. I am just saying that I've noticed changes. I don't move about as fast as I did before. Benjamin also mentioned it to the other evening.' Janet blushed.

Olivia Ashleigh gave the cook an encouraging hug. 'Age catches up with us all Janet, but have you thought about getting fit. Losing a few pounds might help. Maybe, grabbing the opportunities that a future can present will give you more incentive going forward.'

'You mean like finding another love?'

'That as well. I never expected somebody like Bill to walk into my life, but when he did it was like a breath of fresh air. Suddenly everything looked rosy again. Maybe you need to do the same.'

'Maybe, it's not just your age Janet, but your body telling you to take it easy as well!'

'Benjamin's not much better. Christ, if we did it any slower I would fall asleep.'

'Give it time Janet. Everything will fall into place as fate dictates.'

At exactly twenty five minutes past two she walked down the aisle with Janet at her side. Olivia Ashleigh could not decide who to give her away and Janet was the longest, loyal friend so it made sense. Bill also agreed.

Getting close to the altar Janet whispered. *'Bill looks ever so dashing in his naval uniform!'*

Olivia Ashleigh smiled adding a sigh. In his dark uniform, gold braid on his sleeves and cap tucked under his arm he was a vision she would never forget. Behind him Mary Nelson was dressed in her finest white robes and mauve stole. In her hand she had a bible.

Coming alongside Janet stepped away as Bill took Olivia's right hand. He helped lift the lace veil away from her face. 'You're beautiful. My dream come true!'

Mary suggested that the congregation sit allowing the *oohs* and *aahs* to settle.

'We begin this joyful occasion by welcoming guests, family and friends to the wedding of Olivia and Bill to whom I owe so much.

'Their presence here today is not just a union of their love for one another, but an outreaching of their love to all that they know, here in Willow Beck and overseas.'

Mary noticed that the paper tissues were already being passed around. Sat at the end of the second pew was Madame Charron, she had a lace handkerchief.

With the marriage vows over they assembled in the vestry to sign the register. Reg who was Bill's best man, slipped the captain a coin.

'What's this...?' asked Bill.

'It's an old tradition that I once read about,' Reg explained. *'Give the groom a penny and the pounds will come rolling in. Give the bride a kiss and make her dreams and wishes come true.'*

Bill smiled back. 'Perhaps you'd better slip me two coins.'

Olivia looked on with a frown. 'What's that Reg gave you?'

'I'll tell you later!'

Olivia and Bill signed the register, followed by Janet and Reg. It made Janet smile when she watched Bill put retired sea captain as his occupation. She wondered what Charlie would have put, had they been married. Ex-spy, murderer and lover.

Reg shook Bill's hand before he kissed the waiting bride.

Clearing his throat Bill held the hand of his new bride as she sat at his side. He was stood at the head table ready to give his speech.

'I was never one for making formal speeches, not even at school. Most of the time I was ducking the board rubber or walking the corridor to see the headmaster. I could however write poetry and not the verses that you find on the back of a lavatory door. I thought the occasion called for a very special poem for the woman that I love.'

The tent filled with laughter and applause as Bill raised a hand to begin.

'A rose without petals is lost in the wind

But without the breeze who brings forth the birds singing in the trees

And every once in a while, a swan will appear

A graceful vision of beauty and delight

The majestic bird created from lace of innocence white

Today I married my bride

My lovely wife, Olivia my swan

Tomorrow is another day when dreams begin

But today, we dance as long as we can into the night

And so with all my love

I will savour and cherish these precious moments together

Knowing that I am so very lucky to have found this woman

Olivia Willow Lachlan to be my beautiful wife'.

The birds sitting in the branches nearby took to flight as the applause and cheers echoed within the tent, even the catering staff joined in. Rising from her chair and to the delight of the guests Olivia Symons kissed her husband.

'Thank you Bill, that was so beautiful. I love you!'

Bill took a bow above the din of cutlery being drummed on the tables as Reg stood in readiness to give his best man's speech. To his amazement the tent went silent.

Reg grinned. 'That normally happens when I walk into the room,' he said. There were a few whistles and muttered comments. Even Emma Perry found the introduction funny.

Producing a pre-written script and his police whistle Reg placed the whistle against his lips and blew. Nothing happened. The tent was silent waiting a reaction.

'Some bod in the stored gave me this the first day that I joined the force. Today however is the second time that it's been out of the box. I was going to present to Bill for their honeymoon, but there's no way that I'm getting out of bed at three in the morning because he needs help!'

Reg got a sharp dig in the ribs from Emma, but she noticed that Olivia Symons was laughing the loudest joining in with the rest of the guests.

When calm reigned again Reg continued. 'So back to the happy couple in question. You could perhaps look around the room and not find a better suited match. Olivia, as radiantly stunning as ever and Bill, the rugged, handsome catch… or maybe we'd best not bolster his ego too much. Better to just say that they were made for one another.'

Again a round of applause.

'I recently had the pleasure of sailing with them on Bill's boat the *Saucy Belle* where the time spent with them both was an adventure that I will never forget. They make any occasion come alive and now as a married couple, they will enrich this village and the lives of whoever they come into contact with.'

Except nosey customs officers thought Olivia, Bill and Janet.

'Now as best man it was my duty to ensure that the groom got to the wedding on time, however on this occasion it was extraordinarily the other way around.'

Reg felt Emma look up.

'You see to help celebrate the approach of this wonderful wedding the groom and best man had decided to sample a few beers at the local hostelries as the ale is reputed to be some of the best around the county as Benjamin Chapple here will no doubt advocate. After a couple of pints in, I was ready to fight anybody who said different.'

Reg heard Emma tut as some of the men in the tent cheered.

'Luck would have it that being a retired tugboat captain, Bill came to the rescue taking the conscious decision to change to shorts. By this time however I'd definitely lost my sea legs.' Reg looked sideways to where Bill was sat watching. 'If he ever suggests going for a drink refuse!'

Bill grinned, smiling at Olivia.

'But,' Reg said as he read on. 'This captain didn't abandon his crew, finding a greengrocers barrow around back of the pub he took me home, where I was unceremoniously dumped on my doorstep, where my dear wife found me the next morning.'

There was another loud cheer from the men.

Reg waited until the tent was silent. 'Now the moral of the story dear Olivia is that you've a damn good man in Bill Symons and he'll be there for you whatever, come sunshine or storm. Bill got me home and I am confident that he will never let you down no matter what, not unless you decide to ride a white horse through the high street naked…'

The tent fell silent as Olivia, Bill, Emma and Janet looked at Reg and around at confused faces. Reg turned the page of his speech. He showed the reverse side to everybody present holding up the page

'Ride a white horse through the high street naked, whereupon on his charger your knight in shining armour will surely appear. May you both have a long, prosperous and happy life together and any problems be little ones!' Reg picked up his glass and asked everybody in the room to make sure that there glass was charged. 'To Olivia and Bill, god bless you both!'

With the toast over to Reg remained standing. He passed the whistle to Bill. 'You can blow into that as much as you like, but I warn you that whoever manufactured the whistle forgot to put the pea inside!' With that Reg sat back down, he kissed his wife as Emma tried to hide her blushes. Olivia Symons was the first up to applaud Reg.

Eventually the tent went silent again leaving the bride standing.

'It is unusual for the bride to reply, but I feel that I must on this occasion. Bill and I would like to say a big thank you to Reg, Emma and Janet for all the hard work that they've put in, in making our day so very special.

'We would like to thank Reg for the wonderful best man speech and to you all for joining us on this joyous occasion.

'There is however, two amongst you who I would like to thank. The first being our new vicar, Mary Nelson. Without Mary, who I consider a very close friend I would not have had the courage to find God and choose a path of righteousness. The second is my husband Bill. He opened the door of adventure that I believed had shut forever. He brought a love back into my life that I thought had been lost forever and for that I will be eternally grateful. To you all, thank you. Now let the party begin!'

When Olivia Symons sat back down she asked for a tissue to wipe the damp spots from her eyes. Reg signalled to the band to begin playing as the waiters and waitresses moved efficiently between the tables.

Sitting on the same table as the Dupont family and Robert, Madame Charron had already secured a good deal and price with Victor Dupont for a shipment of his best wines. Later come the evening she would get her long awaited dance later with Captain Bill and find the opportunity to congratulate Olivia Symons on a fine catch.

'Where are you honeymooning?' Madame Charron asked.

'Along and around the south coast in the *Saucy Belle*.'

'Mon dieu quelle excitation!'

Olivia Symons agreed. 'We thought so too. Just the sea, the breeze in our hair and anywhere, where the boat takes us.'

'If you should find yourselves lost, say in a sea mist and end up in Dunkirk, there will be a free meal and wine waiting for you anytime!'

Olivia thanked Madame Charron. 'I noticed that you were talking with Victor Dupont earlier, I hope you secured a good deal?'

'Qui, qui madame, I am very pleased. Victor, he tells me that his wine has a certain quality that is assured to invigorate the soul, add vigour to health and give life a new meaning.'

Olivia Symons smiled back. It would certainly do that and much, much more. Holding her glass in one hand sipping at a red wine from the Duponts vineyard she gently held her stomach. Later when they were alone she had a little secret to tell Bill.

Looking across the dance floor to where she saw Mary nod and look back. Mary steepled her hands together in prayer. Miracles were always unexpected.

Other Books by Jeffrey Brett

A Moment in Time
ISBN – 979 - 8642194461
Barking Up the Wrong Tree
ISBN – 978 - 1073495290
Beyond the First Page
ISBN – 978 - 1980681991
Leave No Loose Ends
ISBN – 978 – 1549552984
Looking for Rosie
ISBN – 978 - 1980369400
The Little Red Café
ISBN – 978 - 1980912583
Rabbits Beside the Track
ISBN – 979 - 8635555187
The Road is Never Long Enough
ISBN – 978 - 1794541948
The Moon, Balloon and Stars
ISBN – 979 – 8634519852
Shadow of Blame
ISBN – 979 – 8672633008
The Magic of the Little Red Café
ISBN – 979 - 8576921348

©

Jeffrey Brett, the Author

I was born in London during the middle of the last century, where I lived and worked until leaving for pastures green and wide, with opportunities to write my fictional stories.

Writing is not just a happy pastime, but has become a way of life for me and without it I would feel lost. I feel that there are so many ideas that need to be written although I follow no particular genre creating short stories, romantic and psychological thrillers, and hopefully humorous books.

Now retired after a lifetime of public service I have found the time to make my dreams come true and enjoy my writing, publishing my books. My good friend, award winning writer and author Kathleen Harryman is a great inspiration and encouragement, and through her recent creative artwork, she has helped with some of the book covers. Kathleen's artwork service and books can be found on her website – kathleenharryman.com

I wish you many hours of happy reading. If you have any comments regarding any of my books please email me and let me know - magic79.jb@outlook.com